Tom B   London
and beg   ecoming
a spokesman for Scotland Yard. He later moved into public
healt   here he developed Britain's first r   mpaign
ag   Know   Limits, and ed drugs
awareness programme FRANK. He now lives in Bologna.

The Hunting Season is the second novel in his Daniel Leicester
crime series.

Find Tom on Instagram, Twitter and Facebook at
tombenjaminsays.

Also by Tom Benjamin

A Quiet Death in Italy

The Hunting Season

Tom Benjamin

CONSTABLE

CONSTABLE

First published in Great Britain in 2020 by Constable
This edition published in 2021 by Constable

Copyright © Tom Benjamin, 2020

1 3 5 7 9 10 8 6 4 2

The moral right of the author has been asserted.

A CIP catalogue record for this book
is available from the British Library.

ISBN: 978-1-47213-161-4

Typeset in Adobe Garamond by Initial Typesetting Services, Edinburgh
Printed and bound in Great Britain by Clays Ltd, Elcograf S.p.A.

Papers used by Constable are from well-managed forests
and other responsible sources.

Constable
An imprint of
Little, Brown Book Group
Carmelite House
50 Victoria Embankment
London EC4Y 0DZ

An Hachette UK Company
www.hachette.co.uk

www.littlebrown.co.uk

For Gennaro 'Rino' Zicchino,
un uomo autentico

L'uomo è quasi sempre tanto malvagio quanto gli bisogna.
Man is almost always as wicked as his needs require.

Giacomo Leopardi

Chapter 1

There was no hint of murder that morning; on the contrary, it was bright after a weekend of rain. Autumn had arrived late – floods had hit Spain and a string of Italian cities on the west coast, but Bologna had endured the bad weather with her usual equanimity. This was the city of porticoes after all, and built to withstand extremes.

My daughter Rose had already left for school, so I locked up. From our balcony, an undulating wave of terracotta rooftops swept down towards the centre, russet-damp tiles glowing beneath a sheen of steam and throwing the courtyard, indeed the rest of the city below the roofline, into dark contrast.

But like so much else in Italy, there was always sun if you knew where to look. I walked along our little Via Mirasole, then on to d'Azeglio, crossing the cobbled road and stepping up to the old orphanage – the Bastardini – where warm light flooded between the tall red-brick columns. I slowed along with the other pedestrians to savour every last lick of summer. The church bells, which seemed to keep their own hours, began to peal.

We had arrived at what I liked to think of as our 'English

summer', when the relentless Italian heat had tapered off and the city became habitable again. Rose might mourn the end of weekends at the beach, but I felt like I could finally breathe again, and while for my fellow Bolognese it was a minor tragedy they marked by switching to dark colours, today I stuck to the cream linen jacket of British Summer Time. On the whole, I didn't like to play the Englishman abroad, but it only felt fair to show my appreciation.

Even the broken lift at our office on Marconi did little to affect my mood, and after climbing four floors, I pushed through the varnished double doors, smiling at Alba, who rose from behind her desk. Her look of discomfiture alerted me to the couple waiting beneath the large abstract painting that dominated the reception.

'Daniel. Here is the family Lee. They are American.' She sat down, clearly relieved at having delivered a coherent sentence in English.

I knew instantly this would be about their child – the couple looked at me the way all parents did, as if I was a rescue vessel upon the horizon. But it was hope married with intense anxiety. Would they be able to attract my attention?

'The consulate in Florence sent us.' Mr Lee grabbed my hand. 'They said you were the best English detective in Bologna.' I nodded, although I would have taken it as more of a compliment if I hadn't been the *only* English detective in Bologna.

The Lees were of East Asian origin. Korean, I guessed from the surname, although they were certainly outfitted in the uniform of middle-class America abroad – chinos and Ralph Lauren polo shirts, blue for him, pink for her. Given my current get-up, however, I was hardly one to talk.

'Tell me,' I said. 'How can I help?'

'It's our son, Ryan,' said Mr Lee. 'He's disappeared.'

That English sun was slicing through the blinds into the Lees' eyes, so I pulled them closed. I kept the window behind open: the Comandante's office had had the weekend to rid itself of the old man's cigarette smoke, but I knew that even though he would refrain from lighting up in deference to the Lees, the legacy of his packet-a-day would reassert itself soon enough if I didn't keep the air circulating.

The pair were sitting on the bottle-green chesterfield sofa. I took a matching armchair opposite alongside the Comandante. Between us and our would-be clients was a glass-topped art deco coffee table, upon it a clean crystal ashtray, a pair of rarely opened hardback books on Bolognese architecture and, within a rather beautiful amber-stained Lucite box, fresh tissues. It could have been a gentleman's club or a therapist's. It sometimes felt like both.

'Ryan,' said Mr Lee, 'our boy, he's a *supertaster*.' He looked at me as if this explained everything. I looked at the Comandante, who clearly had no clue either. 'It's like perfect pitch,' said Mr Lee, 'only for taste. It means you've got more, literally more taste buds, but also . . . what are they? Smell? Smell buds? Anyway, cells or whatever's in your nose, and they combine, and, well, you can taste things other people can't, no matter how well trained – and actually, he was really well trained – can. No computer can do that stuff. That's what I said, wasn't it, Mary? No computer's going to be able to do that stuff, so Ryan, our Ryan's going to be just fine.' His voice broke. His wife took his hand and placed it on her lap. She began to explain.

While regular food tasters would sample food to assure its taste, smell, appearance and so on, supertasters, with their rarefied senses, were an elite breed and Ryan was flown in by clients around the world to check the quality of their wares.

The plan had been to meet them at the airport. He was often in Italy for work and they had always wanted to visit. This time they thought it would be great to meet up in Bologna, and maybe, if Ryan had the time, he could join them on trips to Florence and Venice.

Only he hadn't been there when they arrived. They had waited, called his cell but it had gone straight to voicemail. They had sent messages, but he hadn't replied – or even opened them, said Mr Lee – they had emailed from their hotel. That was two days ago, and there was still no trace.

'This isn't the same hotel Ryan's staying at?' I said.

Mrs Lee shook her head. 'Well, it could have been, but we booked it online, it was an offer. We asked the desk if he was there,' she added. 'Just in case.'

'So you don't know where he is staying?'

They looked at each other. 'I know this must seem terrible,' said Mr Lee. Mrs Lee squeezed his hand. 'But we didn't think to ask. I mean, we just expected him to be at the airport, or to get in touch. Ryan travels a lot. He's a freelance, has lots of clients. Always on the move . . . Italy, the South of France. His speciality is truffles.'

'Then his client here . . .'

'Like I said . . .' Mr Lee managed to look both desperate and ashamed.

'So we don't know his client.' They shook their heads. 'Never mind. Has this kind of thing happened before? I mean, a sudden loss of contact, disappearance, that sort of thing?'

'Never,' said Mrs Lee. 'He usually checks in every day. Calls, or at least sends me a message or email when he's in New York. That's his home; we live in the greater Vegas area, where he grew up . . .' She glanced at her husband. 'Even when he did the Appalachian Trail he called every few days and we were able to follow him on Facebook.'

'And there's been no activity there either?' I asked. 'Or on any other social media you're aware of him using?'

'Not since a couple of days before we set off,' said Mr Lee.

'And that was?'

'A photo of a store window,' he said. 'Full of truffles, cheese. Those hanging sausages . . .'

'Salami,' said Mrs Lee.

'Did it say where?'

'Hold on.' Mr Lee checked his phone, showed me the post. 'Boscuri.'

I took a note.

'We would like to have access to your social media, if we may. To see if we can find anything.'

'Of course,' said Mr Lee.

'And you've contacted friends, family . . .?'

'Nothing,' said Mrs Lee.

'In your regular calls, he didn't mention anything about the hotel?'

'Only that it was nice, central.'

'Did he say he was having any difficulties, problems?' They shook their heads once more.

'He never said much about his life,' said Mrs Lee. 'He was always asking us about ours.'

'Ryan's an only child?'

'How did you know?'

Daily phone calls. Dutiful son. The sense that they had cast all their hopes and dreams into the sole life raft that was Ryan Lee. I shrugged. 'You haven't mentioned any other siblings. Well, our experts can check online, and in the meantime we will also contact the police – the hotel should have registered him when he arrived. You haven't spoken to the authorities yet, I presume?'

'The consulate said to get in touch with you first,' Mrs Lee said.

The US consulate was as useless as the UK's, I noted. But their laziness was our gain. 'We'll need his details, photograph, hobbies . . . I take it he isn't married?'

Mrs Lee's eyes widened. 'I think we'd know.'

'Girlfriend, then?' I said. 'Boyfriend?' Now it was Mr Lee's turn to look surprised.

'He had a girlfriend at university,' said Mrs Lee quickly. 'But since he moved to New York . . .' She shrugged. 'So you're saying you can help us?'

I glanced at the Comandante, who gave an almost imperceptible nod. 'We'll get straight on it.'

Relief swept their faces, if only because something was finally being done, I supposed; they no longer felt alone.

'I'm sure everything will be fine,' I added, but I was already thinking about hospitals for Alba to ring around.

As I led the Lees out, I pictured Ryan in a coma somewhere. Secure mental facilities? He was in his late twenties

– the classic age for males to experience their first psychotic episodes. I added homeless shelters to the list. He could simply be sitting babbling and shoeless in a corner somewhere. Or worse. The morgue. She should try morgues first, I decided, if only to rule them out. We were by the lift. I shook their hands.

'Really,' I said, 'try not to worry. I'm sure it's just a mix-up.'

It seemed to help, Mr Lee in particular. I was 'the best English detective in Bologna', after all.

And kind words cost nothing.

Chapter 2

The Comandante's English language comprehension was excellent, but he had kept silent throughout most of the meeting. This was likely not due to his lack of language skills – I had heard him speak impeccable French – but to the importance of *bella figura*: literally cutting a 'beautiful figure'. The Comandante's English might be good, but it wasn't good enough in his opinion, and the importance of making an impression was hard-wired into his generation, even if the young, like his son, my brother-in-law Jacopo, seemed to harbour few reservations about ejaculating English as if it consisted wholly of half-heard pop lyrics.

But the Comandante had certainly understood the Lees well enough and was now surveying me curiously across the table at Epulum, a classic 'old man's' *trattoria* hidden behind a dark door beneath a narrow portico with grimy frosted glass shielding the clientele from curious passers-by. Beside the entrance was a yellowed menu barely legible behind a foggy plastic cover listing the classic Bolognese dishes: *primi* like *tortellini in brodo* and *tagliatelle al ragù*; *secondi* such as *bollito al carrello* – a boiled meat only true Bolognese could stomach

– and *braciola di maiale*; and for the finale, a binary choice between *zuppa Inglese* – a Bolognese chef's rather game punt at Victorian trifle – and 'meringue'. The original prices in lire were scribbled out and replaced in biro with figures in euros slightly above the going rate.

The hunched *padrone*, almost certainly an octogenarian, appeared at our table, notebook at the ready.

'I'll take the *cotoletta*,' said the Comandante. 'With truffles, the white.' The *padrone* nodded approvingly. 'And he will take – pasta, right?' I nodded. 'The tagliolini with porcini mushrooms, and black.'

Without asking, the *padrone* poured a ruby-red Otello Lambrusco into the Comandante's glass. I declined.

'I've work,' I said. 'And you know, Giovanni, I'm old enough to order my own food, thanks.'

An amused smile fluttered behind the curtain of the Comandante's neat grey beard. 'But you like truffles? The white have just come in season, you know.'

'So why, then, did you order me the cheaper black?'

'Well, Alba's always telling us we should make economies.'

'And you thought the white would be wasted on the Englishman. I think that's a little unfair.'

'Can you taste the difference between black and white, then?'

'Probably not,' I admitted. 'Can you?' He frowned: how could I even doubt it? 'If you ask me,' I said, 'it's just marketing.'

The Comandante prodded a *grissini* breadstick toward me. 'And that's precisely why you got black.'

I poured myself a glass of sparkling water. 'So tell me,'

I said. 'To what do I owe this honour?' If he wasn't lunching somewhere like this with one of his old cronies from the Carabinieri, Giovanni usually liked nothing better than to eat alone, accompanied by the latest lengthy comment piece by Ernesto Galli della Loggia in the *Corriere della Sera*.

'I'm concerned about this young man, Signor Ryan,' he said.

I nodded. 'It doesn't look good.'

'Well, perhaps Alba and Jacopo will turn something up.'

'Even Dolores,' I said.

'I remain to be convinced.'

'I know.' And I also knew he wasn't talking about the search for Signor Ryan. 'Although you could greet her a little less like you want to haul her in for questioning every time you see her.'

'Perhaps I will,' he said, 'when she does something about her ridiculous hair and clothing.'

'The fact that she doesn't look like a private investigator is the point,' I said. 'Anyway – Jacopo hardly dresses like Sam Spade.'

'Jacopo is my son. And he works on . . .' he made a vague gesture, 'computers. Dolores Pugliese is your, our, *employee*. And she is, now what is it they say? Client-facing.'

You've been gossiping with Alba, I thought, who was also no fan. 'Jacopo is an *employee* too,' I said brusquely. 'And I employed Dolores because she's bright, energetic, and clearly has an aptitude for our business, as she demonstrated on the Solitudine case.' I sat back as the *cameriere* laid down our meals. 'And anyway, we owed her.'

'We paid her back generously, in my opinion,' said the Comandante. 'By securing her release from gaol.'

'She's a good kid,' I said. 'Your real problem is that she's not a blood relative like Jacopo or Alba.'

The Comandante was leaning over his *cotoletta Bolognese* – breaded veal covered with prosciutto and smothered in melted Parmesan. He drew in the apparently refined aroma of additional white truffle, then looked up at me. 'Neither are you,' he said, although not unkindly, and the whole history of our relationship was conveyed within those steady grey eyes.

I certainly couldn't have got away with addressing any other Italian boss of his age and stature with quite the same licence had he not been my father-in-law, but then, were he not my father-in-law, I wouldn't have been sitting there in the first place.

When I had arrived in Bologna with my late wife Lucia more than a dozen years earlier, I had soon found myself helping out with the family business, first the security side – basically as a bouncer at a homeless shelter – then playing a more active role in Faidate Investigations, especially after Lucia's death, when it had been touch and go whether Rose and I would stay. But the Comandante couldn't bear to lose his granddaughter as well as his daughter, having only a few years previously also lost a wife, so we remained. In that sense – the work, I mean – I was one of the few lucky ones. The chances for foreigners of finding employment in Italy outside teaching English or some highly specialised discipline were approximately zero. The phrase *muro di gomma* – rubber wall – didn't just apply to Italian officialdom's notorious impenetrability, but also to the labour market. Only that weekend I'd read an item lamenting an expat survey voting the country one of the West's worst places to live, despite remaining one of its favourite holiday destinations.

Was that it? Had Ryan Lee confused the two? Behaved like a cosseted tourist in Italy when he had crossed the threshold into the tenebrous ecology of *Italia*? This was apparently Giovanni's fear.

'Supertaster,' he said. 'A sort of food detective, specialising in truffles, that most expensive *fungi*. I wonder if the consul would have been quite so relaxed if an American private investigator looking into the diamond trade had gone missing.'

'You noticed that too,' I said. 'Still, I've heard of "blood diamonds", but "blood truffles"?'

'You smile, my boy, yet it is a largely unregulated business, notoriously beyond the purview of the taxman. And once you step outside the law . . . well, you are always likely to come across unscrupulous individuals. It is not unknown for truffle hunters to take pot shots at each other, indeed for them to enter the woods and never return. Let us hope this is not one of those occasions.

'Signor Ryan arrived just as white truffles have come into season. For a specialist, that doesn't seem like a coincidence. A few shavings, barely a powdering on my *cotoletta* here, has almost doubled the price.' He picked up a *pane comune* – an unsalted bread shaped like a clam that fitted in the palm of his hand. 'Do you have any idea what a white this size would reach? Around two thousand euros.'

I looked at the bun as if it really were that precious.

'And they're currently digging them up in the hills around here,' he said. 'If they're lucky. A really big one could reach ten times that price, or more. Perhaps Ryan had been called to verify a find.' He shrugged. 'One hypothesis.'

'And something went wrong. He discovered something he shouldn't have.'

'Although experienced, he may have got out of his depth. The weak point of the young,' said the Comandante, 'especially, I imagine, individuals of the calibre of Signor Ryan, is confidence. Overconfidence.' He waggled his *grissini* at me again. 'That may be where the danger lies.'

'Why are you looking at me like that?' I said. 'I'm hardly a young man any more, Giovanni.'

'Ah, but if there is one thing we can be sure about,' his eyes twinkled, 'it is that you will always remain considerably younger than me.'

We went to the counter to pay.

'Mr Lee must have been visiting Boscuri for the truffles,' said the Comandante.

'Nothing like the Boscuri white,' said the *padrone*. He gave the Comandante a knowing wink.

'How *is* the market this year?'

The *padrone* made a satisfied smack of his lips. 'Can't complain.'

Giovanni chuckled. 'I bet you can't, you old dog.' He checked his watch. 'As Signor Ryan's photo indicated, they also have some excellent local cheeses. If you leave now, Daniel, you might pick us up a nice piece of truffle-infused pecorino for this evening.'

'Good job I didn't have any wine, then.' I was thinking about the tiring drive across the hills.

'Well,' said the Comandante. 'You did say you had work to do.'

Propped in front of the till there was a delicate model of a pig, apparently crafted out of a single piece of chocolate-brown paper, but without the rigid, automaton-like folds of traditional origami. This may have been down to the delicate paper, a kind of crêpe that creased like tissue, and in consequence the animal appeared much more lifelike. It was quite the work of art.

'Clever,' I said.

The *padrone* shrugged. 'Customer left it.'

Chapter 3

Bologna sits on the edge of the Po Plain, at the foot of the Apennine mountain range which runs along the spine of Italy. In fact the city was constructed upon the skirts of its foothills so the gradient slopes progressively upwards as you head south from the railway station, through the historic centre, until you emerge at Porta San Mamolo.

Cross the Viale, the ring road marking the border of the old city, and within minutes you have exchanged the press of *palazzi*, churches and towers sprung from the city's dark porticoes for jade-green slopes, precariously winding roads, and glimpses of ragged mountain peaks; Liberty villas, spa hotels, private hospitals, and, crowning the crest of almost every hill, monasteries. In a place where the mercury bounces around forty each summer, property prices rise with the gradient, and in the old days the Church had been careful to claim first dibs on the coolest climes. Those monks were no fools.

I had asked Dolores to accompany me to the countryside. She sat back in the passenger seat of the Fiat with her knees up against the dashboard like my fourteen-year-old daughter, although she was actually my twenty-three-year-old trainee investigator, a job title I had invented solely for her in the hope that it might remind her of her place. Some hope.

'You're kidding!'

'Well,' I steered the wheel fully one way, then the other, as we took the torturous route towards Boscuri, 'I'm not going to force you. But I can see what the Comandante was talking about. Don't get me wrong, I like the fact that you fit in with all the other . . . street people. The *punkabbestie, spacciatori* . . .' I meant beggars and drug dealers. 'It's one of the reasons we hired you, but it's not just about them.

'Look, Dolores, far be it from me to advise a lady on her . . . appearance, but you could consider a more . . . universal look.' Her hair was shaved on both sides and blue on top. She had also recently acquired a silver septum ring, and every time I glimpsed it hanging between her nostrils I had to remind myself it was not a sinew of snot.

'It's him.' She meant the Comandante. 'Once a pig—'

'Dolores,' I said. 'It cuts both ways. How can you expect him to treat you with respect if you speak about him like that?' I shook my head. 'I won't have you talk about him, about any of your colleagues, that way. If it's really so terrible, then you can always quit.'

She looked uncharacteristically humbled. 'Sorry, Dan,' she said. *Muro di gomma* didn't just apply to foreigners, and she knew I'd given her a break. But I also knew I was partly to blame – I'd taken a shine to her when she had helped us gain entry into the world of the squatting movement, and I'd hoped to harness the same energy and street smarts to solve future cases. But I'd neglected to take the 'trainee' part of her job any more seriously than she had. I would need to direct that energy if I didn't want to really lose her.

'It's just . . .' she said. 'He looks at me with such . . . *contempt*. I can't help reacting to it.' I couldn't wholly disagree, but there was a lot of stuff to unpack here, from the Comandante's own history battling would-be anarchists not unlike Dolores as an undercover *carabiniere* during the 1970s, to his not unreasonable expectation to be treated with the deference due to his status as the founder, and owner, of the business. They simply rubbed each other up the wrong way, but there could only be one victor in this battle of wills.

'Don't be fooled,' I said. 'In fact, I think he rather likes you.'

'Likes me? Come on!'

'Or rather, disapproves of you to such an extent that he thinks you'll prove his point for him – to me, the naïve Englishman. I may not listen to him, but maybe *you'll* teach me a lesson – why I was wrong to give you a chance, hire outside the family. Not him, but *you*, Dolores Pugliese, will show me how things really work in Italy.'

Dolores seemed about to respond, but thought better of it. She ran her hands through what was left of her hair and began to fiddle with the radio.

The road plateaued through a valley dense with grape vines, only a roofless tumbledown church interrupting regiments of yellow and ochre leaves, before we began to climb another ragged hill, sounding the horn as we turned 180-degree corners and intermittently pulling over when a car came in the opposite direction, or to allow an irritated tailgating local to pass.

Finally, there it was, across an iron bridge straddling a dried-out river bedded with chalk-white stones: Brigadoon – or rather, Boscuri. The Colli Bolognesi hid many such small towns, small worlds, really, given how inaccessible they must have once been. Even today you could still find old people speaking the local dialect, which sounded like a kind of Catalan; places that seemed, despite their bucolic setting, today's blue sky, to exist under a shadow, as if they had never fully recovered from the atrocities meted out by the Germans during the war – the area had been a centre of partisan activity – and now wanted only to be left alone.

But Boscuri, although it had had its fair share of partisans, had been spared a visit by the SS, and was one of the few settlements to actively court the tourist trade. In a few weeks, as it had done annually for almost forty years, it would host a truffle festival attracting vendors, experts, enthusiasts and tourists from across the globe. Sure, the most famous truffles might come from Piedmont or Umbria, but that didn't stop little Boscuri (population: 2,000) taking on the big boys. Throughout October, stalls would line the main street and the modest Piazza Cavour, displaying black and white truffles often laid out in jewel-like display cases, alongside freshly cured hams, local cheeses, and of course the wines of the Colli Bolognesi.

For now, however, the town lay dormant. My ageing Fiat Punto rattled along the cobbled street as shopkeepers, yawning and rubbing their eyes after their post-lunch nap, began to raise their shutters; school kids, having completed their homework, were released by mothers or grandmothers to hit the park opposite the heroically named Grand Hotel – a

three-storey ivy-draped edifice from the nineteenth century
that sat alongside the town hall, both, it had to be said, as
immaculately kept as the rest of the town. Even though it
was ostensibly a rural community out here in the sticks, every
pore of Boscuri reeked of truffle money.

We parked in the hotel car park among Porsche and BMW
SUVs, some bearing British, French and German number
plates, and walked back down the main street with the intention of popping into any likely-looking stores or restaurants
and showing Ryan's photo, a selfie he had taken in New York's
Central Park and sent to his parents: a handsome young man
with a buzz cut, wearing a soft black leather bomber jacket
and a purple T-shirt with partially covered silver script reading: *UN/IL/OO*, one line atop the other. He looked like he
was having a good time. And why shouldn't he? He had the
world at his fingertips, or perhaps that should be his taste
buds. In any case, he was in his twenties, forging a successful career, free of commitments. I vaguely remembered that
feeling.

I took one side of the street, Dolores the other.

Sending her off with her hair like that, in those big boots
and tight jeans, I hoped our conversation in the car would
suffice. We'd see. On the other hand, despite her appearance,
I – and others, I knew – encountered a different Dolores to
the one perceived by our perennially suspicious ex-Carabinieri
capo and his niece, Alba, the company administrator. A gre-
garious, amenable young woman who was about to step into
that *macelleria*, crack into a friendly smile and within a few
moments have the provincial butcher who had initially bris-
tled at her blue hair eating out of her hand.

It didn't take us long to work the street, or me to find the store Ryan had photographed. They didn't recognise him, but recommended I try the hotel – and of course, they had a point. It was likely that if he had made it out here, he might stay the night. But that hadn't been what they meant, explained Dolores as we headed towards it. The people at the restaurant she went into had said it was where the brokers met before the truffle festival came to town. That probably accounted for the foreign cars, and sure enough, the reception of the hotel was buzzing with middle-aged men – and it was only men – dressed in the countryside uniform of the well-to-do: yellow or red corduroy trousers, brogues, Scottish and English woollens. Striped Pink shirts revealed barrel chests beneath ruddy British faces; paisley bow ties and pocket handkerchiefs graced the more dapper French and Italians. Only the white-shirted or black-roll-necked Germans looked as if they really meant business, but the eccentric clothing of the others fooled no one.

Behind the bonhomie, hawkish eyes tracked our progress across the room; whether it was my linen jacket – possibly a somewhat eccentric agent for the Guardia di Finanza, the tax police – or Dolores, an obvious class enemy, which of us they registered as more of a threat was hard to say. Actually, it was obviously the taxman – they had long since won the class war.

I showed the photo of Ryan to the woman at reception, who said he looked familiar – she had seen a young 'Oriental' man here a few weeks ago but she couldn't say for sure; why didn't I ask Il Conte? She nodded towards the tall older man outfitted in a muted version of the clothes of the other Latins, sitting in a high-backed chair stroking a marmalade cat atop his long crossed legs. Although he was clearly Italian – and a count, no less – his thinning fawn hair and beaky, imperious nose were more General de Gaulle than Silvio Berlusconi, and as he looked up to greet us – he couldn't rise because of the cat on his lap – he had that vague yet very definite air of the aristocrat nurtured to view anyone other than their social equal with the forbearance one might grant someone else's children.

'Yes,' he nodded, inspecting the photo, 'the American lad. Extraordinary, a "supertaster". Aurelio had me test him – here, do you mind?' The cat was still sitting, apparently indifferent, on his lap. He indicated a dark wood case. I picked it up and laid it on the table. 'Go on,' he said. I flicked the brass catches. Inside, within velvet-lined padding, was a modern set of digital scales and some accessories.

'Are you really a count?' asked Dolores.

He chuckled. 'Technically, no. As you will know from your history lessons, young lady, the Italian Republic banned titles, so it is merely an honorific, granted to me by those familiar with the Malduce lineage. In today's Italy, a count doesn't "count" for much.'

'Malduce,' she said. 'Like the *palazzo* in Via d'Azeglio?'

'That,' he said, 'was constructed by . . . a later branch of the family.' I cleared my throat. 'Ah, yes,' he said. 'You see those?' Set beneath the scales was a series of glass vessels shaped like pill bottles. I pulled one out. Inside was a white truffle resembling a rather large dollop of used chewing gum. 'The American was able to tell their origin simply from the aroma, right down to the range of hills. Quite extraordinary!'

'This Aurelio you mention . . .' I said.

'Aurelio Barbero,' he said. 'Probably the foremost truffle hunter in these parts. I believe the boy was staying with him, for research or some such.'

Dolores and I looked at each other. 'And where can I find Signor Barbero?'

Count Malduce looked amused, as if he really was addressing a child. 'Il Cacciatore,' he said. He added in accentless English: 'The Hunter.'

Chapter 4

'What a nice old man,' said Dolores as we headed to the car.

'Some anarchist you are,' I said. 'When we first met, you'd have wanted to put his head on a spike.'

'Wrong,' she said. 'I've always been a pacifist.'

I vividly recalled the sight of a certain young lady wielding a machete at a law officer, an act, incidentally, that had almost got her sent down for attempted murder. But I wasn't going to remind her. *Acqua passata*. Water under the bridge.

The *trattoria*, Il Cacciatore, was about a kilometre outside Boscuri, back into the countryside proper, the narrow lane broadening out as it came into view by the roadside. We pulled into a sizeable car park overlooking the hills, an impressive but never pretty view – beyond those cultivated plains and valleys lay the *calanchi*, or badlands. Clay and gravel ridges as creased as elephant hide, crested by swathes of dark forest; spires of churches like outposts in hostile territory. Emilia had never been truly tamed like Tuscany, transformed into one vast ornamental garden. Its wildness remained indomitable. This was, and would always remain, partisan country.

The restaurant was clearly closed, but I had expected that.

It only opened four nights a week, plus lunchtimes at the weekend, which was enough, apparently, to keep it going – pretty impressive when you considered how far it was from Bologna. It was tucked down an unmarked lane, and had no website or listed telephone number.

We walked around the back and I immediately spotted the CCTV camera peering down at us from above a first-storey window, then another on the other side. Ruby lights blinked from both, suggesting expensive systems that were very much operational. Despite the rural setting, it would be a mistake to think it was all backward bumpkins and unlocked front doors in these parts.

The path led into the woods. We followed a ribbon of velvet maple leaves and, increasingly, the sound of barking, to a clearing with a large farmhouse, perhaps a century old, complete with a well at the front covered by a black iron lid. But there was nothing especially picturesque about the building, which, like so many of the houses in these parts, seemed not quite finished – two floors with an ochre facade and a tiled terrace incorporating an open junk-filled garage. Beyond the garage was a high mesh fence topped by barbed wire, at the corner a steel pole as tall as the house itself with a crown of CCTV cameras of the same genus I had seen before. Pressed against the fence, half a dozen excited Lagotto Romagnolo, the celebrated truffle-hunting dogs of the region, were clambering one on top of the other and generally looking delighted to see us, although given the lack of entertainment in these parts, I didn't let it go to my head.

'What's up?' I asked Dolores, who held back as I approached them.

'Nothing,' she said, staying put. 'I'm just not that keen on dogs.'

'Oh come on,' I said, 'how can you be worried by *them*?' Even I, who was agnostic about animals, couldn't help warming to the Lagotto breed. Typically a sturdy, medium-sized confection of dirty-coloured frizzy hair, they were one of the earliest recorded purebreds, originally used for recovering waterfowl in the marshes of Romagna. Once the marshes had been drained, the dogs had found themselves prized again, this time by truffle hunters, for their exceptional sense of smell and keen intelligence, which basically meant being smart enough to drop the truffle between their teeth and not transform a thousand-euro tuber into a tasty treat.

'I had a bad experience once,' said Dolores, edging closer to the fence. 'When I was, you know . . . poor. And everyone had a dog . . .'

'When you were on the streets?'

She nodded. 'Most of the dogs, you know, they were fine.' She was just behind me now, the Lagotto going wild. They had been corralled into a generous stretch of worn grass in front of a line of brick partitions beneath a mini version of the kind of terrace that ran along the front of the house. 'Except there was this one dog – it was one of those gang dogs, you know, I think someone called it a pit bull? Its name was Bruno. Anyway, he was always friendly with me . . .'

There was a metallic snap behind us. I looked around.

' . . . until one day—'

'Dolores,' I said.

'I was playing with him and . . .'

'Dolores.'

'What?' She turned around. 'Oh *shit.*'

The woman was holding the shotgun like a pro, the stock resting in the crook of her arm, both barrels pointing directly at our bellies. Had it been a rifle, she could have belonged to one of those all-female Kurdish army brigades, kitted out as she was in khaki combat trousers tucked into heavy-duty military boots, and a camouflage T-shirt, her only civilian items the red polka-dot scarf tying back her hair and the strings of hippy beads around her wrists.

She was large-boned, like a proper Emilian *contadina*, built for a tough life in the hills. Tall and broad, she had the brown skin that came from spending all year under the sun and not just a month on the Riviera Romagnola.

'What's with the stupid hair?' She tilted the gun towards Dolores, who raised her hands.

'Don't shoot,' she said.

The woman gave a lazy smile. 'This is private property,' she said. 'I could probably get away with it these days.' She meant with the proposed laws advocating for the right of property owners to shoot first and ask questions later. 'Just as long as it isn't in the back.' She looked as if she was genuinely considering it. 'That probably wouldn't look good.'

'We're trying to find Aurelio Barbero,' I said. 'Actually, we want to trace Ryan Lee, and we heard he might be up here.'

'Ryan?' Her face creased with concern. 'Aure!' she called. The dogs started going wild. 'What about Ryan?'

'He's gone missing,' I shouted over the sound of the Lagotto, my hands still suspended warily in the air.

'Missing? Aure! Get out here!'

'Yes, he's—'

'Hell's teeth, woman.' A man emerged from the doorway of the farmhouse in a red tracksuit and unlaced army boots, his tangle of grey hair and beard reminding me of Saddam Hussein after they had pulled him out of his hidey-hole. He looked just as irritable, too. He clumped towards us.

'Can we lower our arms?' I asked above the barking.

'What?' the woman shouted.

'Can we—'

'Oh yeah, yeah.' She looked down at her shotgun as if she had forgotten it was there. 'Shut up, you fuckers.' The dogs instantly quietened down.

'What is this?' Aurelio Barbero stood as sturdy as his partner, and seemed equally built, if not actually rooted, in this place. He had clearly been sleeping, which came as no surprise – although the practice was illegal, most truffle hunters did their work by night to keep the locations of their finds secret.

'He's here for Ryan,' said the woman.

Aurelio looked surprised. 'He's not here,' he said. He looked at her. 'Is he?'

'Of course he's not,' she said.

'Well, I don't know, woman. He might have paid us a visit this morning.' She shook her head. 'Well, where is he, then?' Now he was looking at me.

'That's the problem,' I said. 'He's gone missing. We are private investigators. From Faidate Investigations. We've been asked by his family to see if we can locate him. We traced his recent movements to Boscuri, then were directed here. Someone said he had been seen with you.'

'Hold on,' Aurelio said. 'You're not accusing us of—'

'We're not accusing you of anything,' I said. 'We just went to the Grand Hotel, and they said he was last seen there with you.'

'Yeah.' He looked as if he was finally waking up. He rubbed his face. 'I took the boy there last week. Showed him around, wanted to introduce him to some of the brokers.'

'You wanted to show off,' said the woman.

He snorted. 'Maybe I did. And the boy did well.'

'I heard,' I said. 'I was speaking to Il Conte.'

'Yeah, that's right. Ryan could identify the truffle right out of the jar, just by the smell.'

'So what was he doing with you, Aurelio?' I asked.

He gave me a sharp look. 'Wait a moment. How do I know you are who you say you are? You could be anyone. Do you have ID?' I showed him. 'And how do I know you're telling the truth, that Ryan really is missing or whatever?'

'You'll have to take my word for that.'

'What are you? German?'

'English.'

They looked at each other.

'You don't expect an Englishman—'

'I know,' I said. 'To be able to speak such good Italian. It's my father-in-law's firm.'

'Faidate. Of course. I've heard of him.' The Comandante's reputation as 'Bologna's honest *carabiniere*' lingered even up here after all these years. Aurelio looked at the woman again. 'All right,' he said.

Ryan had stayed with them for a fortnight, heading out with Aurelio and his Lagotto by night. As well as following in their footsteps while they stumbled over hillocks and down crevices in search of whites, he took various soil and plant samples, which he examined in a portable lab he had set up in their spare room.

'Why?' I said.

'What do you mean, why?' Aurelio looked almost offended. 'So he could identify the Boscuri white, of course.'

'But he's not still with you?'

The woman shook her head. 'Left a few days ago.' That made sense – he had told his folks he had a hotel in the centre.

'And he took his stuff, this . . . portable lab with him?' Aurelio nodded. 'And you haven't seen him since?'

They both shook their heads.

'How did he find you?' said Dolores. 'Is it some kind of holiday? Airbnb?'

'What do you mean?' said the woman.

'You know – like "come truffle hunting with a real truffle hunter", that sort of thing.'

'We don't do *tourism*.' She spat out the word, looked at Aurelio. He shrugged. 'My brother sent him,' she said. 'Len.'

'And who's Len?'

'Len Ligabue,' she said, as if that explained everything.

It did.

Chapter 5

I put my mobile on speaker as I drove and called the Comandante.

'Two words,' I said.

'Len Ligabue,' he replied.

'How did you know?'

'Our contact at the Questura provided the hotel details. The security manager kindly let me have a quick look in his room. No trace, although we should revisit with the Lees. I asked who was paying the bill.'

'Len Ligabue.'

'Yes, although interestingly the invoice address named him specifically and used his home address, not the business.'

'So . . .'

'We have already paid Antichi Artigiani del Cibo a visit. He's not there. They haven't seen him all day, although he was due in. We are on our way to the address given on the invoice at present. Would you like to join us?'

Dolores screeched: 'Look out!' I managed to lurch the steering wheel over just in time and our car turned up the bank of the road. A black Land Rover Discovery thundered

past. Sitting upright in the driver's seat, his hawkish pro-
file perfectly impassive, as if he had not even noticed us, I
glimpsed Il Conte di Malduce.

'Are you all right?' It was the Comandante. 'Daniel! Daniel!'

'Yes,' I croaked. 'We're okay. Just some idiot. Came up
behind us. Ran us off the road.'

'No need to rush, my boy,' said the Comandante, clearly
relieved. 'Take your time – we can wait.'

Antichi Artigiani del Cibo. *Antichi* was the equivalent of
'Olde' in English, so the company name could be translated
as Olde Food Artisans, although it didn't sound quite so tacky
in Italian. It was certainly on its way to becoming a cliché in
Bologna, however – *Antica Macelleria, Antica Magnèr* sten-
cilled in the same archaic script upon the same artificially
aged fronts, the same ceilings hung with peppered haunches
of prosciutto, counters heavy with wheels of Parmesan and
rolls of salami, a section reserved for a display of the perennial
black, and seasonal white, Boscuri truffles.

Come evening, these glass-fronted eateries would inevitably
be packed with out-of-towners and tourists, elbow to elbow
over a plate of *salumi* cold cuts and a bottle of Sangiovese.
Many of the traditional, somewhat half-arsed restaurants
like Epulum that had dominated the city centre when I had
arrived years before had simply not been able to compete, and
if there wasn't one of those ripe for a refit, then there were
always the former butcher's, ironmonger's or stationer's that
could no longer afford the rising city-centre rents.

Everyone had heard of the man behind Antichi Artigiani
del Cibo. I'd often seen Len Ligabue on talk shows and in the

weekend sections of the newspapers, where he was habitually pictured beside his chocolate-brown Lagotto, Rufus; more often than not, in fact, cheek to woolly cheek – Len Ligabue was immediately recognisable by his shining bald pate and bushy brown beard with its whimsically twizzled moustache. When set beside the legendary Rufus, with his own dark springy hair, the pair seemed like freaky siblings.

Signor Ligabue's address was in the heart of the city, behind a typically anonymous, albeit grand, iron-studded door along a vaulted portico in upmarket Strada Maggiore. The Comandante was waiting outside, holding a takeaway coffee cup.

'You survived, then?' He nodded cordially at Dolores.

'One of those big SUVs,' I said. 'They drive like idiots.' I looked at the brass plate beside the door. Where there might usually have been a dozen families inhabiting a sizeable address like this, here there were just three names beneath the Cyclops-like camera.

'I've actually tried Signor Ligabue,' said the Comandante, 'but there is no answer.'

I checked the time. Rose had her urban art – read supervised graffiti – group that evening, and I was taxi for both her and her friend Stefania. I bet Philip Marlowe had never had this problem.

I tried the bell myself, waited. The other two names were Ligabue, M., and Laurialo, V. I gave them a go. A woman's voice crackled over the intercom. I looked into the camera. '*Comune info,*' I said.

'You look like salesmen to me,' she said. 'No thank you.'

'She obviously means you,' said the Comandante. 'Would

you mind holding this, dear?' He handed the empty cup to Dolores and pulled a black plastic tube from his pocket. He flicked a switch. A dim blue fluorescent light came on. 'Excellent manufacture,' he said to me. 'It must be fifty years old by now. Brionvega, a fine Italian brand. Can you stand to the side, so you throw a shadow?'

There was a numeric pad set beneath the bells. He ran the light gradually down it to reveal dark smudges upon the numbers 4367. He looked at me expectantly, obviously meaning that I should press them.

'Are you sure about this?' I said. The Comandante's face clouded, then he seemed to understand. He turned to Dolores.

'Would you mind waiting out here, dear? Inconspicuously? If anyone does come in, perhaps you might call.'

'On it, chief.' She walked a few metres along the portico and set herself down cross-legged upon the pavement, tucking her phone beneath the jacket on her lap and placing the empty cup in front of her. She assumed a suitably wan expression.

The Comandante punched the numbers himself and began to push the door open.

'What I meant,' I said, following him through, 'was should we be doing this in the first place? If that woman discovers us, she could call the cops.' The Comandante frowned. 'Giovanni, really – you're not in the Carabinieri any longer.' Now he looked affronted. 'Well,' I said. 'It's the truth, no?'

He shook his head, almost pityingly. Gave my elbow a squeeze. 'Don't worry,' he said, weirdly, in heavily accented English, 'be happy.'

Chapter 6

Ahead of us lay a gloomy flagstone-paved corridor. Classical busts set in alcoves threw silhouettes across our path.

We passed a door that read 'Laurialo, V.' and then a gloomy inner courtyard dominated by a trio of banana trees. At the far end of the passage I could see greenery from a further courtyard, if not an actual garden, enclosed behind a pair of black ornamental iron gates. But before we reached them, the passage opened upon a staircase broad enough to wrap around a glass elevator. Cracked frescoes of skimpily clad mythical characters dashed up *trompe l'oeil* steps, mirroring the real ones, while above them, cushioned upon cotton-white clouds, cherubs and other obscure angels poked fun at their overlords.

The bells had indicated that Len Ligabue would be on the second and top floor, and the sweep of the staircase that it would be some climb. The Comandante didn't hesitate: he called the lift. I looked anxiously back down the corridor, but there was no peep from Laurialo, V.

The doors slid open. We rose through the staircase, passed the *piano nobile*, where I glimpsed a pair of doors topped by an age-worn clay family crest – a rearing goat, or perhaps ram, with the head missing, and a lion, judging by its claws – and arrived at the second. The Comandante expressed his surprise. 'If, as I presume, the *nobile* is home to his son, Marco' – he had clearly done his homework – 'then why live up here?' I understood his reasoning – didn't the Comandante occupy the *nobile* of our own home, the Faidate Residence, while Rose and I inhabited the apartment above meant for lesser relatives? Such was the Italian way – to begin at the top and work one's way down.

The lift doors opened. It was bright up here, with a view towards Bologna's iconic twin medieval towers, looming Asinelli, and Garisenda, her crooked sister. On one side of Ligabue's door stood a cactus – not the tiny sort you buy for the windowsill, but a full-size one you might come across in the American desert – and on the other, in contrast to the classical busts staring blindly from those alcoves below, a misshapen marble sculpture that looked like an elongated Henry Moore, although it was almost certainly by a lesser-known Italian artist.

I heard the jangle of electric guitar music, in fact the unmistakable, hesitant notes, heavy on reverb, opening Vasco Rossi's hit 'Vita Spericolata'. Just those few notes, repeating, like the theme to a Bologna-set spaghetti western.

The front door was slightly ajar. I was about to ring the bell when the Comandante stopped me. He unbuttoned his overcoat and from beneath his jacket produced a compact Beretta pistol.

'You're sure?' I asked. He nodded: he was sure. I rang the bell; the buzz was audible throughout what sounded like a spacious apartment. I knocked. 'Hello?' I prodded the door open. 'Hello? Signor Ligabue?' I pushed it further.

A neon-red question mark faced me through the gloom. As I stepped forward into the corridor, the light became brighter and the question mark cooled to a kind of ice blue. Framed sketches lined the walls. Some were modern scribbles, others finely detailed. I recognised one, I believed – a view of the Po Marshes, by Bolognese artist Mario de Maria – although as with the sculpture outside, it was just guesswork.

'Signor Ligabue,' the Comandante called. 'We are coming in!' He added to me: 'Keep trying, in case he's in the shower . . . or otherwise indisposed.'

'Signor?' I shouted. 'Signor Ligabue?' I followed the corridor to the right and found myself looking down upon an open-plan warehouse-style living space. A huge sofa faced an open fire set within a bare red-brick wall, logs slotted inside a rusted-iron holder sculpted like a wave. At the far end of the room, a glass staircase curved up to what I presumed was some kind of loft space.

'Signore? Hello?'

I descended the three steps into the *soggiorno* proper. The music was louder here. I looked around. There were expensive standalone speakers, but no visible sound system. Through the tall windows, the bulk of the church of San Petronio rose like a fortress above the red roofs; beyond, the hills – the monastery of San Michele fringed by trees and even distant San Luca were visible through the haze.

'When you've finished admiring the view,' called the Comandante. He gestured for me to join him by the stairs. I'd been wrong – they didn't lead to a second false floor, but kept going directly upwards into a tower.

'Well,' I said. 'You've got your answer.'

'What?'

'Why he isn't on the *nobile*.'

The Comandante peered up the glass steps as dubiously as he had the ones at the entrance. 'You check there, I'll do downstairs.' He tried to press the gun on me.

'It's fine.'

'Please,' he said.

'I don't even know how to use it.'

'It's simple,' he said. 'There's no safety catch, just point and shoot.'

I shook my head. 'Honestly, I'm safer without it.'

I began to ascend. I'd grasped immediately that Len Ligabue had nothing less than one of the city's legendary towers *in his living room*.

Before the grand *palazzi*, before even many of the great churches, Bologna had been a kind of medieval Manhattan, its ruling families building dozens of stone towers throughout the city to protect themselves and project their power. Over time, many had collapsed, while others had been torn down, recycled or topped off for safety reasons. I guessed this tower had been one of the latter, although as I continued to climb, glancing through the glazed medieval windows, I began to wonder quite how high I was going. I was still below Asinelli, which stood at around a hundred metres, but I seemed to be coming level with Garisenda. Yet Garisenda had to be fifty metres. Was that possible? Could I be *that* high up, despite nothing being visible from street level? Of course I could. Bologna was the city of hidden places – gardens blooming behind graffitied doors, porticoes masking *palazzi*. Why not a tower cocooned by one of those palaces? I looked up through the twinkling steps and kept going.

Then the music stopped.

'Hello?' Perhaps the Comandante had found the record player. 'Hello?' I emerged through a wooden hatch into an office.

Did I see the stopped turntable first, or the man? Either way, I instantly regretted declining the Comandante's offer of the pistol.

He was behind a glass and metal desk, his back to me – in fact, his arse. Bent out of the window, looking down. Although I could see neither bald pate nor beard, I knew instinctively that this was not Len Ligabue.

He straightened up. Turned. His face was pallid beneath cropped, prematurely grey hair. He looked like he had just thrown up. He lurched forward, slamming his palms flat upon the desk.

'It's Dad,' he said. 'He's down there.'

Chapter 7

'Marco Ligabue?' I said.

'He's not moving.' Then a look of terror crossed his face. 'Who are you?'

'Daniel Leicester,' I said quickly. 'Private detective. We found the door open. We were looking for Signor Ligabue. Your father, you say? Are you Marco?'

'You're not one of them?'

'Them?'

'Whoever did this!' The office was not as it should have been – papers, photos, pens and pencils were scattered on the floor. Half the desk was swept clean. Some books, too, had clearly been dislodged from the shelves.

I shook my head. 'He's outside, you say? On the ground?' I reached for my phone. 'I'm calling the police.'

'Call an ambulance!'

The operator came on. 'Ambulance,' I said, still watching him. 'There's been a fall.' Then I probably broke every rule in the book – I handed the phone to Marco. 'You explain,' I said.

He grabbed it. 'My father . . . What? Who am I? Marco

Ligabue. My father – he's in the courtyard. He's fallen . . . Where? The tower.' He shook his head. 'What? . . . It doesn't matter. He's not moving . . . *I don't know*. Look, I'm up in the tower and he's below, but he's not moving. That's the tower in our house. Strada Maggiore, 23b . . . Yes. Please. Please come quickly.'

He passed the phone back to me. Our eyes locked, then he made for the stairs. I made a half-hearted attempt to stop him, but I didn't really think he was trying to escape.

I listened to his feet clang down two steps at a time, then made my way over to the window and leaned out. Below – far, far below – a human shape lay crooked, face down, in the courtyard.

Really, Marco, I could have said, there's no hurry.

I found the Comandante waiting at the bottom of the stairs.

'At least you didn't shoot him,' I said.

'Marco Ligabue? He just ran past me. What happened? Did you find his father?'

'In a manner of speaking.'

We left the apartment. By the time we had arrived on the ground floor, Marco was at the end of the passage, trying to unlock the gate. An elderly woman was standing beside him, Laurialo, V. by the sound of things.

'Not that one. The other, you see . . . Oh, it must be the third. That's right.'

He finally got the gate open and rushed over to the body.

'It's you!' said Lauriola, V. to me. 'Did *you* do this? I'll call the police.'

'We *are* the police, *signora*,' said the Comandante. Lie or no, it seemed to do the trick. Salesmen, police – all tradesmen looked the same to her.

We crossed the courtyard towards Marco, and the body. Not a pretty sight – Len had clearly hit the dry fountain at the centre first, demolishing part of its oval bowl, before ending up at the bottom of the marble steps, covered by chunks of masonry. He was wearing jeans and a white T-shirt, I noted, although no shoes or socks. But then he had set out from home.

Marco was pawing ineffectually at his father's corpse, that bald pate dusted by debris, famous beard almost indistinguishable from the raspberry puddle around his head. His son tried to lift it up even as the Comandante was saying *no, lad*.

Too late – one side of Len's face had caved in, warped like a melted waxwork. In his horror, Marco dropped it before holding up his own bloody hands.

I heard an ambulance approaching. 'Better call the police,' I said to the Comandante. 'The real ones, I mean.'

He nodded. 'Of course, the lad is contaminating the scene with his own DNA. You should stop him.'

'Do you really think he did it?' I said, not moving.

The Comandante looked up at the tower, then back at the body. 'It hasn't just happened, if that's what you mean. The blood has congealed. Look.' He pointed to a line of ants trooping to and from the body.

'There's not much of a smell,' I said.

'It's been cool, with the rain.'

'You mean it happened over the weekend?' I said. 'But wouldn't the rain have washed the scene clean? It was really coming down.'

'It did,' he said. 'That's seepage. There was much more.' He drew shapes around us with his finger. It was true – we were about four metres from the corpse and standing upon crimson tidemarks. And the fragments of what I'd imagined to be the shattered fountain crunching beneath my feet as we had neared the scene turned out to be human teeth.

I looked away, anywhere. Back up at the window.

'An accident,' I said. 'Maybe he just slipped. Or jumped.' As if that made it any less gruesome.

'What do you think?'

I shook my head. 'There had clearly been some kind of altercation.'

'Terminal velocity,' said the Comandante. 'At such a height, there's no hope. Like being hit by a truck at a hundred and thirty kilometres an hour. If they meant to kill him, it was as sure as a shot to the head.'

I could hear the ambulance people running through the passage. Giovanni held up his hands. If they didn't recognise him personally, they recognised his authority.

'Crime scene,' he said.

Dolores was close behind. She froze, transfixed by the corpse. I tried to shield her, but she sidestepped me. 'It's fine,' she said.

We watched the male medic move Marco Ligabue gently aside while the woman crouched and, snapping on a pair of rubber gloves, felt for a pulse at Len's neck and wrists before reaching for a stethoscope. But there would be no surprises – that was clear to everyone, except perhaps his son.

My phone rang. It was Rose.

'Dad! Where are you? We'll have to leave soon!'

'I'm . . .' I looked back at Len Ligabue. 'A bit tied up at work, love. But I'll be there in time, don't worry.'

'Promise?'

'Promise,' I said.

'O-*kaaay*.' She sounded unconvinced.

'Her painting?' said the Comandante, who imagined he was coughing up for fine-art lessons. I hadn't had the heart to explain. 'You go.'

'You're sure?'

'There's nothing to keep you here that I can't . . . Oh.' He lowered his voice. 'I don't suppose you had time to photograph . . .'

'The office? As it happens, I did take a few snaps before coming down.'

'Good – it's my legs. The stairs.'

'Not your lungs, the cigarettes? You could always have asked Dolores.' I looked around. 'Now where's she got to?'

The Comandante pointed to a shady corner below the tower, dense with shrubs. 'At least the hair makes her easy to spot.'

I walked over. She was kneeling down, reaching into the plants. 'Dolores,' I said, 'I've got to go. I want you to stick with the Comandante. Do—'

She looked up. There was a dark form lying in a nest of flattened leaves. I instantly recognised that famous Lagotto, Rufus. His eyes were closed, a pale tongue poking from the corner of his mouth.

'I think he's alive,' she said.

Chapter 8

Another English summer morning, but today I had less of a spring in my step. I was on my way to meet the Lees.

I walked down the kilometre-long portico of Via Indipendenza, Bologna's Oxford Street, where the usual global clothing chains abutted local curiosity shops like La Coroncina, which had been supplying the Bolognese with nose-hair clippers and Scopa playing cards since 1694, rehearsing what I would say and how I would respond to their questions. Of course they had a right to know everything – they were paying, after all – but I didn't see how revealing that we had stumbled upon a murder as part of our investigation was going to help them, at least until we knew for sure that it was related to the disappearance of their son.

Ryan had been staying at I Portici, one of the most upmarket hotels in the city, apparently at the expense of the late Signor Ligabue. The Lees were sitting upon a black leather bench in the otherwise white marble reception, Mrs Lee again clutching Mr Lee's hand in her lap. They looked out of place in this largely business-fashion hangout, as if they had strayed from their tour group and should have had radio receivers upon orange lanyards around their necks. What a nightmare, I thought – not only losing your child, but doing so in a foreign city, every alien, albeit grandiose, setting now invested with malevolence, peril.

'We're here to see if there's anything you notice that might help,' I explained as we stepped into the lift, accompanied by the black-suited head of security, complete with transparent ear coil.

'You said you've already checked his room?' said Mr Lee.

'Briefly. Mainly to . . . make sure he wasn't there.' They apparently failed to pick up on the true purpose of Jacopo and the Comandante's initial visit – to check that Ryan hadn't been hanging by his neck inside the wardrobe or lying dead in the bathtub. 'Did your son mention anything to you about an Aurelio Barbero, by the way?' They shook their heads. 'Len Ligabue? No? You're sure? It's just that he paid for the room.'

'You found that out?' said Mr Lee. 'Have you spoken to him?'

I pictured Len Ligabue's smashed face, his son bent over his corpse. 'It's a lead we're following.'

'Thank you for everything you're doing,' said Mrs Lee. 'We're so relieved you are "on the case".'

'You're welcome.' I smiled awkwardly. The lift door opened.

'You saw the news then?' the head of security asked me in Italian. 'About Ligabue? Think this is connected?'

'I've no idea,' I said, grateful that the Lees couldn't understand.

'Are you going to inform the cops who was paying for Signor Lee, or do you want me to?'

'It's already done.' I smiled again at the Lees.

The security guy unlocked the door. It was a smart room overlooking the park. Not quite a suite, but large enough for a king-size bed, small sofa set and a writing desk by the window. In the ample bathroom there was a Jacuzzi-style tub with enough knobs and buttons to confuse all but the most experienced bathers, and a separate walk-in shower. Ryan Lee was obviously considered worth the expense. Not a bad job, supertaster.

'You say no one entered until yesterday?'

'He had "do not disturb" on his door,' said the security guy. Yet the place looked as if it had had a thorough tidy in any case – even the bed was made, with the sheets neatly turned down and the pillows plumped and placed side by side. 'I checked the CCTV between the time he last entered his room and when we were informed about his disappearance. Not a soul.'

'I'd like to have a look at the film of him leaving,' I said. I turned to the Lees. 'I imagine he's a very tidy young man?'

'Oh yes,' said Mrs Lee proudly. 'Ever since he was a boy, he's hated a mess.'

There was a series of guidebooks neatly stacked, by order of size, upon the desk. On top, a slim black plastic slab – a Kindle. I had been expecting to see a food or travel title on its screen, so was surprised to find the cover was Roberto Saviano's *Gomorrah* – an exposé of the Campanian mafia.

I paced around the room. No briefcase, computer ... I wondered what this 'portable lab' looked like. Whatever it did, I couldn't see any trace of it here.

I heard the sound of the wardrobe doors being drawn back,

followed by a little gasp – but it was just Mrs Lee finding her son's clothes all neatly hung up. She ran her hands through them as if they were divine relics.

I went over to the bedside – a phone charger, I noted, but no phone – and opened the drawer. Empty. I pulled it fully out, checked beneath the drawer and behind it. Crouched and peered inside, then got down and looked under the bed.

I came over to where the Lees were standing in front of the open wardrobe, asked if I could move the door across.

There was the safe.

'Could you?' I asked the head of security. He got out a card and punched in the long number that would unlock it.

Anyone hoping for revelations was going to be disappointed. There was a computer power lead, Ryan's house keys, his passport, and a credit card, which I took to be a spare for emergencies, precisely the kind of things a seasoned traveller would place here. All of this, in fact, only delivered bad news – that he hadn't planned to travel outside Italy, he certainly wasn't returning home; the computer and telephone leads showed that he wasn't thinking about going anywhere too far or for too long.

There was no sign of erratic behaviour. I checked the minibar – untouched. No note . . . I went back to the pile of books. Beneath the Kindle was an Italian dictionary, a thick red and black hardback titled *Truffles of the World: Soil Ecology, Systematics and Biochemistry*. The Lonely Planet guide for Italy. I flicked through it to the Bologna section and out fell a folded piece of I Portici embossed paper. A hand-written list of restaurants. I glanced towards the others. They hadn't noticed. I slipped it into my pocket. My phone rang.

'*Salve.* Signor Leicester?'

'Yes.'

'*Ciao.* Oriana de Principe. I'm a reporter for *Occhio Pubblico.* I hear you have a missing American.'

'Who did you hear that from?' I asked, playing for time.

'That's not important,' she said. 'Surely you'd like some publicity. Perhaps we can help.'

'That sounds like a definite possibility.' I looked at the Lees. 'How about you give me your number and I'll get back to you.'

'No need,' she said brightly. 'I'm downstairs.'

Chapter 9

Oriana de Principe, by contrast, did not look at all out of place in the reception of I Portici, despite being dressed in what I tended to think of as *Occhio Pubblico* combat wear – smart boots and jeans, a tight designer leather jacket and sweater, the kind of thing the TV show's female reporters sported on location, usually beside a police cordon, or harassing the husband (and implied murderer) of a missing woman.

Signora de Principe was sitting cross-legged and alert on the sofa by the exit. She carried herself with a self-possession I recognised from my own days as a reporter, and which instantly put me on guard. She must have sensed it too – she rose to her feet and waved as we came out of the lift so there would be no avoiding her.

'Someone you know?' said Mr Lee meekly. With her long raven hair and classic Italian good looks, Oriana de Principe was the kind of woman who made married men meek.

'Not exactly,' I said. 'She's an Italian journalist. There's a programme on national TV called *Occhio Pubblico – Public Eye*; it covers crime and missing persons. It's quite a big deal,' I admitted, 'that they're taking an interest.'

'You don't seem very enthusiastic, Daniel,' said Mrs Lee.

'It's not that exactly,' I said as Oriana approached us. 'It's just . . . Well, you have to be careful when you deal with the media.'

'But any publicity's got to be good publicity, right?' said Mr Lee.

'Let's see what she has to say.' We went to sit down.

'Would you mind translating for us?' Oriana asked.

'Then before we begin,' I said in Italian, 'who told you about the Lees?' Her cheerful expression didn't budge, but her eyes hardened.

'What's the problem, Daniel?' she replied. 'We're all on the same side, aren't we?'

'I was just surprised to find you here, that's all.'

'Oh, your office told me.'

'Who?'

'A woman. It's not a big deal. She was only trying to help.'

'Okay,' I said. 'And about the Lees? Since we're all on the same side.'

'A contact,' she said, looking me straight in the eyes, 'at the US embassy.'

'Consulate,' I said.

'Yeah,' she said. 'That's it.' She raised her eyebrows almost mockingly. We both knew that whether she was telling the truth or not, I was trapped. 'Anyway, why so worried, Sherlock? It's a great way to put the word out, unless you don't actually want to find this kid – you know, string the relatives along, milk them for some cash. Frankly, I've got a list of private snoops begging for exposure.'

'I just want the best for my clients,' I said. 'They're nice people, I want to protect them. You understand. Tell me: what makes our boy so interesting?'

'American. Supertaster . . . truffles. It's a real mystery, right? You used to be a journalist – it's a great story.' Ryan wasn't the only one Signora de Principe had done her research on, I thought.

'We've really no idea what's happened yet,' I said. 'We're at the beginning of the investigation.'

'And I'm here to help you.'

'But what if . . . and I'm definitely not saying this happened, but what if, for example, Ryan has been kidnapped?'

'Have you received any demands?' I shook my head. 'Well then.'

'But if he's been taken and you begin to publicise it, it could be worse for him – they might decide he's too hot to handle.' I glanced at the Lees. They were talking to each other while we babbled in Italian. 'They might even kill him.'

'*Dai*,' she said. 'You're being dramatic. *Occhio Pubblico* has a sixty-five per cent clear-up rate, way better than the police. You should have faith in us.'

'You'll press ahead regardless, then,' I said. She shrugged – of course. 'And Len Ligabue?' I asked.

'What about him?'

'It's all over the news this morning. You've not come up from Rome solely for Ryan Lee.'

'So are you saying there's some kind of connection?'

'No,' I said. 'And I hope you're not either.'

'Why should I?'

'Because it makes for a better story. All right, by all means talk about Ryan missing in Bologna. Go to town on truffles, supertasters, the lot, but don't explicitly connect the two – it won't help us find him.'

'Okay.' She gave me that hard look again. 'Unless there's an explicit connection. And you'll let me know if there is, right?'

'Right.'

The business with Signora de Principe concluded, I walked the Lees back to their hotel. It was as much caution as a courtesy because I didn't want the *Occhio Pubblico* reporter pouncing upon them once they were alone, regardless of her apparent lack of English; she was plainly no fool, a top reporter in fact, and I was sure she would find a way to communicate if she needed to.

From the Lees' hotel opposite the railway station, it was a direct, if unprepossessing, stroll back to the office at the other end of Via Marconi.

Marconi was a fascist relic – a boulevard that had been constructed over one of those grand canals that had acted as an artery into the city before the advent of the motorcar. Although it had taken a battering during the Second World War, many of the Futurist edifices remained, complete with Mussolini-era friezes featuring muscular Italians labouring in arms factories, or noble farmers baling hay, although casual viewers might be forgiven for thinking the buildings were from the fifties, sixties or even seventies – remove the bombastic art, and the style had survived the test of time. Even my late wife, no right-winger, had grudgingly observed that fascist aesthetics – which shaped every Italian new-build for twenty years between the 1920s and 1940s – could be pleasing on the eye. In any case, as in so many other Italian cities, the country's dirty architectural secret stood hidden in plain view – the tactical bombardment by the Allies that had preserved so much of Italy's patrimony had also served Mussolini's legacy.

Our building, however, was a genuine child of the sixties, which probably explained why the lift was always out of order. I took the stairs, wondering how the Comandante managed the climb. Alba looked up from her desk as I entered.

'Did you speak to the lady from *Occhio Pubblico*?' she asked excitedly.

'Oriana de Principe.'

'She's one of their star journalists,' said Alba. 'Covers all the big cases.'

'Yes,' I said. 'I thought I recognised her. When she called, what did she say precisely?'

'She just asked for you – said she wanted to talk about Ryan Lee. I gave her your number. I hope that was okay.'

'Of course,' I said. 'Did you mention where I was?'

'No.' She shook her head. 'I just said you were out. Why?'

'It doesn't matter.' I checked my watch. 'Is everyone here?'

'Except Dolores.' Alba smirked.

'Be nice.'

'What do you mean?' She was a picture of wounded innocence.

'I'm sure she has a good reason.'

'She always does,' said Alba. She snapped her laptop closed and followed me into the meeting room. The Comandante and Jacopo were already there.

'We may as well get started,' I said.

'Signorina Pugliese?' said the Comandante.

'Late,' said Alba.

'Like I said, I'm sure she has a reason. Well, a lot has happened since yesterday – not least the discovery of Signor Ligabue, who hired Ryan.' I looked at the Comandante. 'I suppose it's being treated as murder?'

'The dog, the mess in the office . . .' He nodded, then turned towards Alba. 'Dear?' She switched on the projector.

'You mean throwing the dog out of the window?' I said. 'What a nasty thing to do. It seems very . . . vindictive.'

'Or perhaps the contrary,' said the Comandante. 'The sign of a professional – the dog's barking; out it goes. All it really tells us is that it is unlikely to have been an accident or suicide . . . Ah, here we are.' The photos I had taken in the office. It wasn't my best work – I had been in a hurry to get downstairs – but it did the job. 'You see,' continued the Comandante, 'apparently some kind of struggle. I presume the Ispettore . . .'

'Alessandro?' I asked. The Comandante didn't really need to confirm – who else would he call but his old number two from the Carabinieri?

' . . . will carefully examine the corpse for defensive wounds, forensics and so on. You will note the desk is only partially bare, as if a body has been pushed against it in the struggle. The fact that the desk and cabinet drawers are closed suggests the office was not subject to a search, a hurried one at any rate. This reduces the probability of a robbery gone wrong. Furthermore, the Ispettore tells me Marco claims to have let himself into the apartment after failing to receive a response from his father, so the door was closed, and a lock like that could not have been easily picked. If the son is telling the truth, this implies that Signor Ligabue let his assailant or assailants into his home.'

'Where was the son over the weekend?' I said.

'Their house in the countryside, near Boscuri,' said the Comandante.

'Witnesses? Wife? Girlfriend?' The Comandante shook his head. 'Not looking good for Marco, then,' I said.

'Technically, although murderers usually take the trouble to fabricate more elaborate alibis.'

'And what does Marco know about Ryan?'

'The Ispettore has assured me he will ask him. Moving on, here we have enlarged some of the photos in an effort to see the documents, but those we can make out seem relatively innocuous—'

'I'm sorry!' Dolores burst into the room. I saw immediately that her septum ring had disappeared and the remainder of her hair had been cut to a short crop, now dyed black. Her face was smudged black too, and her hands were filthy. 'Someone stole the lock on my bike!'

'Surely, dear,' said the Comandante, 'you mean someone stole your bicycle?'

'No.' Dolores looked desperate. 'My lock. I wouldn't mind, but it cost more than the bike!'

We all burst out laughing.

'First,' I said, 'get your breath back and go and clean up. Then for heaven's sake tell us what happened.'

It had been at the animal hospital in Bolognina. She had gone over first thing to check on Rufus – I had meant for her to simply telephone, but I should have known, animal lover that she was, she would actually go and see him – and when she had come out, her bike was lying there with its rear wheel detached and the lock gone.

'Aurelio had some tools in the back of his van, so he helped me fix it. But that's why I'm late.'

'Aurelio who?'

'Barbero. He was there when I arrived. He had dropped Stan with Marco, then, as he didn't have a permit to park in the centre, he had gone on to see Rufus.'

'Stan . . .'

'Ligabue,' said the Comandante. 'Len's sister. I presume she uses that rather than "Stalin".'

'*What?*'

'Oh yes, it's quite common in Bologna. Have you never wondered why there are so many Ivans, Olgas and Nadias? The Ligabues' father was a particularly ardent communist, I understand, and went the whole hog – Lenin for Len, and Stalin for his sister.'

'Is that even allowed?'

'Well, technically,' said the Comandante, 'one cannot give a child a name that will expose them to public ridicule, but this was the early sixties, and everyone was a communist in that neck of the woods – former partisans, and so on. Any decision about the name would have been made at Comune level . . .'

'And everyone in the Comune was a communist.' I nodded. 'Poor Lenin, poor Stalin! No wonder she calls herself Stan. And how about the famous Lagotto, Rufus?' I looked at Dolores. 'What's the prognosis?'

'They're keeping him sedated,' said Dolores. 'They've

given him a scan. They think he will survive, but both front legs are broken and the skull is fractured. He did seem to perk up when Aurelio stroked him, though, so he must be able to recognise people.'

'Truly a silent witness,' I said.

'They could have a line-up,' said Jacopo. 'And the one he barks at, or cocks his leg against, could be the murderer.' Dolores shot him an angry look.

'Were the police present, dear?' asked the Comandante. Dolores glared at him too, then realised he was being serious.

'A van arrived when I was leaving. It had "Forensic Services" on the side.' The Comandante nodded.

'So,' I said. 'We can't ignore the obvious coincidence of Ryan Lee's disappearance and Len Ligabue's murder. But let's not lose sight that we are being paid to find Ryan, not get justice for Len. And if they are connected, this makes our search even more urgent.

'We have to ask ourselves: what could Len's murder actually tell us about what happened to Ryan? Why would someone want them both out of the way? What had Ryan discovered?' I looked at Alba. 'Where are we with his mobile records?'

'The Caserma said it would take more time because it was an American phone number.'

'Get back to them and drop Alessandro's name.' I looked at the Comandante. 'How likely do you think the Ispettore is to have tipped off *Occhio Pubblico* about Ryan Lee?'

'That reporter,' said the Comandante drily.

'She intercepted us at the hotel.'

'The Ispettore and I went for an *aperitivo* afterwards. She called Umberto then. I am quite sure he did not initiate contact with her, but there were a number of uniforms at the scene, and she is very well connected. You understand these journalists.' He looked at me knowingly. 'They can be like a dog with a bone. I suppose it is not beyond the realms of possibility that he threw her another, so to speak, to get her off his back.'

'Well, she's got her teeth firmly into the Lees now – there'll be a piece about Ryan on the programme, direct from Bologna, tomorrow evening.'

'You couldn't . . . dissuade her?' said the Comandante. 'If Ryan is alive . . .'

I smiled. 'She's well aware of that, but his safety palls in comparison to a prime-time slot.' I checked my watch. 'With that in mind, I suggest we get moving.' I pulled out the list of restaurants I'd found in Ryan's hotel room. There were more than twenty. 'They'll be opening for business soon.' I pointed at Jacopo and Dolores. 'We'll split up.'

Chapter 10

Despite the faux-aged fronts of the Antichi Artigiani del Cibo franchises dominating the prime positions in the city centre, down *vicoli* – narrow lanes – in basements or along back streets, Bologna's old restaurant culture clung on. Much of this was due to the sheer scale of a city that boasted the largest intact medieval centre in the world – it had been the Manhattan of the Middle Ages in more ways than one – but it was also because of all the business that flooded in from 'outside the walls', as anywhere beyond the old city gates was commonly termed. Living within the walls, it could be easily forgotten that Bologna was Emilia Romagna's capital, with a greater metropolitan population of over a million, many of whom came into the historic centre for work or play. Added to that, of course, there were the dozens, if not hundreds, of restaurants spread across the conurbation.

Based on this, twenty-four restaurants seemed a rather modest hit list for our supertaster if his intention had been to sample the dishes in every one, although I supposed there was only so much tasting even an expert could do. I noted there was not a single Antichi Artigiani del Cibo restaurant on the list.

What precisely had Len Ligabue been trying to discern from his competitors? And why?

I gave Jacopo the restaurants furthest afield – he could get there on his Vespa – with Dolores the ones around the fringes of the walls, because she did still actually have her bike. 'But before you begin,' I told her, 'buy another lock. Make sure you get a receipt – we'll put it on expenses.'

'*Thanks*,' she said. This had clearly never occurred to her.

'And compliments, by the way, on the new look.'

She gave me a little bow. 'Maybe I should put that on expenses too?'

'I don't think I could get it past Alba. But thank you anyway.'

'What for?'

'Making my life easier.'

'I realised you were right,' she said. 'Sitting outside Ligabue's place, pretending to beg. That's what I'd only ever be good for in the Comandante's eyes unless I did something about it.' She climbed onto her crappy bike and headed off down Marconi.

I looked at the list and tried to make a mental map of my route. It would be *very* roundabout, but if I did it properly, and didn't get held up, I could make it to the final restaurant on the list – Da Mauro on Via Solferino, close to where we lived – by lunchtime. I sent Rose, and Alba, who would usually be doing the cooking at home, a message telling them to meet me there for half past one, then got going. We weren't called gumshoes for nothing.

***

The first place I visited was Da Norma in Via Polese, a street running diagonal to Via Marconi.

In Bologna there were restaurants you went to and restaurants you didn't. I couldn't see any particular reason for this most of the time – Da Norma appeared much like every other restaurant I visited (and I visited a lot; in Italy they filled the social and physical vacuum of the pub) – but there were just some restaurants that you had either never been invited to, or that were too close to your regular places, so that after a while it seemed almost improper to enter them. Da Norma was one of these places. I had often passed it, packed with its own regulars with their own favourite dishes (albeit the *primi* and *secondi* would be much the same as at the establishments I frequented), glancing in as if it was a sort of alternate universe, perhaps one in which another me ate with a different social circle, in a different life.

I stepped inside feeling vaguely sheepish, as if they only had to look at me to know my secret. Would I be welcomed after spurning their attentions for so long?

It was still early, not even midday yet, and they were just setting up for lunch. The waitress held up a hand and said to me – in English, I noted, as if only a stupid foreigner would think they could eat this early – 'We no open yet.'

'I'm not here for that,' I replied, in Italian. 'I'd like to see the owner; are they about?'

'What do you want?'

I pulled out the photo of Ryan. 'I've been asked to trace this missing person. An American. Ring any bells?' She was shaking her head before she had even looked at it. 'Please,'

I said. 'Take a careful look. His mother and father are very worried.' Mentioning family to Italians is always a helpful emotional prompt, just as telling someone they are *maleducato* – badly brought up – is the ultimate insult.

'No. I mean, I can't say for sure, but . . .'

'He would have been here at some time over the past five days.'

'How do you know?'

'He's a . . . restaurant reviewer. For an American website. Big food fanatic. He specialises,' I picked up the menu, 'in truffles.' A piece of paper had been inserted announcing the special dishes featuring Boscuri whites. 'You were on his list.'

A waiter came out, and I explained again. Then an elderly woman – this must be the *padrona* – a clearly tough cookie who softened the instant the waitress mentioned Ryan's mamma but couldn't help either. It was only as I was making my way out, leaving behind one of the batch of photos I had made, that a young guy arrived – another waiter.

'Domenico! Do you know this guy?'

'Him? Yeah, of course! The weird American.'

'Did he say anything to you?' I asked. 'Other than his order?' Domenico shook his head. 'And *what* did he order?'

'*Primo* and *secondo*. Both with white truffles. Pretty crazy. And . . . he didn't eat that much – in fact, I asked him is everything all right because he'd left half the pasta, two thirds of the *cotoletta* – that dish alone, thirty-five euros! – and he's, yeah, yeah, fine, I just love the taste. I was thinking, crazy American, but it was true, he really seemed to take his time over every mouthful. Even though he barely ate his food, he was there as long as if he had. And he had nothing to drink

– just fizzy water, I mean, which he rolled around his mouth after every taste as if it was fine wine. Oh, and he made this incredible paper monkey.'

We followed him to the cashier's desk. Behind it, there it was, clinging to the neck of a bottle of Sicilian *amaro*, its broad face sporting a contented, if unsettling, smile.

'Can I take a look?' I asked.

He reached over and plucked it off. 'Mad, isn't it,' he said. 'How he did it, I've no idea. There he was, I thought, just playing with some paper between courses, and then at the end he presents me with this! Really, a work of art . . .'

'He didn't give you a tip, then,' said the waitress.

'Come on,' said Domenico. 'This is a thing of beauty.'

'I'd prefer the money,' said the woman.

'When was this?' I held it up to the light. There didn't appear to be any messages concealed in its creases.

'Last Thursday . . . No, what am I saying, Thursday I'm off. Must have been the Wednesday.'

'Was he with anyone?'

'No, alone. I guess that's why he had plenty of time to do the model.'

'I don't suppose I could have it?' I said.

He snatched it back. 'It was a gift.'

I took a photo. As I left the restaurant, I forwarded it to Jac and Dolores, telling them to look out for something similar.

As it happened, Epulum, where I had seen the model of the pig, was next on my list. I arrived as they were opening up.

The *padrone* was not quite as accommodating as he had been when I had been accompanied by one of his long-standing customers. He clearly had the restaurateur's innate sense – as refined as any Lagotto's nose – of the whiff of scandal. He shook his head.

'Not that I recall,' he said.

'But he left that paper model,' I said. 'Where is it?'

'Oh, yeah. *That*. Him. Yeah.'

'The model?'

'No idea.'

'I gave it to a little girl,' said an elderly woman, quite possibly the *padrone*'s wife.

'Do you remember this guy?' I said. 'He's missing. His mother is very worried.'

The woman frowned. 'I think I may have glimpsed him.'

'Do you know when he was here? Day, time?'

'The Saturday lunchtime,' said the *padrone* immediately. He looked over my shoulder at a well-dressed elderly couple entering. 'Now, if you please . . .'

'*Signora*?' I said to the woman. 'Anything else?' She looked as if she was really thinking about it, but shook her head. 'I'll pray,' she whispered. 'For his safe return.'

I arrived at Da Mauro more or less on time. Following my initial success, I'd struck out at the other places on my list, which had no recollection of Ryan, or any of his artwork, except for Solferino, the *trattoria* in the same street as Da Mauro, where the *padrone* remembered the polite young man who had consumed just half of his braised beef, garnished with Boscuri white, and left a finger-sized model of the Statue of Liberty, which the cleaner must have thrown away.

'So that's a mystery,' I said to Alba, who was positioned

with Rose by the window. Despite it being well into lunch-time, Da Mauro was half empty – the empty half in question being occupied by a long made-up table in the middle of the restaurant, presumably awaiting a party. I looked over at the bar to see if I could spot any more paper models.

'Not if you had bothered to actually read the questionnaire you asked the Lees to complete,' said Alba. 'It's his hobby – a Korean form of origami called *jongi jeobgi*.' Her pronuncia-tion made Rose giggle. 'That's how you say it! I was interested so I looked it up online. It's amazing what they can do.'

'Well,' I winked at Rose, 'that's one mystery cleared up.'

'Have you noticed,' Alba addressed Rose, 'how forgiving he is of his own mistakes? He's not like that when you don't do your homework, is he?'

'No.' Rose shook her head. 'He's *not*.'

'Watch and learn, dear. There's one rule for men in this country, and one for us.'

'That's a bit harsh,' I said. 'We don't have to be here. I invited you because I thought you'd like a break from the kitchen.' I regretted my words even as I said them.

Alba smiled. 'See how they use their economic power to think you owe them something?'

Rose nodded, drinking it in.

'Is this really necessary?' I said.

Alba assumed a rather Teutonic accent that I believe was supposed to be mine. '*Is this really necessary?*'

Rose clapped. 'That's just like him!'

'You've got to be kidding.' I tried to signal the waiter.

'They hate it when the shoe's on the other foot,' said Alba. 'When they're the butt of the joke.'

'Next time I won't bother.'

'Next time I won't cook you lunch!'

I decided it was best to steer clear of the minefield of Italian feminism. I knew Lucia had emigrated to the UK, where we had met, at least partly to escape the kind of macho behaviour Alba was accusing me of, but had I really imbibed the culture to the extent that I had begun to ape the average Italian male? I told myself no, but couldn't escape the uncomfortable feeling Lucia was up there somewhere applauding her cousin from a women-only cloud.

I ordered a simple *primo* of *orecchiette ai broccoli* – I was already getting sick of truffles, though not so Alba, who somewhat deliberately ordered the tagliolini with Boscuri white as we were on company expenses, and was joined in her choice by Rose, her new protégée.

'Save some space,' said the waiter. 'There's cake too, on the house to our regulars.'

I glanced towards Mauro, looking particularly grave behind the bar. 'That's very generous,' I said. Generosity was not a quality for which Mauro was renowned – 'regulars' we might be, but we usually didn't even get our coffee *offerto*.

'There was a *laurea* party today,' the waiter said in a low tone. 'Only it was cancelled at the last minute.'

'The student failed their final exam?' I asked. *Laurea* meant graduation, commonly marked by an oral exam in front of a panel of professors with friends and family – who had often travelled to the city for the first time – in attendance. Although it sounded like an ordeal, in reality, providing the student had completed their thesis to the satisfaction of their tutor, it was usually only a formality.

The waiter tutted. 'They'd made the whole thing up – the parents only found out when they came up from Molise for the ceremony.' There was a collective intake of breath around us; the other tables had been listening in. The faked *laurea* was every Italian family's worst nightmare, and not uncommon in Bologna, the oldest university city in the world.

'And how is the child?' said an elderly man sitting with his wife.

'Oh, all right apparently,' said the waiter. 'At least the mother didn't say worse.' We all knew what that meant – *Occhio Pubblico* regularly featured young people who had gone missing after having faked a university career right up to the moment of the supposed *laurea*. In a nation where education remained the pinnacle of accomplishment – and the title *dottore* was employed as a real mark of respect – few had the courage to confess to proud parents that they had failed to make the grade.

These kinds of disappearances were common – we dealt with two or three a year – and a pretty easy source of income, because the kids usually wanted to be found, even if they didn't realise it themselves. It was more a cry for help. But these were the happy endings – reconciling the young person with their relieved parents. For some desperate individuals there appeared to be no escape, and the entire restaurant knew what the waiter really meant by 'worse': suicide.

Still, we appreciated the free cake.

Mauro looked blank when I showed him the photo of Ryan, along with the model from Da Norma. Alba then headed back to the office, while Rose and I went home. I was pretty wiped out after almost three hours on the street. I could access everything from my home computer or mobile anyway, and although my calendar was free for the afternoon, that evening I had another work appointment. It would be good to spend some time with Rose now her school day had come to an end, even if that meant her doing her homework on the kitchen table then shutting herself in her room to play on her tablet.

We turned into quiet Via Mirasole – literally, 'Look-at-the-sun street'. There may once have been a time when you were able to feel the sun on your face in Mirasole, but not for at least half a millennium, as the buildings shot up and squeezed together. In fact, despite its historically sought-after position in the south of the city, it had been notorious for brothels until they had been shuttered in the late 1950s, almost every one of the doors in the tunnel-like gloom of the low-slung portico running along the south side once containing a house of ill repute.

Although perhaps this was less than coincidental – most of those pretty-as-a-postcard *palazzi* on Via Solferino had contained secret exits onto Mirasole, while in the other direction, across the Viale, were the great monasteries that had once been packed by holy men with vows of celibacy.

And sandwiched in between the aristocrats, the whores and the Roman Catholic Church had sat La Famiglia Faidate, origins obscure, but ownership of La Residenza dating back to the seventeenth century. The building long preceded the family – the ground floor and the four-metre-high bricked-over battlements fronting Mirasole had been constructed in the late fourteenth century by a family of traders, undoubt-edly upon ruins left by the great earthquake of 1346 that levelled much of the city. Further down, in the *cantina*, there was recognisably Roman brickwork, and an archaeologist commissioned at the insistence of the Superintendent of Fine Arts when we needed to strengthen part of the foundations to deal with subsidence had found Etruscan remains, although apparently nothing of historical significance, which at least meant we were able to stop the floors parting from the walls.

The ground floor of the Residence was a mix of impractical spaces; once used as stables, workshops and servants' quarters, they now housed storerooms, Jacopo's 'space' (variously a rehearsal room for friends' bands, a studio for artists, and a photography gallery, but mostly left cold and empty), and an apartment converted in the 1960s for Lucia's great-grandmother's carer but now occupied by Alba. The rest of the family lived on the first and second floors, which had been added during the late Renaissance, with their part-frescoed (those parts that hadn't crumbled with age) Romeo and Juliet balconies. The Comandante was on the *nobile* and Rose and I above, along with Jacopo on the other side of the landing.

La Residenza was the kind of place our Anglo-Saxon guests inevitably gasped had *tons of potential*, and the Briton inside me still felt a little guilty every time the automatic courtyard doors opened and my inner home-renovation TV show kicked in. But the Italian I had become closed the automatic gates behind us and followed his daughter up the time-worn steps in the certain knowledge that no amount of transformation would change the fact that we were all little more than custodians of the place. The Faidate Residence, even those fractured frescoes, would persevere long after we had left. In a city that often seemed like a stage set for Shakespeare, we truly had no more permanence than players.

I closed the front door behind me. Rose unloaded her books onto the kitchen table with a long teenage sigh.

My phone buzzed: it was a message from Dolores.

I think I've got something.

Chapter 11

I sat down in my office, which was really just a stretch of hallway between the kitchen and the living room, and switched on my computer to Skype Dolores.

'Hey.' She was sitting on a park bench somewhere in the suburbs puffing on a roll-up cigarette – well, some things hadn't changed. 'I'm in San Donato.' She meant the quiet, post-industrial workers' area in the east of the city. 'It could be nothing.'

'Tell me.'

'Didn't find a thing at the other places I visited, but this one – Tavola Felice – they had a model, of St Francis.'

'St Francis?' I said. 'Is it a figure with its arm raised? A guy told me it was the Statue of Liberty.'

Dolores shook her head. 'I didn't see that. I saw St Francis of Assisi. There was the bird in his hand – right?'

'I didn't see it. The guy must have thought it was a torch.'

'Well, the manager and I both thought it was St Francis. Anyway, he just found it there when he came in. But that wasn't the thing.'

'What *was* the thing?'

'When I showed him the photo, he didn't recognise Ryan, but he thought his T-shirt seemed familiar.'

'Really?' I reached for the photo, peered at the purple T-shirt beneath Ryan's bomber jacket, the silver lettering: *UN/IL/OO*.

'He said he's seen one of the kitchen staff wearing it, or something like it. He couldn't remember what it said exactly. Just the English words "sun" and "moon".'

'This guy . . .'

'One of the cooks,' she said.

'And . . .'

'He wasn't there – he's supposed to come in this evening. I know,' she said, judging my reaction, 'I told you it was a long shot.'

'Not at all,' I said. 'Good work. Along with the model – St Francis – it's quite a coincidence. I mean . . . this T-shirt. How common could it be?'

Dolores shrugged. 'I've no idea.'

'Did the manager have any other details?'

She shook her head. 'At first he seemed keen to tell me, but then . . . I don't know. Apparently the cook is from India. Ishaan, he said his name was. But then he clammed up. Said he didn't know his surname, phone number, and so on. I didn't want to push it.'

'You did well,' I said. 'Look, it may be nothing, but would you mind heading back there when the evening shift begins?' I thought about it. 'Get Jacopo to join you.'

'I can do it.'

'I know you can. But just to be on the safe side – you never know.'

She took another appreciative puff. I wondered: was that *only* tobacco she was smoking?

'Jacopo doesn't need me to look after him,' she said.

'Maybe he can keep an eye on that new bicycle lock of yours,' I said. She rolled her eyes.

I googled *sun il moon* and the first entry was a Wiki on Sun Myung Moon, founder of the Unification Church – or Moonies, as they were more commonly known. My world froze. I pictured the Lees sitting in the hotel reception hand in hand, the personification of the unassuming middle-class American couple. Had that just been a ruse? Was their son actually on the run from a *cult*? I pushed myself back from the desk.

'Are you all right?' Rose was standing there with a pencil in her hand. 'You gasped.'

'Fine.' I thought back furiously over the preceding forty-eight hours. No, that wouldn't make any sense. None at all. 'Nothing to worry about.'

'Then why did you shake your head when I asked?'

'To be honest,' I said, 'for a moment I thought I might have made a dreadful mistake.'

'With this missing man?'

I nodded. 'But it's fine.'

'You're sure?'

'I think so, yes.' There really was nothing to suggest the Lees were anything other than the concerned parents they said they were. For a start, if they had wanted to track Ryan down and return him to a cult, that still wouldn't explain why he had gone missing from his hotel room, or point to any connection with Len Ligabue.

Expelling a relieved breath, I looked back at the computer.

In the line above the entry I noticed the query: *Did you mean sun* kil *moon?*

I clicked on the link, and things began to make a little more sense. Sun Kil Moon turned out to be the stage name for a San Francisco based singer-songwriter who had taken inspiration for his name from Korean super flyweight Sung Kil-Moon.

I searched Ryan Lee and Sun Kil Moon together and immediately came up with a smattering of social media – a couple of Twitter posts, a fan forum.

Jacopo had already plunged into Ryan's digital presence but drawn a blank vis-à-vis his work trips, whether they were in France, the US West Coast, or Italy; he was professionally reticent about his movements. It appeared that with leisure, however, he was as enthusiastic as any other twenty-something, and a big fan of Mark Kozelek, the artist behind Sun Kil Moon, even though the singer-songwriter was old enough to be his father. But that was not the point: with his heritage, I could see why the fusion of Korea and America in the name might have attracted his attention, and why he would like the music, too. Many of Kozelek's songs were imbued with the kind of world-weary melancholia I could imagine a frequent-flying American, perhaps something of an outsider, a romantic even, relating to.

Nonetheless, Kozelek was hardly a household name, and his milieu seemed, quite literally, half a world away from what I might expect of a migrant kitchen worker. Italy was not exactly what you could call multicultural – I couldn't think of a single non-white Italian currently above the lowest rungs of society. Not one black or Asian doctor, lawyer, journalist or showbiz celebrity. Italy's immigrants tended to be new, and as a consequence, confined – if not through choice – to their own culture.

So while it was not inconceivable that this cook was simply another Sun Kil Moon fan with precisely the same T-shirt as Ryan Lee, given that even I had never heard of the chap – and he was from my generation, apparently banging out precisely the kind of morose melodies I enjoyed listening to and that drove my daughter crazy – it seemed a bit of a stretch to imagine the lad was also an admirer. If so, perhaps we could begin a Bologna chapter of his fan club. But Dolores had a point – less reassuring scenarios seemed worthy of investigation.

Chapter 12

Cross most piazzas and you could be forgiven for believing that Italy remains ethnically homogenous, yet the country has a similar level of immigration to other western European states.

Most of Italy's newcomers are 'invisible', hailing from Eastern Europe – Albanians, Romanians, Ukrainians. They are known as *extracomunitari*, a term that in the stratified northern Italian consciousness has substituted the old pejorative *terrone* – 'people of the soil' – once aimed at their southern compatriots. (Indeed, *extracomunitario* – meaning literally 'outside the European Community' – has very similar connotations, even if some, like the Romanians, are now EU citizens.) These are Italy's builders, cleaners, carers, manual labourers – tolerated, exploited and, on the whole, viewed with the kind of suspicion that used to attach itself to anyone who came from south of Rome.

My Italian friends derived a great deal of amusement after the Brexit vote by teasing me that I too had now become an *extracomunitario*. The truth was, however, that although it was technically accurate, it didn't really apply to me any more than to Americans or Australians. The small British community in Italy remains at the top of the immigrant tree along with foreigners from other wealthy countries.

Non-white people, however, exist mostly out of the corner of one's eye. You might be approached by an African lad begging in the street while his application for asylum is being processed. Rejection will rarely spell physical removal – you glimpse him now from the train or *autostrada* bent in the fields for twenty euros a day. Tens of thousands of undocumented Africans are left to labour in this legal purgatory, presumably because of their contribution to Italian agriculture.

Paler skins signify a slightly more privileged place, albeit usually maintaining at least one foot in the shadows. The restaurant's kitchen door swings open as the white Italian waiting staff navigate between courses, and there, behind the scenes, are the Indians, Sri Lankans, Bangladeshis, Pakistanis. And they're not just washing up. Away from the gaze of diners, those traditional dishes – that signature lasagne or *tagliatelle al ragù* – are often being prepared by someone raised eating not Nonna's *tortellini in brodo* but her curry dhal.

This was the group to which Ryan's T-shirt wearer appeared to belong, and although I was ready for it all to be a wild goose chase, I had a bad feeling. Racism wasn't the only reason such people were kept out of public view – human trafficking had taken off in a big way in recent years. And where you had trafficked people, you were only one remove from people traffickers – and hardcore criminality.

'You could at least look pleased to see me.' Oriana de Principe had ditched her combat gear for a slinky silver dress and heels, but I wasn't fooled; it was simply a different form of armour. We were in the foyer of her spa hotel, a plush, if somewhat soulless, spot on the outskirts of the city commonly used for business conventions and, I knew from our frequent visits here, extramarital affairs. It was close enough to the outer ring road to facilitate quick and easy access during *aperitivo* time, so that adulterers could report at the family dinner table by eight o'clock.

'Just nerves,' I said. 'I always look this way when I'm about to dine with a beautiful woman.' Alba might not have approved of the compliment, but Oriana de Principe seemed happy enough.

'You're married.' She nodded at my ring.

'Widowed.'

'Oh.' She frowned. 'I'm sorry.'

'How about you?' I meant the impressive diamond.

'I was engaged,' she said. 'He let me keep it.'

'He was generous,' I said.

'He felt guilty.' She nodded towards the dining room. 'Shall we? I'm starving!'

The hotel restaurant had been one of the places I had left off Jacopo's list once I knew I would be meeting Signora de Principe. If the Ispettore had decided to use our case as a ploy to distract the reporter from the Ligabue investigation, I might as well see if we could get anything out of it ourselves.

'So how's it going with Len Ligabue?' I asked.

'We've been all around town,' she said. 'My feet are so sore! Don't you miss it? The journalism?'

'It feels like a different world,' I said. 'In more ways than one. I was a print journalist and now it's all online. Anyone can call themselves a journalist these days.'

'I know!'

'And living in Italy, the changes that have occurred in my life . . .'

'Your wife?' she said. 'How long ago did it happen?' I appreciated her lack of pity or confected compassion. I liked that she didn't pretend.

'Around four years now, almost five.'

'Kids?'

'A daughter, fourteen.'

She winced. 'That's tough. To lose her mother like that. I mean, however she did . . .'

'Traffic accident.'

'At that age.'

'Do you . . .'

She looked amused. 'Kids? How old do you think I am?'

'I didn't google *you*.'

'You mean you can't tell?'

'Twenty-eight?' I had aimed about five years low.

She flashed me a TV-bright smile. 'Who said Englishmen can't be charming?'

'Not James Bond.'

'Don't push it!' She looked down at the menu. 'So this is one of the places on your list. How many did you say there were?'

'Twenty-four,' I said. 'We've been all over the city today. You're not the only one with sore feet.'

'Leads?'

I shrugged. 'Nothing specific. Except this.' I found the photo of the *jongi jeobgi* St Francis that Dolores had sent to my phone. 'Turns out he likes to leave these behind at places he's visited. I don't know if he does it everywhere, or just now and then, but it's a definite . . . *thing*.'

'It's beautiful,' she said. 'What did you call that? *Joji-jo*?'

I laughed. 'You mean you've never heard of *jongi jeobgi*?'

'*Jogli-jogli*?'

'Well, you'd better try and get it right for tomorrow night.'

'*Jobli-jobli*?'

'Now I know you're not trying.'

'Honestly,' she looked wryly over her menu, 'I'll just say "origami"; what does it matter?'

'You'll probably get a complaint from the Korean embassy.' Oriana did not look as if this would trouble her.

In the spirit of Ryan Lee – 'although let's hope not literally,' she said – we decided to have the Boscuri white dishes. I didn't really fancy more truffles, but at least I had had the *orecchiette* earlier in the day, and *Occhio Pubblico* was picking up the tab.

We both went for *secondi*. I took a seasoned steak and she went for the *cotoletta Bolognese*. 'When in Bologna . . . Actually,' she added, '*he* is from Bologna.'

'He?'

'My ex. He would always go on about the *cotoletta Bolognese* being the font.'

'The what?'

'I'm Milanese, you see, so he would say that the *cotoletta Milanese* was,' and now she put on a pompous voice, '"nothing but a crude cousin of the *Schnitzel*, the dish of your former colonial masters, the Austrians!" He would shake his head and moan: "Yet the whole world knows the *cotoletta alla Milanese*, whereas the Bolognese is the *source*." It went all the way back to the Renaissance, apparently.'

'Very Italian,' I said. 'Falling out over food.'

'Oh that's not why we broke up,' she said. 'He slept with my best friend.'

'Ah,' I said. 'Sorry.'

'It was doomed anyway. I mean, we met at university in Rome. He was my first proper boyfriend . . . we were the perfect couple. Him the lawyer, me the reporter . . . Too perfect. We got bored. If it hadn't been him, it would have been me.'

'But you got to keep the ring.'

She held out her hand. 'Pretty, isn't it? And it has a super-power – it repels sharks.'

I felt my phone vibrate. It was Dolores. I called her back from the bathroom.

'He didn't turn up,' she said. 'We've been waiting, hanging around, but there's no sign.'

'You went in and asked?'

'Of course,' she said testily. I had forgotten that this was Dolores I was dealing with, not Jacopo. 'The manager said he was supposed to be there, but . . .' I could almost see her shrugging. '*Boh.*'

'What about the other kitchen staff?'

'They say they don't know. I wanted to press them but the manager said he didn't want to spook them.'

'It was probably one of them that tipped him off. They may all live together. It could be worth trailing a couple of them . . . You could ask the manager who he's closest to.' I checked my watch. It was nine. They'd been at it for twelve hours, and *they* weren't sitting eating expensive food while working their way through a bottle of Sangiovese. 'But it's a long shot. Look, if we're going to do this, we'll leave it until lunchtime tomorrow. In the meantime, call it a day.' Dolores didn't rush to complain. 'Did you get Ishaan's surname?'

'The manager's still playing dumb, or else he genuinely doesn't know.'

'They're employing the guy . . .'

'He said he got him through an agency.'

'Perfect! The agency can tell us then.'

'He wouldn't give us the name. I didn't want to press him because I thought he might throw us out.'

'One of *those* agencies,' I said. I went back to the table.

'You took your time,' said Oriana. 'Phoning your girl-friend, making excuses?'

'One of my staff,' I said.

'Oh?' I could almost see her antennae quiver.

'They were just calling in – another dead end.'

'So,' she said. 'What do *you* think happened to Ryan?'

'Honestly, at this point I really don't have a strong idea. Being an ace reporter for *Occhio Pubblico*, I suspect your guess is as good as mine.' I lifted my glass in salute. We had got through almost the entire bottle of wine, I realised, and I appreciated Signora de Principe afresh. I always bemoaned my Italian friends' relative sobriety – they could keep a glass of wine or a small beer going all night, making me feel like an alcoholic every time I refilled my own – but perhaps I was just mixing with the wrong crowd. Finally, I thought, I really was beginning to miss journalism.

'Psychotic episode, most likely,' said Oriana. 'He's prob-ably fallen into the river.'

'That would take some effort – the rivers here are all underground.'

'Ah yes, you were involved in the Solitudine case, the anarchist who ended up in the canals.'

'You really have taken an interest in me,' I said.

'Purely professional. Know your enemy.'

'The truth is out!'

'Just an expression.' She emptied the bottle into our glasses. 'We're collaborators, after all.'

'So, given that you think it's probably all just a tragic accident, what are we going to do on TV tomorrow?'

'Oh,' she frowned, 'but it's a great *story*. Truffles, an American, Ligabue's murder . . .'

'Where's your connection?'

'Do I really need one?'

'No,' I admitted. 'The coincidence is enough. Good TV. So . . . we're live from the auditorium at Santa Lucia. I presume most of the item will be on Ligabue.' She nodded. 'How long will our slot be?'

'Around ten minutes. There's the intro, then a bit of background on Signor Lee – the glamorous lifestyle of the supertaster and the risky business of hunting truffles.'

'Nice.'

'Thank you. Then some CCTV footage from the hotel, then cut to you and the Lees.'

'You got the film? We're still waiting.'

'I asked nicely,' she said.

'Anything that might be useful to us?'

'I don't think so . . . It's literally just some film of Ryan leaving the hotel, there doesn't seem anything remarkable about it.'

She showed me the black-and-white video of him closing

his door and walking down the corridor. He seemed relaxed, wheeling a case behind him, a kind of superannuated briefcase that I immediately understood to be the mobile lab. I peered closer.

'Anything?' Oriana asked. Ryan was wearing a light jacket, beneath it what seemed like some kind of plain dark T-shirt or sweatshirt. 'What's wrong?'

'I'm sorry?'

'You look disappointed. Was there something you were looking for?'

'I'm disappointed precisely because there isn't anything,' I said.

'Well, maybe the programme will help.'

'Maybe.'

'You don't seem convinced.'

'Oh, I expect we'll find him, but as you know, these things rarely end well.'

'And what about the dog?' she said.

'I'm sorry?'

'Rufus, thrown out of the window like that.'

I drained my glass. That was one detail that had not been released to the press, but obviously Oriana had her own sources, if not half the Carabinieri. Which made me realise she probably also knew who had discovered the body. I thought: *fuck*.

'Is that what happened?' I said carefully.

'Bastard, or bastards. Why would they want to do a thing like that?'

'Barking, maybe?'

'Killing people,' said Oriana, 'that's horrible, obviously,

but somehow it feels like fair game. But murdering animals.' She shuddered. 'That's the mark of some kind of psycho.'

I could have echoed the Comandante's comment that it might simply have been the sign of a professional, but I didn't want to dwell – not least because it seemed that Oriana's sources weren't as on the ball as I'd feared. Rufus, after all, was still alive.

Unless she knew that, and was trying to catch me out?

The *cameriera* came to collect our plates. It may have been my disappointment that our tenuous T-shirt lead had proved to be just that – after all, if Ryan hadn't been wearing it when he went missing, then it seemed the clothing choice of this kitchen worker *had* simply been a remarkable coincidence and he hadn't swiped it from our boy – or the dead bottle of wine between us, but, after getting a blank look when I showed her pictures of the monkey and St Francis, I said: 'I don't suppose you've got a guy in your kitchen today called Ishaan?'

'Ishaan,' she said. 'I was just saying, isn't that a beautiful name? Turned up this evening. Why?' I could feel the heat of Oriana's gaze.

'I was wondering if I could have a word.'

'What? With one of the kitchen staff?'

'Friend of a friend.'

She frowned. 'I'd have to ask the *padrone* . . .'

As she went off, Oriana asked me: 'Who's this Ishaan?'

'Really,' I said, 'it's just the smallest thing. It could be a guy we thought might be connected, but as it turns out, it's almost certainly nothing. I don't even know why I bothered, to be honest, but since we're here . . .'

'So he's connected with Ryan?'

I saw the *padrone* calling me over and shook my head. 'Probably not.' I got up.

'Is there a problem, *signore*?' He stood behind the long bar as if it was a final redoubt.

'Not at all, an excellent meal.' I handed him my card and pulled out the photo of Ryan. 'I believe your cook may know something about this missing person, an American.' There was no point beating around the bush – niceties are usually lost on Italians.

The *padrone* shrugged. 'Come with me.'

I stepped behind the bar and followed him through the swing doors into the restaurant kitchen. Here was the hotel engine room – a strip-lit gleaming metal and marble-topped expanse as large as the restaurant outside. Almost all the staff were Asian apart from a big-bellied, grey-bristled Italian in a tall chef's hat walking the aisles overseeing the preparation process. The *padrone* called him over and asked about Ishaan.

'How should I know?' he said grumpily. 'They come and go. Hey – Reyansh.' He turned to an older Asian with a moustache, who I couldn't imagine wearing a Sun Kil Moon T-shirt in any circumstances. 'They're looking for some guy, Ishaan.'

The man indicated a younger bloke at a chopping board, a white doily perched on top of his rather bountiful jet-black quiff. 'The replacement sous.'

'That's him?' The head chef turned to me. 'What's he done?'

'Nothing,' I said. 'I just want a word about a missing person, Ryan Lee.'

The chef turned to the *padrone*. 'This kid, he's a keeper.'

'Won't take a minute,' I said.

The chef gave me a hard look but nodded to Reyansh. 'All right.'

I watched Reyansh approach the young man, who was apparently responsible for a batch of white truffles in a small Tupperware tub. He was using a flat-sided tool like a cheese grater to shave the truffle over dishes of pasta and meat with what appeared to be the greatest care and precision.

Reyansh had a word in his ear, and pointed over at me. Ishaan listened, the grater poised above a dish of tagliolini. He nodded, finished covering the glistening dish of pasta with a layer of truffle flakes, then laid the grater down on the board and began walking in the opposite direction.

'Where's he going?' I asked the head chef.

'Where's he going?' the chef shouted at Reyansh, who had returned to his own bench. Reyansh looked panicked.

'Sorry, boss!' He went after him.

'May I?' I said to the *padrone*.

'You see what's happened?' grumbled the head chef. 'He's bloody spooked him!'

'It's important,' I said.

'Go ahead then,' said the *padrone*.

The head chef began to complain loudly as I set off after the two men through the kitchen. 'Now what am I supposed to do?'

Chapter 13

By the time I had caught up with Reyansh, he had exited the far door, turned down a bare white corridor and reached some kind of changing room where Ishaan already had a locker door open and was stripping off his kitchen whites, beneath which he was wearing jeans and that Sun Kil Moon T-shirt.

'Hold on,' I called in Italian. 'I just want a quick word.' At the sound of my voice, he grabbed a blue puffa jacket and ran the other way. I shouted after him again, this time in English. But he was through the exit at full pelt, leaving the older guy ranting in Hindi.

I pushed past Reyansh and followed Ishaan through the open door. We were at the rear of the hotel. I spotted a form dashing past an empty illuminated swimming pool before plunging into the wooded borders.

I went after him, crashing through the pine curtain and onto a mini golf course, almost barrelling into a replica of the church of San Petronio on Piazza Maggiore. In fact, I was standing in the *middle* of Piazza Maggiore, a tiny rendition of Giambologna's Fountain of Neptune perilously close to my feet, Bologna's highlights laid beneath me as mini golf.

A tangle of porticoes, along which golfers could putt, formed a sort of path through the city. Appropriately, the longest led up to the wedding cake-shaped church of San Luca, set upon a great mound above the course just as she stood above the city. Only behind the outline of her cupola, I saw the shadow of another dome.

I began to move towards it, Gulliver-like, stepping between Piazzas Maggiore and Minghetti, careful not to tread on the statue of an old statesman as I attempted to creep up on the other giant crouched behind the hill.

I was passing the two towers, clutching hold of the crenellated top of the taller Asinelli, when San Luca's second dome rose. Ishaan sprang from behind the church and made for the treeline before I could get between them.

'Please,' I shouted in Italian. 'Stop. You don't have to be scared.' But there was no hesitation from the lad – he took one lolloping stride into Montagnola Park, another over the railway station, and was through the next screen of trees. I tried to grab him, but I trod on a discarded golf ball and crashed sideways into San Luca, the unyielding concrete shivering through me.

I scrambled upright and pushed forward through the trees, finding myself on a path running beside a tennis court. One way clearly led back to the hotel. I went the other way, arriving at the hotel car park, and spotted Ishaan up ahead, weaving between the parked cars.

He was younger, nimbler than me, and in sneakers. Still, I pressed ahead, swerving through the cars until I arrived at the private road that reached around the hotel. At least we had rid of obstacles, I thought. Then I saw headlights gliding towards me, Ishaan's shadow flitting beyond them, back into the darkness.

A horn blared; the car was coming on more quickly than I'd expected – of course, I was running towards it – and I veered to the side, an ankle twinge reminding me that my stumble on the golf ball would not be forgotten, or forgiven, so easily.

I carried on, the soles of my shoes slapping upon the asphalt as the kid gained distance. A flash of glamour – the road had led me back to the front of the hotel and its fake Liberty-style facade. I spotted Ishaan dart past floodlit fountains, hurdle a shrubbery. I scrambled after him. Couples who had stepped outside for a smoke or a romantic clinch paused to watch us as if we were part of the show; one or two even raised their phones to record the occasion – a house detective chasing some delinquent who had stolen the silver, perhaps.

Ishaan slipped through the ostentatious black-and-gold-painted iron gates and turned into the gloomy slip road. I made off after him, but he was getting further and further away. The sound of my own footsteps began to slow, and I finally came to a halt, watching as he disappeared into the darkness. I walked back to the hotel gates, breathing heavily.

'Hey!' Oriana was waiting for me at the entrance, hands on elegantly adorned hips. 'You're not going to let him get away?'

'I'm not going to catch him,' I panted.

She pointed at the hire-bike station just outside the gates. 'You've got the app?' she asked.

I nodded. 'I've got the app.'

I followed her over. She was already pointing her phone at

the bar code upon the bicycle's mudguard. The lock snapped open. She looked at me.

'Well, what are you waiting for?'

Picture the pair of us on those orange and silver bicycles – me in my suit and tie, Oriana barefoot, her shoes kicked beneath a bush, and that slinky silver dress hitched up to her thighs – cycling silently along that gloomy side road illuminated by amber pools of lamplight.

We arrived at a small, almost superfluous-seeming round-about. One exit led to a gated-off patch of wasteland, another to a narrow road by a railway line that Google Maps suggested accessed an underpass and an industrial estate.

We began to follow it, passing a rickety camper van, seemingly abandoned, then another.

We came across a woman, a girl really, standing by the pavement in black vinyl hot pants and a boob tube. Her jet-black hair was tied back, her pale make-up caked on like a clown's. Dark eyes that might once have defined her beauty dully registered us on the orange hire bikes with nary a flicker of surprise.

'Have you seen a man?' Oriana asked her. 'An Asian man, running this way?'

Now the girl looked startled. 'You want fuck?'

'An Indian,' I said in English. 'Young guy?'

She looked equally blankly at me. 'Want suck?'

'We're wasting our time.' Oriana took off. We came across more girls scattered along the road, but they were similarly monosyllabic, and by the time we had arrived at the empty, graffiti-riddled underpass, it was clear that even if Ishaan had come this way, he was long gone.

'Well,' said Oriana. 'It was worth a try.'

'I suppose this sort of thing happens to you all the time at *Occhio Pubblico*.'

'Grist to the mill,' she said. 'So your guy turned out to be important after all.'

'Possibly,' I said. 'Maybe he was just frightened. Thought I was with immigration or something.'

'Maybe,' said Oriana. 'But not as good a story.'

A man stepped in front of us. Short glossy black hair shorn bare at the sides, heavy gold earring, a carefully cultivated beard framing his round, almost babyish face.

'What you want?'

I steered my bike, and myself, in front of Oriana, planting my feet down on either side of it. I noticed we had finally managed to stimulate the interest of the prostitutes across the road.

'What you want from my girls?'

'Nothing.' I tried to push past, but he clamped his hands on the bike's handlebars.

'Why you hassle my girls?'

I shook my head. 'We weren't, we were just asking—'

'Go fuck yourself,' Oriana said coolly behind me. The pimp's attention snapped toward her.

'You dressed like whore. Careful, bitch.'

'Hey,' I said.

'Come on then,' said Oriana. 'You worthless *son* of a bitch.'

He made a move towards her. I blocked him, half with my bike and half with my shoulder. A bolt of pain shot up from my elbow as he grabbed hold of it and, with a sharp two-handed move, twisted it in opposite directions. I followed the pain, downwards, and fell on top of the bike in a dull clatter. A further charge of pain shot up my other arm. He had hold of my upraised wrist.

'Stay down.' He let go and stepped over me. I grabbed hold of his ankle, but he whirled around with his free foot and kicked me in the stomach.

Twice. With a metal-tipped toe cap.

It felt like I'd been stabbed. But instead of blood, I tasted truffle, then fine wine. I launched it into the gutter.

As I doubled up, I heard a smattering of applause from the girls. Followed by a scrape, a gasp. A sort of surprised wheeze.

A body thudded down beside me. The pimp, his baby face bloated and pink, was clutching his throat.

'You're lucky I didn't have my heels on, you shit,' I heard Oriana say from above. 'I would have put one through your eye. And you know why? Because you're nothing. Less than nothing. They would give me a fucking medal. Back off . . .' The girls had begun to close in. 'Or I really will kill him. In fact, do you want me to? Say the word and I'll do it. No problem. I mean it.'

'Better no,' said a woman's voice. 'There's more than one. They brothers. Make more trouble for us.'

'Have it your own way.' Oriana helped me to my feet. 'Are you all right?'

'I'll live.'

She brushed me down and we began to walk our bikes along the slip road. She paused. 'Damn it.' She examined the grimy soles of her feet. 'I really *should* have brought my shoes.'

I began to get my wind back. 'Jesus, Oriana.'

'Don't blame yourself,' she said.

'I'm *not* blaming myself.'

'A lot of these gangsters are ex-military,' she said. 'They're not complete fools. They know how to look after themselves.'

'Then . . .?'

'Krav Maga, Israeli self-defence technique. No messing. Had I been a guy, he might have seen it coming. But *this* helpless female? He's lucky I didn't stick a blade between his ribs . . .' She pouted. 'But I didn't have my knife.'

'You're kidding, right? You don't carry a knife.'

She looked at me as if I was mad.

'I hunt murderers,' she said.

We arrived back at the entrance to the hotel. Despite the trash talk, in that dress Oriana still managed to look perfectly in context before the fountains, although I must have appeared a little the worse for wear. 'Well,' I said. 'It's been an interesting evening.'

'Don't tell me it's over.' She took my hand. 'I need to have a shower, get rid of this dirt, and we should clean you up too before we have a nightcap.' She drew me closer, pulled a face. 'But maybe we should do something about your breath first.' She ran a long index finger along my jawline, stopped it at my lips. 'I think there's a spare toothbrush in my room.'

Chapter 14

'You can stay, you know. It's all paid for.'

'I would love to,' I said, beginning to pull my clothes on. 'But I have to be there for when Rose wakes up.'

'You couldn't just . . . make it for breakfast? Come back here.' Oriana opened her arms and I lowered myself back down to give her a lingering kiss.

'I'd love to,' I said again, breaking off. 'But even though she plays it cool, she's not really. She's just a kid.'

'How are you feeling?' She touched the pair of dark weals upon my stomach.

'Just a bit sore,' I said.

She smiled. 'No lasting damage, then.'

'Purely cosmetic,' I said. 'Well, I don't need to ask for your phone number, because I already have it, and I'll be seeing you very soon.'

'You will.' She blew me a kiss. I watched her roll drowsily over as I closed the door, her long, naked back wrapped in the white sheets.

I woke in my own bed a couple of hours later. Despite losing

Ishaan, I felt energised after my night with Oriana, by simple human contact – intimacy – probably. I'd only had a few dates, usually set up by well-meaning friends, since Lucia, and none had felt right, but this had been different, unforced, as if I had actually been a normal person, not a grieving widower, a needy individual hauling all their baggage to the dinner table. And Oriana had felt . . . well, she had *felt*, obviously, fantastic, but it was not only that. We seemed to be coming from the same place, something I thought I might only truly find again with an English girl, but perhaps it wasn't so much about the national culture as the professional one – journalists understood journalists, just as teachers teachers, chemists chemists . . . Of course, nothing much could come of it – she was a high-flyer in Rome and I was definitely rooted here in Bologna – but maybe that was also a good thing – there wasn't any pressure. And I certainly wouldn't say no to seeing her again outside the TV studio.

'What's that song?' said Rose, already eating her Coco Pops.

'What song?'

'You were humming.'

'Was I?'

'You seem happy. Is something wrong?'

'I'm not sure I like the sound of that.' I reached for my own bran flakes. But I only filled the bowl halfway before topping it up with Coco Pops.

'Hey! They're mine!'

'You're sweet enough as it is.'

'I didn't hear you come in last night.'

'You never hear me come in, Rose,' I said. 'You're always wearing your headphones.'

'No I'm not.' She raised her hands to her ears.

'You are,' I said. 'It's just that an angel usually floats into your room and takes them off after you've fallen asleep. How else do you think your iPad manages to magically recharge itself, indeed, move itself from whatever precarious position it has found itself upon your bed?'

'You mean you come into my room?'

'I am careful to knock on the door, *signorina*.'

'Anyway,' she looked sly, 'that's how I knew you came in late – I woke up this morning with my headphones on!'

'Ah,' I said. 'Dammit. Hoist with my own petard.'

'What does *that* mean?' We always spoke English when we were alone together, but even her bilingual ability had its limits.

'Caught in my own trap,' I said.

'I meant – what does it mean *literally*?'

I shook my head. 'No idea.'

'I'll look it up. How do you spell "petard"? ... Oh, *Shakespeare*. So,' she said as I dug into my much-improved bran flakes. 'Did this woman hoist you on her petard?'

I looked up. Her expression was blank, but her eyes were drilling into me.

I continued with my breakfast. What the hell. 'Yeah, I met someone for dinner, Rose.' I looked back up. 'In fact, she's on the TV.'

'Really?'

'A reporter on *Occhio Pubblico*.'

'Who?'

'Oriana de Principe.'

'*Wow*.' She held her phone up to show me a photo of Oriana. 'Her?' I nodded. '*Wow*.'

'It was just work.'

'You don't usually seem so happy after "just work".'

'Look, for a start, she lives in Rome . . .'

'So it *wasn't* just work.'

I squirmed like a source, or a suspect coughing up a confession. 'I won't deny I had a nice time.'

'Then she could take the train, we could—'

'Rose.' I held up my hand. 'I shouldn't have said anything. Look, we're just friends; a relationship is out of the question. You should know that, all right? *All right?*'

'But you're still *friends?*'

'Oh yeah,' I said. 'In fact, I'm going to be on the show tonight.'

'Really? When did you find *that* out?'

'Just last night,' I said. Actually, I had known since the previous morning but had wanted to minimise the teenage anticipation.

'*Wow.*' Rose gazed at me with the look of frank admiration I imagined other fathers received on a daily basis from their daughters. 'She must like you too.'

'Look, Rose,' I said. 'It was strictly business. I don't even *want* to go on TV. I didn't want our clients to go on TV. It was the very last thing I wanted.' My daughter's look of admiration had been replaced by one of bemusement.

'Why wouldn't you want to go on TV?'

I was locking up when Alba called, sounding excited. 'We've been contacted by Liana Benvenuto.'

'You're sounding as if I should know who that is,' I said.

'Liana Benvenuto – Bologna's Queen of Truffles. I was

reading about her in the *Carlino*.'

'All right,' I said. 'And what did she want?'

'Well, it wasn't her exactly, one of her people. But she wants to see you.'

'Did she – or her *person* – say what it was about?'

'Only that it was connected to Ryan Lee.'

Chapter 15

I borrowed the Comandante's limo for the visit to the head-quarters of Benvenuto SpA, which was not actually in the city of Bologna, but around twenty kilometres up the A1 in the direction of Modena.

The stretch between Bologna and Modena boasted on one side of the road, in Sant'Agata Bolognese, the headquarters of Lamborghini; on the other, in Maranello, Ferrari's HQ, leaving me feeling somewhat underpowered in the Comandante's, albeit spotless, ten-year-old Lancia.

Dolores was sitting beside me; Dolores version 2.5, that is, the additional 0.5 consisting of her houndstooth grey suit, which she had held quizzically up in the doorway when I arrived at her apartment in Via Pratello. It had once been home to her late friend and mentor Paolo Solitudine – the anarchist who had suffered a watery demise – but was now rented to her at 'mate's rates' by an obscure leftist organisation that had somehow managed to squirrel away its assets in the same time-honoured Italian tradition as banking foundations, political parties, and the Catholic Church.

'I found it when I was clearing his stuff out,' she said,

meaning Paolo. 'Obviously it wasn't his. Maybe a girlfriend left it here? It's pretty clean and there are no holes.'

'Does it fit?'

'More or less. I wore it once. For an eighties-themed party.'

'Go on then.'

She had emerged ten minutes later wearing a black roll-neck jumper beneath the wide-shouldered jacket, along with a matching knee-length pencil skirt. With her new hair and big looped earrings (she explained she had bought them especially for the party), she could have just stepped through a portal from 1983, possibly from the set of a Robert Palmer video. Fortunately in Italy it's rarely about *what* you're wearing so much as about how you wear it.

And I had to admit, Dolores wore it well.

The GPS bade us take the turn-off for Crespellano, and we followed it along increasingly minor roads, drawing us deeper into the rolling Emilian countryside, sloping fields and vineyards on either side, until we began to skirt an ancient red-brick wall and the satnav announced we had arrived at our destination.

I continued slowly along the road until we reached a kink that I had taken to be a place for traffic to pass but which turned out to contain a gate with intricately decorated ironwork featuring the Benvenuto crest – a long-nosed dog standing tall against the trunk of a tree. Security cameras were placed high on either side of the gate, and before it there was a metal pillar with an intercom. I lowered the window and announced our arrival.

'Wait in the car,' came the response.

Part of the gate opened and out stepped a uniformed

security guard, a sub-machine gun strapped across his front. He asked to see our ID, then checked our names against a clipboard. He spoke into his chest mike.

'Stop on the other side,' he said. The gates began to open and he waved us through.

Another guard, similarly attired and armed, was waiting with his hand raised. I stopped the car and watched in the rear mirror as the gates closed behind us. He went through precisely the same process with our IDs and I was then asked to open the boot while the one from outside checked beneath the car with a steel pole topped by a mirror.

'OK.' The second guard leaned in. 'Go ahead.' He pointed down the single road bordered on both sides by vineyards until it disappeared into an unbroken line of pine trees.

We drove into the trees, our path marked by cypresses placed on either side of the lane like a security detail. Standing discreetly between every half a dozen, I noticed, were lamp posts topped, as they had been at Aurelio and Stan's, with a nest of CCTV.

We pulled up at another gate. A high fence weaved through the trees on either side. There was no intercom, but as soon as we stopped, the gate began to open and another pair of armed men – although these were only sporting holstered pistols – waved us forward and came to stand on either side of the car. They had hand-held devices and appeared to be checking our identities against them; we must have been filmed coming in, I realised. Then the metal bollards ahead of us sunk into the ground and we continued on.

We turned a corner. Up ahead was an opening in the treeline, and we emerged to find ourselves at the top of a lush valley; beneath us, set among further vines and fields burnt brown by a summer of sun, stood a sprawling old *palazzo*. I glanced back. That line of trees continued in a crescent for at least a kilometre on either side until they met cragged, cradling hills that no doubt concealed their own security measures. We had entered a hidden valley, a secret place.

We drove down towards the *palazzo*, which stood at the apex of a topiary that might have traced its origins to the Renaissance. A setting worthy of the Medici, although they hadn't come quite this far. But the Sforza? Or another of the grand old families? Now, of course, it belonged to relatively new money, albeit that their fortune stretched back over a century and a half.

Behind the *palazzo* was a red-brick complex that, apart from the car park ahead, was the only visible note of modernity – a tinted glass facade upon the entrance of what I imagined would once have been stables large enough for a small regiment of cavalry, which stretched back until they abutted the beginning of the hills.

I pulled in and a white-jacketed guy directed us to a generous space between a monster Lamborghini SUV and a gold Aston Martin Vantage.

'Signor Leicester,' he shook my hand as I got out, 'and Signora Pugliese. Welcome to Palazzo Benvenuto.' We glanced at each other. There was an unmistakable aroma of truffles in the air. Not overpowering, but strong – that earthy, mouthwatering tang as pervasive as jasmine in season.

The man led us out through the rear of the car park, which was bordered by high laurel hedges, to a grey gravel path. He stopped there. 'If you will just continue upwards and straight

ahead, Signora Benvenuto will meet you in the *salon dell' oca*.'
As we left, he spoke into a walkie-talkie.

'Do you think that's all he does?' said Dolores. 'Show
people out of the car park?'

'I'm sure he would say it's not that simple.'

The path towards the house was punctuated by steps up
through the terraced garden, with its trickling time-worn
fountains set among geometric beds of flowers, box hedges
trimmed into cones, obelisks and spheres. A gecko darted
across my path. Up ahead, a pair of green-shuttered doors
opened. A woman emerged from the *palazzo*, waved and
came down to greet us.

'I *adore* your suit,' she told Dolores. 'Is it Dior?' She leaned
forward and inspected the buttons. 'Goodness, it's original.'

I was no expert on female fashion, but I somehow intuited
that Signora Liana Benvenuto's suit was a Chanel, which,
unlike the suddenly self-conscious Dolores Pugliese, she wore
as if she wore nothing else.

An attractive blonde in her early forties, she did not seem
weighed down by her wealth – she had a firm grip, a healthy
complexion and looked as if she played a lot of tennis. As she led
us into the house, she apologised in British-accented English
for the security – 'It can unnerve people, but it was Papà's
doing, and I suppose he had good reason' – and pointed out
the bucolic frescoes in this, the 'salon of the geese', in which
rosy-cheeked Marie Antoinette figures played the peasant. I
got the impression she was happy to meet us. I suspected that
in this rarefied, truffle-infused atmosphere where her time
was undoubtedly parcelled out minute by expensive minute,
we were something of a novelty.

She checked her watch, an incongruous Fitbit. 'You're actually a bit early – or rather, being English,' she smiled, 'you're right on time. Our other guest is late. Would you like a quick tour?'

'Thank you,' I said. 'Your English is superb, by the way, accent and everything.'

'School,' she said. 'A couple of terms in England. The British were one of our main clients in the old days. Now it's,' she waved her hand, 'everyone else. My children are studying Arabic, Russian and Mandarin. On top of English. Poor darlings!'

We followed her through the *palazzo*, which was truly worthy of the designation – a proper palace, the chevron parquet creaking beneath our feet as we passed through further frescoed salons arranged variously as reception rooms and offices, with Benvenuto staff tapping away at their computers beneath dark canvases while mythical figures frolicked overhead.

Finally we arrived at the far end of the building, another salon similar to the goose room, where instead the countryside had been transformed by the hand of Progress, at least from an early-nineteenth-century perspective – a great horse-drawn baling machine was harvesting wheat, with the *contadini* labouring cheerfully beside it, apparently unperturbed about their displacement by new technology. In one corner, a young man in a blue tailcoat was presenting a bashful maid with a bunch of wheat as if it was a bouquet of flowers.

Signora Benvenuto opened the terrace doors. Across the gravel was the building I had seen earlier. It had definitely been stables at some stage, but it was clear that even before it had been converted to meet modern requirements it had been expanded to fulfil the process of industrialisation depicted upon the ceiling behind us. As we walked towards it, gravel crunching beneath our feet, I experienced a sudden vertigo-like sensation. It was something to do with my sense of perspective – I realised that the building, which had seemed from the opening of the valley to end just before the undulating slope behind it, actually drove into the hill.

'Have you noticed the smell, by the way?' said Signora Benvenuto. 'I barely do, of course – I grew up with it and I think my olfactory senses must have been ruined by now. But poor Ryan was almost knocked over!'

'You mean Ryan Lee?' I said.

'It was me – well, us, my company – that selected him. He's one of the very best supertasters in the business, if not the world.'

A pair of smoked-glass doors slid open and we stepped into a sunny atrium. A pair of women smiled at us from behind the reception desk. Visible through the glass wall behind them was a scene that would have pleased any Bond villain – a cavernous factory-cum-warehouse.

'You wouldn't have thought it, would you?' said Signora Benvenuto. 'To be honest, I'm not a hundred per cent sure it would be allowed today, but when Papà began work in the seventies, everything was a bit slacker. After that, it was just a question of adding on.'

'But how is it possible,' I said, 'to have all this activity here, and yet the *palazzo* accessible only by those tiny roads?'

'There's a railway,' she said. 'Can you believe it? Papà was inspired by the British post office, and their railway beneath

London. It cuts straight through the hill to the depot where everything's shipped out. But we're getting ahead of ourselves. First I should ask you: what do you actually know about truffles?'

'Seeing all of this,' I said, 'probably a lot less than I thought. All I really know boils down to the white being seasonal and more expensive, and Emilia Romagna being a player in a multi-billion-pound industry centred on Italy.'

She nodded. 'A gram of Boscuri white truffle comes to around six euros, and your typical restaurant dish will contain around ten grams. Black truffles are pretty valuable too, hence the security. What you may not be aware of is that truffles are not only native to these parts. There's a rich source in the Balkans – Albania, Bulgaria, and some parts of the old Yugoslavia. It's not widely known, although it's no secret to anyone in the business, that for years there's been traffic in these foreign truffles. A connoisseur would spot them straight off, but a casual diner . . . maybe not. Think of it like wine – the difference between a glass of top-tier Sangiovese Superiore and,' she shrugged, 'something from Bulgaria.

'In the past, it was a rather ad hoc thing. You'd have stalls in the local market passing off Albanian truffles as Boscurili, a guy turning up at a restaurant with his pockets bulging with counterfeits, that kind of thing – the locals would all know the stalls and people to avoid and the legitimate restaurants wouldn't touch them, but they would manage to flog them to the chancers and tourists who couldn't tell the difference, and no one complained.

'In the meantime, the price of truffles has risen ever higher and so has the incentive to pass off these foreign imposters as the real thing. We employ tasters on a permanent basis to sample products and visit restaurants, rather like secret shoppers, to ensure customers are getting what they're paying for. If they discover fakes, they'll squirrel away a sample for us to test back at our labs. We then approach the vendor ourselves, or contact the Guardia di Finanza.

'Recently, however, we have come across a new strain of truffle that somehow manages to ape the characteristics of Italian truffles, and particularly the Boscurili. It might be something to do with the soil biology. . . it's hard to tell, but someone certainly knows what they're doing. It was only picked up when a world-renowned expert who was testing a truffle purchased for a restaurant in Tokyo—'

There was a ping on Signora Benvenuto's Fitbit and she checked her wrist. 'Ah, our Italian guest has arrived,' she said. 'Ironic, really – you would think he, of all people, would be able to keep to a timetable.'

We began to head back to the *palazzo*.

'So that's why you employed Ryan,' I said. 'A supertaster to sniff out a supertruffle.'

'Ha! Yes, though I'm not sure I'd call it a supertruffle precisely; more like a superfake.'

'*You* hired Ryan?' said Dolores. 'But we thought Len Ligabue—'

'Yes,' said Signora Benvenuto. 'I arranged it through the Triumvirate.'

At the end of the corridor, through the open doors to the *salon dell' oca*, a moustachioed man rose to his feet and gave the approaching *signora* a small bow.

Chapter 16

In keeping with a certain kind of well-to-do Italian in late middle age, Signor Dante Millefoglie was outfitted as a parody of the British gentleman. From his Church's brogues and his red corduroy trousers to his yellow silk paisley bow tie, Harris Tweed waistcoat and blazer, he appeared to signal his position in society – an ample *palazzo* apartment, a place in the hills, membership of a dining and *buraco* club. He was a university professor, the head of a banking foundation or a senior journalist.

In fact, he was a haulage boss. He took Liana Benvenuto's hand as they kissed on both cheeks.

'*Cara Liana*, my apologies for the delay.'

'I was just saying,' said Signora Benvenuto, 'I would have expected you of all people to be on time. Were you just as bad when you were delivering parcels?'

Dante Millefoglie laughed, although I wasn't sure he found it funny. 'Worse! But the important thing was I got them there in the end, which was more than could be said for some of my competitors.' He turned to me, his expression behind that generous moustache turning suitably grave.

'Signor Leicester,' he took my hand, 'and . . .'

'Dolores Pugliese.' She gave his hand a perfunctory shake.

We sat facing each other on separate sofas – Dolores and I on one side, Dante and Liana on the other. I looked at Signora Benvenuto.

'You said you arranged it through the "Triumvirate"?' I said. 'That sounds very . . . mysterious.'

'It was Len's little joke – he loved his Roman history. You know, Pompey, Caesar, Crassus?'

'That didn't end well,' said Dolores, who had a degree in ancient history. 'Caesar got stabbed, Pompey beheaded, and Crassus choked on molten gold.'

'Well,' said Liana uncomfortably, 'as I said, it was just a little joke.'

'And you are certainly taking plenty of precautions,' I said.

'A fact of life,' she replied. 'Even back in Papà's day you would hear stories, whispers . . . hunters who had disappeared, an argument over a find . . . someone discovered in the forest with a blow to the head . . .'

'I think I'm beginning to understand,' I said. 'You're a producer, Signor Ligabue a retailer, and Signor Millefoglie. . .'

'Distribution,' he said.

'And Marco? Shouldn't he be here?'

'We thought it best to leave him in peace for now.'

'Lad's got enough on his plate,' said Dante. He looked at Liana. 'Probably have a word at the funeral.'

'You said you hired Ryan,' I said. 'Then why was he on Len's books?'

'As you know,' said Liana, 'we harvest on a large scale on managed land. It seemed most likely that if fakes were being infiltrated into the supply chain, we would be the most likely source, so we wanted to keep the investigation under wraps. But,' she assumed a solemn expression, 'what can *you* tell us about Len's death? Does it really look like murder?' I nodded. 'And Signor Lee? How far have you got with him?'

I hesitated. In this setting, their fine clothes, Liana Benvenuto and Dante Millefoglie exuded such authority it was as if I was reporting to them. But it was the Lees who were actually my clients.

'Not as far as we would like,' I said. 'We will be appearing on *Occhio Pubblico* this evening.'

Liana looked alarmed. 'But you won't mention us, any of this.'

I shook my head. 'I'm only interested in your superfakes and the unfortunate Signor Ligabue in as much as it affects our search for Ryan Lee. Frankly, I think that should be the most pressing priority – Signor Ligabue is dead but Ryan may still be alive.' They looked a bit surprised to be told what their priorities should be, but indicated their agreement. Still, they also looked as if they were holding something back. I leaned towards Liana. 'What is it you're not telling us, Signora Benvenuto?'

She appeared startled. 'What do you mean?'

'It's always difficult to get the full picture, but some people see a bigger one than others. There may be things you know that would help us, things you don't even realise could help. Tell me, for example, why do you think Ryan would be reading a book about the Camorra?'

'Well . . .' Liana looked at Dante.

'You said it was something your father was behind,' I

continued, 'but I confess I've never seen quite so much security anywhere outside a government building. It seems like an awful lot of trouble to go to, to protect yourself from an Emilian hill farmer armed only with a shotgun. They're not given to planting bombs, are they?' She frowned. 'At least that's what I presumed they were checking for beneath our car.'

Dante shifted in his seat. 'It's not the fake truffles per se that worry us, lad,' he said. 'It's their level of sophistication. These aren't just plucked off Albanian hillsides; they were developed after a hefty chunk of research into the precise composition of the soil, humidity and so on. They may have been "found" outside, but they were farmed in conditions designed to replicate Boscuri whites. That's not something ordinary smugglers could achieve. There's organisation here, and where there's organised crime . . .'

'There's the mafia,' said Dolores.

'Quite so, signora. If the mafia is into trash, then why not truffles? The rewards are considerably higher, and they're businessmen at heart.'

We sat in silence. Then I said: 'So you think Signor Ligabue might have been the subject of a mafia hit, and Ryan was caught up in all this?' I thought of the Comandante's comment about Rufus going out of the window – *the sign of a professional*.

Dante Millefoglie nodded.

'Have you mentioned this to Ispettore Alessandro of the Carabinieri?' They had. Well, at least it was all now well within the purview of his Special Operations Group, along with the considerable armoury of black arts they had at their disposal. 'And how did this superfake get to Tokyo in the first place? You must have some kind of chain of provenance . . .'

'Everything appears above board,' said Signora Benvenuto. 'Which is why we felt the need to take the extraordinary measure of hiring Ryan through Antichi Artigiani del Cibo. The truffle came through a legitimate broker who sourced from us. The thing to understand, Signor Leicester,' she said, leaning forward, 'is that reputation is *everything* in our business. It would mean ruin for a broker or established hunter to pass off a fake. They would never be able to work again.'

'They would never be able to show their face in Boscuri again,' said Millefoglie. 'People have long memories in this land, and bear even longer grudges.'

'And the broker?'

'Count Malduce.'

'He didn't mention any link with Ryan and the fake truffles when we met him,' I said.

'We didn't inform him about our enquiries,' said Liana.

'He may have guessed.'

'The Count has worked with this family since my father's time. He would never do anything to harm our reputation.'

'Or his own,' added Millefoglie. For Italians, I thought, this pair were extraordinarily trusting. What was that most common Italian saying? *Fidarsi è bene, non fidarsi è meglio.* To trust is good, to distrust is better.

'Well,' I said. 'Whoever is behind this, the Lees – Ryan's parents – deserve an answer, and it seems to me that if we can find out what happened to him, what sparked all this, we may even get to the source of your superfake.'

'We will pay you to continue your investigation for as long as necessary,' said Liana Benvenuto.

I nodded, thinking of the Lees in their budget hotel by the railway station. At least I had a tiny piece of good news to convey.

'And if it does turn out to be the mafia behind the death of Signor Ligabue and the disappearance of Ryan Lee . . .' I looked between the two of them. 'Would you pay a ransom for the recovery of the kid?'

They did not need to confer. Evidently this had already been discussed. Signora Benvenuto nodded. 'We would also be prepared to consider financial terms,' she said carefully. 'If it led to the cessation of their activity.'

I understood. Perhaps I could persuade the kidnappers to release Ryan as a symbol of goodwill, although negotiating a kind of protection arrangement on the Triumvirate's behalf . . . That was never likely to end well. Once I had got hold of the kid, they could count me out. I had no intention of being caught in the crossfire. Or, I glanced at Dolores as we rose to leave, being choked on fake truffles.

Chapter 17

We headed along the A1 towards Bologna in silence. The carriageway was busy with traffic, a line of trucks hogging the inside lane, dozens of cars jostling for position along the other two – slowing as the overhead 'traffic tutor' came into view, changing lanes or gliding down the middle lane in an attempt to fool it, then speeding up straight after.

We passed an Autogrill, a Sarni service station, an almost unbroken strip on either side of the highway – ceramics manufacturers, light engineering firms, kitchen outlets, gym equipment suppliers, vast hangars containing packaging companies . . . This was, after all, Europe's 'packaging valley', where giant mechanised production lines added the final touches to much of the continent's manufacturing output before sending it on its way, often via Millefoglie SpA juggernauts.

On the other side of Bologna was 'data valley', home to the European Union's largest supercomputer. I thought of the languid English prejudices I had grown up with about 'jolly Italy' with its pizza and pasta and coffee shops, its exuberant waiters and beautiful women who everybody knew would transform into fat mammas at some mysterious stage; the chaotic Italians who couldn't even rule themselves – all those prime ministers! – and their army whose tanks only had one gear: reverse. I thought of a childhood beach, the swirling confusion of the *pasticceria*, ice cream before I knew it as *gelato*, spaghetti with clams, Pompeii under the sun. That beating sun that presumably accounted for the Italians' tardiness, their fiery nature, chronic corruption. An Italy every bit as authentic as the England of Big Ben, Stratford-upon-Avon and afternoon tea.

I felt humbled by the implications of what we had learned at Palazzo Benvenuto – how the tentacles of organised crime may have extended to the counterfeit truffle trade and by implication touched upon the death of Len Ligabue and the disappearance of Ryan Lee.

In our ageing Lancia, Dolores and I were just one among this mass of other automobiles and jostling trucks; our little company, our little family, just one among the millions of others. The mafia, meanwhile, if it was involved, had more combined economic clout than the entire German automobile industry; was as much of an economic powerhouse hidden in plain sight as the host nation itself.

'You know,' I said quietly, 'if you want to take a step back from this job . . . even take a break from the company, you can.'

'Why would I do that?' Dolores looked at me. 'You mean because of the mafia, right?'

'It would be okay,' I said. 'I mean, I understand how it is.'

'How is it?'

'I mean with the mafia. People don't want to get involved,

be associated . . . and understandably so. They're afraid of retribution.'

She shook her head. 'I want to find Ryan as much as you do.'

'Of course,' I said. I looked back at the road. And here was another Italy you didn't see depicted at home much, either – the fortitude of ordinary people confronted by the monolithic evil of organised crime.

I signalled to exit. 'Where are we going?' she asked. I nodded towards the glass-topped development ahead.

It was the latest Antichi Artigiani del Cibo venture, and by coincidence as we neared the building, an advert for it featuring the deceased restaurateur came on the radio.

'At any Antichi Artigiani del Cibo restaurant you can expect the very best food Italy has to offer,' Len Ligabue said with his reassuringly authentic Emilian lisp, 'but now you can even create your own meals by going to the source: Cibo d'Italia.'

It had been a characteristically bold Ligabue enterprise, albeit that it was whispered to have been born out of a monumental act of pique when Turin's Eataly had opened a food theme park, FICO, in Ligabue's Bologna backyard. Certainly, although vast FICO dwarfed the supermarket-size Cibo d'Italia, what the two venues had in common was that very modern food meme – 'authenticity' – whether it be 'artisanal', 'ethical' or 'biological', although personally I didn't care a great deal if my prosciutto came from pigs fed on 'forest-found' chestnuts or the *mozzarella di bufala* buffaloes were 'hand-massaged'. But it was easy to sneer. In a country where cynicism could have been a part of the school curriculum, I couldn't help respecting Len Ligabue's ambition – he had clearly been driven by a genuine passion for his homeland's gastronomic heritage, even if it had coincided with the opportunity to cash in.

We pulled into the half-empty car park, a couple of rows back from the entrance, where there stood a three-metre-high transparent obelisk containing the semi-holographic iconic image of Len cheek-to-cheek with Rufus. It had been intended to signal to visitors the provenance of this great enterprise, but now immediately called to mind a huge tombstone.

Behind it were ranks of trolleys, but I stopped Dolores from taking one. We weren't here to shop.

'Why, then?'

'To understand,' I said, and stepped through the sliding doors.

It was not a supermarket on the plan of a Tesco or Carrefour, more like a food court or indoor market, with dozens of islands decked with varieties of ham, cheese, pasta, bread . . . I had heard some good things – that, despite the competition from FICO on the other side of the city, Ligabue had not lost his magic touch. And it was true, there were a few people in Cibo d'Italia this morning apart from the ones behind the counters – some retired couples, a couple of becalmed-looking tourists – but this didn't do much to distract from the sense of being trapped in a windowless airport terminal building between shelves of Pugliese Canestrato cheese and Dolomitian *Apfelstrudel*, killing time before a flight that would never arrive.

We wandered past counters piled high with Parma hams

and Romagnan cheeses, Sicilian salami and Abruzzo sausage. Boscurili truffles – little open boxes of black and whites shaped like diseased kidneys – sat on presentation pillows.

We stopped at a *bruschetteria* (the first time I had heard of one of these – I suspected it had been invented for Cibo d'Italia), where Dolores ordered freshly chopped Piennolo tomatoes, 'DOP-certified, grown on the slopes of Mount Vesuvius' – stall 21 – plus *bocconcini* of mozzarella 'from the artisanal dairies of Caserta' – stall 18 – while I went for prosciutto Friuli-Venezia Giulia, 'dry cured using only salt from the pans of Cervia' – stall 3 – and olive oil, DOP, 'from Frantoio in Tuscany, known for its fruity flavour' – stall 12. The bread was 'milled from 100 per cent Umbrian wheat', which could be found at stall 11. Above the menu was the Antichi Artigiani del Cibo logo – a sketch of Len and Rufus's ugly mugs. Running along the bottom, in a longhand font: *Food is our philosophy.*

A man turned the corner of an aisle with a TV camera on his shoulder, creeping ahead as if he was stalking game. A security guard came up behind him, another came the other way. They began to move the man towards the entrance, although he continued to film even as they tried to block his shot. We followed them through the shopping aisles, *bruschetta* in hand.

The cameraman was finally ejected outside. Dolores was about to follow him, but I stopped her – I could see Oriana de Principe, back in her combat gear, holding her microphone like a baton.

'Who's she?' said Dolores.

'*Occhio Pubblico.* Probably doing a b-roll for the programme this evening.'

'B-roll?'

'You know, background shots to illustrate the story, that kind of thing.'

'Jacopo said you're going on with the Lees. Are you nervous?'

I shrugged. 'I used to be on the telly from time to time when I was a reporter. Promoting an investigation or to comment on a news piece. I was once actually offered a job for a TV production company, but turned it down.'

'Why?'

'Because I thought print journalism had more integrity. More fool me: it was just a few months later that the paper went online and I got the elbow. Hold on.'

A small group of men was approaching from the car park, all dressed smartly in black, their raincoats flapping behind them like the wings of crows. Oriana and her cameraman headed towards them, confronting the man in the centre, who I could tell from his cropped grey hair and ashen face was Marco Ligabue.

He shook his head, tried to get around her, but she had more moves, managing to block his path while thrusting the microphone forward. He was forced to stop, and there was a brief exchange before another member of his group moved between them and Marco was able to sidestep Oriana, making it through the sliding doors into the building, where he almost barrelled into me. He drew up, a flicker of recognition appearing upon his lips as if I was an old friend out of context, until he remembered. His face fell and he barged passed me, along with his entourage.

'It would be much easier if you would just speak to us,

Signor Ligabue,' called Oriana, who had followed him into the building. 'If you've got nothing to hide, what are you hiding from?' She stood there coolly watching them go while her cameraman shot over her shoulder. 'Okay.' She drew a finger across her throat. 'Cut.' She broke into a dazzling smile and came to greet us. '*Darling*. What are you doing here?'

'We just stopped by to have some lunch,' I said. Oriana looked amused.

'Really? Just lunch? Are you *sure* you're telling me everything, *Mister* Leicester?'

'Honestly,' I said. 'We were outside the city, following up a lead about Ryan, and dropped in here on the way back.'

'And what lead would that be? Or will I have to ask you this evening?'

'I can tell you,' I said. 'But it would have to be off the record because it's a question of client confidentiality.'

She seemed to consider this, then considered me. 'All right,' she said. 'But don't break my balls if we come up with the same information from other sources.'

'I won't break your balls,' I said. 'Considerable though they may be.'

Oriana looked at Dolores. 'Anyone would think he'd seen me naked.' Dolores turned crimson.

'Congratulations,' I said, 'for managing to embarrass my young colleague. I never thought I'd see the day.'

'I'm not embarrassed!'

'Anyway,' I said, 'we were coming back from a visit to a truffle company . . .'

'Benvenuto Truffles?'

I smiled. 'I couldn't say. But it turns out she had hired

Ryan to check the work of her food tasters. A sort of quality review. A supertaster to check the tasters. It doesn't get us much further, but it does help explain why he was doing the rounds of the restaurants.'

'It does,' said Oriana. 'Nothing more? Have you managed to get anywhere with this missing cook?'

'Not as yet. I'm following it up this afternoon.' I shook my head, almost as if to shake off Oriana's spell – as usual, she was asking all the questions. 'But what are *you* doing here? It's a bit extreme, isn't it, monstering the grieving family?'

'Ah, but who's to say they're grieving?'

'Who's to say they're not?'

'Did you know Antichi Artigiani del Cibo is massively in the red? This place,' she meant Cibo d'Italia, 'shot a huge hole in their finances. Marco has been on at his dad to get rid of it for ages.'

'So you're saying it was suicide now?'

'With all that mess in the office? No note? I hardly think so. And Marco was found at the scene of the crime.'

'Really?'

'Yes, darling, really. With his dad out of the way, he might be able to get rid of this place, cut his losses, save the business . . . or at least walk away with some money in the pot. Motive enough for you?'

'That's *Occhio Pubblico* – judge, jury and executioner.'

'In this country, somebody's got to be. And tonight – the Lees are ready? You've got all the details?'

'I've got all the details.'

'*A dopo*, then.' She gave me a semi-formal kiss, Dolores a little wave, and went on her way.

'You two seemed to get on well,' said Dolores.

'Your face!'

'What? It's just hot in here . . .'

We went to the exit, headed to the car. As we drove out, we got stuck at the barriers behind a line of trucks bearing the four staggered red lines of Millefoglie SpA.

Chapter 18

'Ishaan . . . no,' said Luca Monza. 'Never heard that name, but that doesn't mean anything.'

'I was thinking he may have registered at the shelter. Maybe you could check on the system . . .'

Luca raised a bushy black eyebrow. 'Now why would I want to do that?'

I gave him an even look. 'Why indeed,' I said. 'Can I buy you another drink?' He looked down at his three-quarters-full glass of beer and shook his head. I looked down at my empty wine glass.

'But you go ahead,' he said.

We were sitting at a chipped table near the bar at a Bologna institution, Osteria della Luna, which was as obstinately decrepit as usual, its owners apparently determined to hold out against the encroachment of the Antichi Artigiani del Cibo-style eateries that now lined the lanes around it. That was not to say that stray tourists didn't occasionally come and loiter at the entrance – it had begun to pop up in those ubiquitous insiders' guides – but they rarely remained. With its tatty tiles, cracked walls, yellowing notices and photographs, limited drinks choice and the only food available that which the customers had brought in themselves, it was certainly a curiosity, but it didn't exactly fit the image of Bologna promoted in the weekend travel sections. As Len Ligabue might have observed, there could be such a thing as too authentic. And it got pretty boisterous at times as well.

But not now – La Luna was empty except for us and a couple of old guys who really needed a drink at three o'clock in the afternoon.

I tried to attract the attention of the woman leaning behind the bar, chin resting upon her palm, a picture of boredom. She had a pretty typical look for La Luna – all in black with a faded tattoo running up one of her forearms. Her curly hair was chopped to an uneven dark bob, leaving her long neck bare. A grave powder-white face was dominated by a striking Roman nose; large brown eyes were rimmed by charcoal. Finally I called across.

'Can I have a Coke?'

She looked insulted. 'No Coke here.'

'Something *like* Coke, then?'

She shrugged. She would see what she could do.

'Coke?' Luca looked amused, which was a bit cheeky for someone who could get through an entire evening nursing a small beer.

'I'm on that TV programme tonight.'

'Looking forward to it.'

'You and Rose both.'

'But not you? I would have thought it would have been a blast from the past. Maybe you're nostalgic for the old days.'

I shook my head. 'You can't go back.'

Luca understood. As my oldest friend in Bologna, and boss at the homeless shelter I'd worked at when I'd first arrived in an effort to pick up the language, he knew my history. Even though he, on the other hand, *had* gone back – after a spell behind a desk at the Comune, he had managed to return to his old job, and as a consequence was well acquainted with the current state of Bologna's underclass. But whether he would help me track down an immigrant was another matter – and we weren't talking about some kind of bribe. With Luca Monza it was always about principle.

'Hey!' The woman nodded at a dubious-looking dark bottle in front of her. I realised I was meant to get up and fetch it myself.

'Can I have a glass, please.' She could do that much, at least. 'And some ice.'

'Tastes shit with ice.'

'I'd like it with ice.'

She shrugged and filled the glass with ice, then looked at me with those big eyes. 'You want me to pour, or can you do that yourself?'

'I'm fine, thanks.' I took the bottle and the glass back to the table.

'I think she likes you,' whispered Luca.

'Romance is not dead. Anyway,' I said, 'this is purely a private matter – it's got nothing to do with Ishaan's immigration status, the authorities. I simply need to track down this missing American kid. After Ligabue's murder . . .'

'So it was a murder? There was speculation in the press.'

'It's being treated as one. Between the two of us, Ligabue hired Ryan, and now he's dead and Ryan's vanished.' I checked my phone, took another look at Alba's email. 'Ryan's last mobile signal was from a mast near Ligabue's home on the day he is believed to have died. Ishaan was seen wearing a T-shirt Ryan had been pictured in . . .' Luca gave me a sceptical look. 'I would be inclined to agree with you, particularly as Ryan did not appear to be wearing the T-shirt when he went missing. But as soon as I approached Ishaan, he fled.'

Luca shook his head. 'He's an immigrant, possibly illegal. I'd probably run if I saw you coming.'

'*Dai.*'

'You look . . . well, you *could* look like a cop . . .'

'I had the impression he was tipped off,' I said. 'At the other restaurant, which is why he wasn't there. And he really ran for it, Luca. He seemed terrified. It was like he knew something . . .'

'It means nothing.'

'Maybe,' I admitted. 'But if I could only,' I smiled at the cliché, 'eliminate him from our enquiries . . .'

'No police?'

'No police.'

'Tell me what you know,' he sat back, 'and what he looks like.'

'Well, he's a good-looking young guy,' I said, 'with something of a quiff. You could say a kind of Indian Elvis. The youthful, good-looking one, I mean, not the old fat one . . .' I gave him the best picture I could.

'I'll see what I can do,' said Luca. 'The name could be false, you know. Really, even with the description you've given me, it'll be like a needle in a haystack.'

'Anything you can find out . . .'

We got up and went to the bar. The woman unfolded from her angular pose to stand tall, at least for an Italian. She rang in the payment on the old-style till, which, like much else in La Luna, was antique more through entropy than design. Along with the receipt, she handed me a napkin.

'Maybe this will help find your supertaster,' she said. I looked down; upon the napkin was a sketch that almost perfectly captured my description of Ishaan.

'That's brilliant,' I said. I took a photo of the picture, then handed it to Luca. 'How did you do that?'

She looked annoyed. 'I'm an artist.'

'Everybody is somebody else in Bologna,' said Luca.

'Then what else are you?' said the woman.

'Married,' he said plaintively.

I thought of something. 'Do you have a card?' The woman and Luca exchanged a look – as if she would have a card! She took another napkin and wrote her name and email.

'Stella Amore,' I said. 'Is that a real name?' She gave me that offended look again.

'It's *my* name,' she said.

Chapter 19

Via Castiglione is one of the most venerable streets in Bologna. Beginning beneath the two towers, it runs beside the medieval guildhall before gradually climbing south past Palazzo Pepoli, complete with its portcullis and battlements, crossing Via Farini and assuming embowed porticoes as elegant as the Renaissance aristocracy who once stepped out beneath them, before it curves upwards towards the old city gate.

But the porticoes are interrupted midway by an old lady, venerable Santa Lucia, a squat box of a church founded in the fifth century and taking its current form a few hundred years later, the stubbly brick facade echoing big brother San Petronio in Maggiore, the main square. The pointy brickwork was designed to carry a smooth facade but, like the geological gradations that mark the advent of the Ice Age, so these crocodile-skinned Italian churches inevitably memorialise the coming of the Great Plague, when building work was halted due to labour and financial shortages. They mark Catholicism's historical high-water mark: before the Renaissance, Reformation and Darwinism forced other, less grandiose priorities.

Napoleon kicked the last priests out of Santa Lucia at the turn of the nineteenth century, and it had had many incarnations since, even, in the 1950s, as a gaol for female prisoners who had campaigned for equal rights. Now, like so much else in Bologna, it had been swallowed up by the university for use as an auditorium, hence *Occhio Pubblico* hiring it as the venue for their 'Bologna special'.

I picked up the Lees in a hired limo from their hotel, sitting in the front as we drove through the centre. I turned to inform them that another client had offered to contribute to the financial burden of the investigation. From now on, we would charge them the bare minimum for retention of our services.

'Why would they do that?' asked Mr Lee.

'They hired Ryan in the first place and are obviously keen to help however they can.'

'Who are they?'

I explained about Liana Benvenuto, and the purpose of Ryan's assignment, although I left out the bit about the mafia. I did add, however: 'You should know, when you go on TV this evening, the focus will be on the death of an Italian celebrity, a well-known restaurateur, probably murdered. A link may be made to Ryan's disappearance.'

They looked startled. 'Do you think it's connected?' asked Mrs Lee.

'There is no way of knowing,' I said. 'It could be entirely coincidental. However, this person, Len Ligabue, was one of the people who hired Ryan.' They seemed to almost physically deflate at the news. 'But I want to emphasise,' I went on, 'I don't have any reason to believe Ryan is dead. And it would not surprise me at all if the two incidents were completely unconnected.'

'Do you *really* believe that, Mr Leicester?' asked Mrs Lee with a mother's intensity.

'I admit that there are elements about our case that are . . . a concern, but I certainly wouldn't give up hope. If you are looking for connections – and *Occhio Pubblico* certainly will, although as far as I'm aware they don't know anything about the specific link with Ligabue – it's always easy to find them, but sometimes you see things that aren't there. There may be a perfectly mundane reason why Ryan has gone missing, and even if it is connected with another crime, I don't see any reason to believe he's not still alive.'

'But if it's to do with criminals . . . murderers . . .'

'A request for a ransom is not inconceivable,' I said. They looked at each other.

'I'm not sure we could afford . . .'

'Don't worry about that now,' I said. 'If they ask for a ransom, then at least we will know something, and of course the police are very experienced at dealing with that kind of thing.'

'But surely kidnappers would tell us not to go to the police,' said Mrs Lee.

'Let's cross that bridge if we come to it.' I was beginning to wish I hadn't said anything, but at least it had distracted them from thinking the worst.

We pulled up outside Santa Lucia. I got out and opened the passenger-side door. Mrs Lee stepped onto the pavement, looking up at the large church. Again I was struck by how strange all this must seem to them – but then I supposed if your child has disappeared, unusual surroundings, strange events, even people like me are little more than scenery.

We crossed the small cobbled square, past mobile units bleeding cables through the church's double doors. We followed them up the stone steps and inside.

It was a huge space that seemed more appropriate for a political rally or conference than a TV show, rows of seats sweeping back from where once would have stood an altar but were now set arc lights, scaffolding and TV cameras orientated towards a stage. Rising upwards was the traditional platform on which *Occhio Pubblico*'s on-camera audience would sit like a jury in a provincial court. At a right angle, the seats and table for guests. In the middle, a raised stool.

There was the usual chaotic activity that accompanied TV shows, which, despite the running, shouting and arguing, would magically resolve itself at the last minute to produce something impeccably professional, although at this early stage in the countdown they were still in the full throes of apparent mayhem.

'No no *no*,' said a young woman approaching us with a clipboard. 'We're closed.'

'We're guests,' I said.

'Who are you?' She looked as severe as one of those six-foot *corazzieri* that guarded the president of the republic, although she was only tiny.

'These are the Lees. I'm their translator. There's an item on their son, Ryan Lee.'

'Oh! The Oriental!'

'They're Americans,' I said.

'You know what I mean.' She checked her Apple watch,

giving me an irritated look before assuming a fantastically insincere smile as she turned to the Lees. 'Welcome,' she said in English, shaking their hands. 'Welcome to Italy!' The Lees smiled uncertainly. She turned back to me.

'You're early,' she said in Italian.

'We're on time.'

She looked at her clipboard again. 'I suppose you are, but no one else is.' She gave the Lees that smile again, and turned on her heel. 'Come on, then,' she said, leading us down the empty centre aisle.

'So how does this show work, exactly?' said Mr Lee as we sat in the front row and the machinery of the studio continued around us.

'I guess there will be some kind of introduction,' I said. 'Then they'll kick off with the main item, which will inevitably be the murder I mentioned, before they come to the other more high-profile stories.'

'But if they want high-profile cases,' said Mrs Lee, 'why are they interested in us?'

'It coincides with their visit to Bologna,' I said. 'The fact that Ryan's a foreigner, and probably the truffle element too – we can't rule out them trying to connect it all together, even if they don't know anything about the Ligabue link.'

'Well,' said Mr Lee. 'Just as long as it gets the information out there – if someone has seen, knows something . . .'

'That's right,' said Mrs Lee. 'I mean, how many Korean Americans can there be in this city?'

'You're already here?' It was Oriana in yet another incarnation – a smart blue trouser suit and heels. We got to our feet. 'Thank you so much for coming,' she said in English to the Lees. She gave them both a lingering hug. 'You are both very brave.'

'Anything for our boy,' said Mrs Lee.

'Daniel.' She gave me a semi-formal peck on both cheeks.

'You suddenly appear to have acquired perfect English,' I said.

'Oh, it's not so good, is it?' She was a picture of innocence – a look that didn't suit her at all.

'It's very good,' I said. 'So much so that I doubt you even need me here to translate.' The Lees looked alarmed.

'Oh no,' said Oriana. 'You can translate my questions for the TV audience.' She turned again to the Lees. 'Obviously everything will be in Italian on air. Now, has it been explained to you how it works?'

As Oriana laid out the programme schedule in fluent English, part of me felt like stepping back into the shadows of the auditorium . . . then out into the evening air. Perhaps I could make it home in time to watch the programme live. It wasn't that I minded playing the translator on TV; it was that I'd suspected from the off that Oriana was more proficient at English than she had been letting on, and I wondered how much more she had kept to herself. I felt like a fly caught in a web. The spider was still out of sight, but I could sense the silk quivering. Oriana caught my eye and flashed me an amused smile that left me feeling like dinner.

Now everything happened quickly. We were whisked to a make-up area behind the stage. On the other side of canvas screens we could hear the auditorium beginning to fill, the stage manager corralling the uncomplaining on-screen audience into position and explaining how when the red lights went on, they were live, and 'the whole of Italy can see you, so think about where you're putting your hands' (this, I thought to myself, was clearly why so many of the middle-aged and elderly women who usually filled the screen behind the host looked so constipated).

The green room for guests in a standard TV studio exists to insulate them from the behind-the-scenes whirl, but at Santa Lucia there were no such facilities and we sat making awkward conversation, through me, with other guests – ordinary people like the Lees who had been the victims of crime or lost loved ones, while production assistants, journalists, gaffers and the rest dashed around, and often into each other, as they prepared to go live.

A hush fell in the auditorium, and backstage. The production crew froze; in fact we all did, looking up at the screen rigged in the area in front of us. The news faded and *Occhio Pubblico*'s police-blue credits came up, and with them the face of their statuesque flame-haired presenter announcing, 'Tonight, in our special from Bologna, city of porticoes, city of shadows, we feature a case that has enthralled the nation – the mysterious death of famous restaurateur Len Ligabue, discovered at the bottom of one of the red city's iconic towers, and explore the circumstances that led to his gruesome end. We also feature cases throughout the city and region, including a young American supertaster, whose strange disappearance, which occurred at the same time as Signor Ligabue's death, adds a further dimension of mystery to the murder that has shocked all of Italy.'

I softly translated to the Lees, cutting out the hyperbole

and playing down the link to Ligabue.

The challenge for Italian public TV shows is to keep their audience tuned in for the duration of the programme, which often stretches for up to three hours or more across an evening. Italian television has nothing approaching the funding in the UK, so fills its airtime with lengthy, low-cost programmes. Most evenings these are talk shows, typically featuring politicians – the only people they can get on for nothing – so almost every night is dominated by parliamentarians shouting over each other before a studio audience amid eccentric sets created, I suppose, to distract from the tedious subject matter. Imagine BBC's *Question Time* on the deck of the Starship *Enterprise*, three or more hours a night, every night.

Game shows, old dubbed Hollywood movies and true-crime programmes fill the gaps. *Occhio Pubblico* was one of the most venerable *Crimewatch*-style shows, parachuting its investigative teams into locations that had experienced a particularly noteworthy crime, and throwing local missing people into the mix – always a source of grim fascination in such a family-orientated society.

The death of Len Ligabue had a lot going for it – celebrity, mystery, murder. Here was an event that could be strung out across the entire three-hour programme, which would naturally include numerous ad breaks.

I wasn't sure how to read the fact that the slot on Ryan was scheduled midway through. Did this mean that they would specifically link him to Len's death? Probably. It would be prime viewing time. But also, to be fair, this would mean he received maximum exposure. Now we were here, I was coming around to the idea that getting Ryan's face out there might move us forward – yes, we had a tenuous lead in Ishaan, but little else to show for our efforts except ominous connections with the late Ligabue and the counterfeit truffle trade. If he *had* been seized, if he *was* still alive, a random witness might provide us with the breakthrough that could help us – or the police – save his skin or at least recover his body. If the mafia really had got hold of him, short of ransoming him off, he would be lost to us in any case.

To their – and particularly Oriana's – credit, *Occhio Pubblico* had been all over the Ligabue story, to an extent that would have been unthinkable in the UK. *Paparazzi* was not an Italian word for nothing, and in a culture where there sometimes seemed to be a law against everything, conversely anything appeared to be permitted *Occhio Pubblico*, perhaps in the knowledge that few would consider resorting to Italy's notoriously backlogged justice system to sue for recompense.

The opening, narrated by Oriana striding in front of a screen in the studio, focused on the discovery of Len's body – a shot of the cordoned-off front door on Strada Maggiore, then some shaky phone footage of the bloodstained rubble by the fountain, which had presumably been obtained from someone at the scene. Next came highlights of Len's career: his rise to prominence after inheriting his father's restaurant – I recognised Il Cacciatore – then going on to develop Antichi Artigiani del Cibo, which he had managed with his son, Marco. The slot wound up at the peak of Len's accomplishments – Cibo d'Italia – but finished with a shot of Oriana pursuing Marco toward the entrance, asking: 'Was this a step too far?'

'So they think he got into money trouble?' said Mr Lee as the show cut to *pubblicità*.

'That seems to be the direction they're taking,' I agreed.

'Dirty money, loan sharks, it adds up,' he said.

'But where does Ryan fit into this?' asked Mrs Lee.

'As I was saying,' I said, 'he probably doesn't.'

'Are you ready?' It was Oriana, in the flesh, in English. 'There will be a slot on other cases in Emilia Romagna, then you should come on in around ten minutes. Someone will collect you.'

'You were very good, dear,' said Mrs Lee. 'I mean, from what we could tell. Daniel translated.'

'Thanks!'

'Run us through what you will need from us again,' I said.

'Oh.' She waved her hands vaguely. 'We'll talk about Ryan, show his photo. We have some stock footage of truffle hunting and the trade, and then we will ask Mr and Mrs Lee about the kind of boy he was, and to make a plea for anyone who knows anything, et cetera.' She smiled at me. 'Or you can, for them.'

'That's it?'

'It should be about . . . eight minutes.'

She disappeared again and we sat there, the nerves beginning to jangle as the commercial break came to an end and a production assistant – the rude one we had met earlier – materialised, ready to accompany us on set.

Then we were up and on our way towards an audience of millions.

It's a rarefied atmosphere beneath that sun-hot lighting and the camera's pitiless eye, subject to the whims of production crew and presenter alike, but apart from advising the Lees to dress lightly because of the heat, I had not given them any particular pointers – I would be the translator after all, and would try to soak up the pressure, even if Oriana's sudden grasp of English had unsettled me. For now, I chose to take her at her word – that my role was all part of the theatre.

We were seated on high stools and miked up while the adverts ran. The on-camera audience shifted, stretched and coughed, making them appear considerably more human than they did on screen, while beyond the white lights I could see the shapes of dozens, if not hundreds, in the auditorium. Oriana was standing centre stage, having some make-up applied at the same time as holding an apparently two-way conversation with the production team hidden beyond the lights.

The make-up girl scurried away. Oriana straightened herself up and turned ninety degrees towards the camera, placing one foot slightly forward. The angry red light came on, signalling we were live.

'At the same time as Len Ligabue met his tragic fate, Bologna's restaurant world would be rocked by further mystery – the disappearance of a food taster, an American hired by Signor Ligabue.' So she did know, I thought. My mouth went dry but I tried to keep my expression as passive as possible. 'Now we have in the studio the parents of Signor Ryan Lee, accompanied by the private detective who has been hired to find him. Tell me, Mr Lee, what happened?' She looked at me, and I felt the gaze of the whole of Italy, including my daughter.

'She would like you to tell her what happened,' I explained to Mr Lee. He looked at his wife, who gave him a reassuring nod, and he explained what they knew, which I then relayed to Oriana.

'Doesn't he think it is a strange coincidence that Ryan disappeared at the same time?' she asked. I turned to Mr Lee and translated.

'Well, yes,' he said. 'Now you come to mention it.'

'Would you be even more surprised, Mr Lee,' she said, 'if I told you that your son, Ryan, was the last person to see Signor Ligabue alive?'

'How do you know that?' I asked her.

'Please, Signor Leicester, translate the question.'

I turned to Mr Lee. 'She's saying that Ryan was the last person to see Ligabue alive.'

'How does she know that?' he asked.

'He said how do we know that,' Oriana translated before I could get there. She turned back towards the camera. 'There were clear signs of a struggle in Len Ligabue's office,' the screens switched to photos far more professional than mine, 'but while many of us now keep our movements up to date via our computers or phones, Signor Ligabue was a traditional man and wrote his appointments in a desk diary. The police found it on the floor.' Cut to a large black leather embossed diary among the papers. Then another shot open at the page for Sunday. At 15.00 was scribbled quite clearly *Ryan Lee*. 'Mobile records also indicate that Lee's last signal was close to the home of Signor Ligabue at 14.40. Meanwhile the autopsy states that Signor Ligabue had been dead for at least twenty-four hours, which means he most probably fell to his death on the Sunday afternoon. It's all beginning to add up,' she concluded.

'What's she saying?' whispered Mr Lee.

'What I am saying,' Oriana di Principe said in English, swinging around to face Mr and Mrs Lee, 'is that your son is the prime suspect in the murder of Len Ligabue.' She then turned back to the camera and repeated herself in Italian. Members of the studio audience gasped. One old lady even crossed herself.

'Judge, jury and executioner,' I said in English. Then added in Italian, 'That's not proof.'

'He's in the diary!' a man from the audience called.

'Maybe they took him,' I said loudly, looking straight at the camera. Oriana got between it and me.

'So,' she said, 'this mysterious "they" murdered one of Italy's most famous restaurateurs but decided to kidnap an anonymous American?' She turned to the audience. 'Does that seem likely?' They wagged their heads. 'How much more likely that the pair had some kind of argument, a fight, and Signor Ligabue was the victim? Ryan Lee then panicked, fled the scene and went on the run.'

'Where's your motive?' I said. 'Where's your evidence, other than an entry in a diary? It's rubbish. Irresponsible journalism.'

'There we have it.' Oriana placed her hands on her hips as she turned back to the camera. 'A failed English journalist lecturing *Occhio Pubblico*, Italy's greatest investigative programme. Fortunately we will not be diverted from our search for the truth, wherever it leads. Now, we have to ask all our viewers,' the photo of Ryan flashed up on the giant screens behind us, 'to call or write to us immediately if you have any information on the whereabouts of Ryan Lee so we can get to the bottom of this mystery and deliver justice for one of Italy's most beloved restaurateurs and his family.'

Chapter 20

The red light flicked off as the programme went to a recorded segment and Oriana de Principe strode away from us like a boxer who had landed a sucker punch. As a pair of production assistants pounced to relieve us of our mics, I went after her.

'What the hell was that?' I said in Italian – I wanted everyone to hear this. 'You accused their missing son of murder live on air!'

Oriana whirled around. 'I followed the evidence – something you should be doing.'

'I didn't know about this appointment.'

'There we are – and if you had, what conclusion would you have drawn?'

'Whatever it might have been, I wouldn't have leapt to judgement on live TV! And in front of the parents!'

'It's a shame,' she said, glancing over to where they were being led away. 'But you have only yourself to blame.'

'What do you mean?'

'You shouldn't have let them on if you were so concerned. You knew all about the Ligabue link, which you concealed from me, and God knows what else. Come on, you must have known we would link the two.'

'But this . . .' I said. 'It was such a . . . leap. Where did you get the diary from? The access?'

'You know I can't reveal my sources.'

'Alessandro?'

'You mean Ispettore Umberto Alessandro? Your boss's old number two? Surely you can ask him that yourself.'

'And what about Marco? The business being off the rails?'

'Oh yes,' she said. 'There's still that.'

'Well?'

She gave me a curious look. 'This isn't a one-off, Daniel. There'll be plenty of time to get to that . . . This story's going to run and run, a little like your supertaster.'

I caught up with the Lees at the rear exit. Mr Lee looked drawn, Mrs Lee looked furious.

'What *happened*, Daniel?'

'I'm sorry,' I said. 'I thought they might link it to Ligabue, but I had no idea they were going to make that accusation.'

'Ryan's no murderer.'

'I'm sure he's not.'

'You'll be the only one – the whole of Italy must think he is now. What is this business about the diary? How did she find that out, and you not? We thought you had connections.'

'I'll follow that up immediately,' I said.

'And the police – if they really think he's responsible, they haven't even approached us.'

'That may indicate their true feelings about his guilt.'

'Have we made a mistake with you?' said Mrs Lee. 'We

only want to find Ryan. Can you really help us, or should we be looking elsewhere?'

'You can always try someone else,' I said. 'But I don't think another agency could move more quickly.'

'Because if the worst has happened to him,' she said, her voice trembling, 'I would want to think we had given it our all. Can you look me in the eye and promise me that you're the best, Mr Leicester?'

'I can promise you, Mrs Lee,' I said, 'that I will *try* my best.'

She gave me a searching look. 'I suppose that will have to do.'

We stepped outside. It had begun to rain, and the cobbles gleamed jet under the lamplight. I walked them to their taxi and they got in without saying goodbye. As soon as the cab had passed beneath the narrow arch of the gatehouse marking the old inner city wall, I called Ispettore Alessandro.

'You had better come over,' he said.

'Where are you?'

'Paradise.'

Chapter 21

Paradise was in the quarter between Via Indipendenza and the university area, in one of the few unporticoed streets in the neighbourhood. It was a two-storey red-brick *palazzo* that was giving nothing away with its somewhat bland, albeit well-maintained, medieval facade, dark oak door and iron lion-head knocker. There was only a single brass button beside a faintly illuminated nameplate that read, as the Ispettore had said it would, *1256*.

I rang and waited. Waited and rang. Finally there was a scraping sound and the door slowly opened.

'Yes?' It was a sinewy old woman clad entirely in black.

'I am here to see Ispettore Umberto Alessandro.'

'And you are?'

'Daniel Leicester.'

She nodded and stood aside to let me in.

I stepped into a huge frescoed hall. Even for someone who had become accustomed to the constant aesthetic barrage that comes with living in Italy, this was something else. It was like entering the mouth of a baroque whale.

'I don't know much about art,' I said, as I followed her up the grand marble staircase, 'but the fresco . . .'

'Yes, it's Carracci,' she said, without turning around.

She pushed through a pair of frosted-glass doors into a long, dark library with a wooden ceiling displaying dingy hunting scenes upon each panel. The walls were lined with books, the windows set high like a scriptorium in a monastery, presumably to afford maximum light and minimum distraction, although the only light this evening came from the orange glow of the huge fire roaring at the far end of the hall.

We walked along the central aisle towards another set of frosted-glass doors, into a second hall with a high vaulted ceiling. Beneath it, studded leather armchairs and sofas were arranged in discreet clusters, with suited men talking quietly to each other. Another huge fire cast a comforting glow.

Ispettore Alessandro was sitting alone reading a hardback book, *sans* dustcover, looking as resolutely elegant as usual, with that swept-back mane of grey and strong, deeply tanned Roman face; the double-breasted navy suit, striped shirt and plain bottle-green tie kept in place with a thin silver clip. A white cotton handkerchief rose like Mont Blanc from his top pocket. He placed the book down to greet me. On the spine it read *Leopardi*.

'You're lucky to have caught me.' He shook my hand, his grip smooth yet unfeasibly strong. 'I was just passing my phone over when you called – the club has a no technology policy.' He gave me a meaningful look. I dug out my own mobile and handed it to the old woman, who bowed and went on her way.

'I would have thought you would be the first person they would have wanted to call in an emergency.'

'Oh, in a *real* emergency they would know where to find me. Drink?'

'You know, after the night I've had, I could do with one. Scotch?'

He went over to a drinks trolley and poured a generous finger for us both into a pair of crystal glasses.

I took a seat. '"Paradise"?' I said.

'After the *Liber Paradisus*, which is Latin for *Heaven Book*. It was a law passed by the Comune in 1256 abolishing slavery and freeing the serfs, the first mass manumission in Europe.' He opened his arms. 'And it began here, in this very hall, on the initiative of a group of concerned citizens. Bologna's progressive credentials stretch back a long, long way, Daniel.'

'What were these citizens so concerned about precisely?'

'Oh,' he smiled, 'that they were running out of taxpayers. *Voilà.* Instead of having to pay for labour in the slave market, they got the labour to pay for itself and called it "freedom".'

'You had me worried.' I raised my glass. 'For a moment I thought you were unequivocally on the side of the good.'

The Ispettore frowned. 'I have missed your Puritan disapproval, Daniel. Have you forgotten you're in a Catholic country? Here, good is nothing *but* equivocal.'

'So you didn't see *Occhio Pubblico*?' I said. 'What your pet reporter got up to?'

'My wife is hosting her book group this evening, the latest Ferrante novel. I thought it best to make myself scarce . . . But don't worry, I have actually recorded it. "Bologna special", and so on. I was curious to see how they presented the murder of Signor Ligabue.'

'They pinned it on Ryan Lee.'

'Ah, *a serial-killing supertaster on the loose . . .*'

'You mean there's been more than one murder?' I said, alarmed.

'Just a manner of speaking. Are you any further on in finding the boy?'

I shook my head. 'But it would have helped if you had told us about his appointment with Ligabue.'

'She got hold of the diary, you mean? She's good, I'll give her that.'

'So you didn't feed it to her?'

'Why would I do that?'

'I don't know . . . to distract from the true direction the case is taking? Just like you put her on to us in the first place to get her off your back?'

To my surprise, Alessandro pulled out an e-cigarette from his inside pocket. It looked like an expensive pen between his fingers. 'The final straw,' he said apologetically, 'was the no-smoking policy at the Caserma. The writing was on the wall.' He expelled a puff of watery white smoke. 'It's a valid lead,' he said. 'Your boy *did* have an appointment with Signor Ligabue, and his signal was lost nearby around the same time. Everything points to a connection between the two – and here is something Signora de Principe's mole in our department does not know, as I have purposely kept it to a tight circle: we also found Mr Lee's prints at the scene.'

'He could have met Ligabue there at any time,' I said.

'Indeed, but still . . .'

'Surely you don't think he did it. He had only been in the country for a few weeks. There was no previous record of conflict between the pair of them. Ryan has no criminal record, history of aggression or mental illness. It just doesn't make any sense.'

Alessandro nodded. 'It seems most unlikely.'

'Then . . .?'

'Something to do with Ryan's assignment,' he said, 'on behalf of Liana Benvenuto but also connected to Ligabue – the truffle trade and the infiltration of counterfeits into the Italian market.'

'The mafia?' I said.

The Ispettore smiled. 'There's always the mafia. We're looking into it.'

'What about Ligabue's son, Marco? The lack of an alibi, AAC's financial woes?'

He shrugged. 'It could explain his father's death, but it doesn't really help with your missing American, at least not if your focus is on finding him alive. A financial trawl will take time. What about this cook?'

'We've got a sketch.' I showed him the photo on my phone. 'We're going to ask about.'

Alessandro took another puff on his e-cigarette, then pulled out a small notebook. He wrote down an address, tore off the sheet of paper and handed it to me.

'You might like to begin here.'

It was midnight. The students had returned to the city but were yet to start their lectures. They packed the bars and porticoes, propping themselves against the ancient columns to sup beer, smoke pot, reacquaint themselves with old friends and show off new tattoos. The business conventions had begun to reappear, untidy crocodiles of northern European engineers and salesmen boggling at the graffiti, the kids, the contrast to their utilitarian homelands.

But despite the shadowy womb-red porticoes, the girl riding past perched upon the handlebars of her lover's bicycle, there was an edge in the air – studies were about to recommence, there was business to be done. Summer might wish to linger, reluctant to say its goodbyes, but autumn was in the hall, hanging up its coat.

I stepped into the courtyard of the Faidate Residence and looked up. All the lights were out except for a dim glow from Rose's room. I walked up the two flights to our apartment, my humiliation on national TV only now seriously beginning to sink in as I thought about my friends and colleagues witnessing it, most of all my daughter.

I left my stuff in the kitchen and went to tap softly on her door. When she didn't reply, I opened it and peeked inside. She was asleep in front of her iPad, still churning out *Occhio Pubblico*. I switched it off and backed out.

'Dad,' I heard her say, propping herself up and rubbing her eyes.

'Go to sleep,' I said. 'We can talk about it in the morning.'

'What happened?'

I could see that wasn't going to work. I returned to sit on the end of her bed.

'I'm sorry,' I said. She looked surprised.

'What for?'

'For what happened. I know you'd told your friends . . . I'm sorry if I disappointed . . . embarrassed you.'

'Oh!' She wrapped her arms fiercely around me, as I should have wrapped my arms around her, then pulled back.

'It wasn't your fault. What a horrible cow! It was clearly an ambush. And to have the parents on, too. It was a terrible thing to do. Exactly like you said, "irresponsible journalism". I was so proud of you for standing up to her.'

'Really?'

'Of course! Really, really proud.'

I looked into those earnest brown eyes, her mother's eyes, then stood up – I had to get out of there before I burst into tears. 'Now you get some sleep,' I said. 'You can give me another pep talk in the morning.'

'O-*kaaay*.'

I closed the door, returned to the kitchen and spotted the Laphroaig. Hell, another wee dram wouldn't do any harm. I took my glass to the balcony and wished, for the first time in quite a while, that I had a cigarette to accompany it.

I thought about Oriana and felt a damn fool. Such a bloody fool – for being so complacent, as if the intimacy we had shared had meant anything. As if even if it had, it could possibly have got in the way of a good story. And there was me thinking that maybe that would be my salvation – to find another like-minded individual, another journalist. I'd conveniently forgotten I'd never been that kind of hack in the first place. I'd always been too much of a bleeding heart, which is precisely why I had found a soulmate not in some hard-bitten hack but in Lucia, who had provided me with genuine salvation in the daughter we had made together, whose love for her father was strong enough to overcome what surely must have bordered on social disaster in her teenage universe.

'She's your girl through and through,' I said out loud.

'Thank God for you, Lucy, Lucia. I miss you. You know that, don't you?'

I leant forward to hear her reply but, resting upon the balcony, my forearms settled into grooves smoothed by previous generations, I received the usual oblique response: a sole chime from the tower of San Procolo, and beyond, the low purr of the city, its shutters closed, claws sheathed.

Patience as long as centuries.

Chapter 22

We checked the location Alessandro had given us on Google, detaching the little golden man from the traditional map and dragging him to the road in question, Via Ercolani, in the north-west of the city, which, although within the walls, occupied that quarter beyond Via Marconi that had been destroyed by Allied bombers trying to take out the railway station during the Second World War. Reconstruction had not led to the return of medieval-style dwellings. Instead they had been replaced with a series of tidy brick low-rises, bland but not unpleasant – what British new towns might have looked like had they been designed by Italians.

The road itself was off the roundabout by the basketball stadium (Bologna's Virtus being the true recipient of the city's sporting pride, given that the only pleasure to be derived from the soccer team was its annual struggle to remain in Serie A) and consisted of residential property above squared, glass-fronted commercial premises: estate agents, a watch repairer, a butcher, a bar. Around a third of the fronts were shuttered and up for sale. Between one such shuttered property and a pet shop was an employment agency – People Mover, a name that struck me as ironic given that it was plainly named after the airport's chronically delayed monorail into the city centre.

From the bar on the corner I sent Dolores to check out the agency. Meanwhile I would wait at the table, nursing my hangover. It had turned out my additional wee dram had led to another, then another . . . I ordered a large glass of sparkling water with my coffee and knocked back a strong aspirin.

Dolores wasn't long. 'Well?'

'I got a job.'

'You see what a decent haircut will do?'

'Yeah,' she said. 'Great career prospects: "hostess".'

'Tell me.'

'There was this creepy guy at the desk and two Asian men just sitting there as if they were waiting their turn. I sat beside them but he called me over straight away.'

'Why was he creepy?'

'Oh, you know . . . the way he looked at me.'

'Italian?'

She nodded. 'Anyway, I said I was looking for work, handed him the CV' – we'd composed a fake one for her, mainly around unskilled service stuff – 'and he immediately offered me this job greeting visitors to some kind of truffle expo. I thought there might be something in it, so I said yes. Starts tomorrow. But that's not the interesting thing.'

'What *is* the interesting thing?'

'The location,' she said. 'It's in Palazzo Malduce – the one in Via d'Azeglio.' She gave me a frustrated look. 'You know – the one I mentioned when we met the Count. The one he said belonged to a later branch of the family.'

'Well, that *is* quite a coincidence.' I thought of Ispettore

Alessandro sunk in that soft leather chair, his face flecked amber through the crystal of his whisky glass.

You might like to begin here . . .

I finished my coffee and got up. 'How do I look?'

'All right,' said Dolores. 'You could tuck your shirt in, though.'

I checked myself in the bar mirror. I straightened my brown knitted tie – I had given in to peer pressure and was wearing a seasonal corduroy jacket and dark jeans – but was otherwise presentable enough by Italian standards.

'Wait here,' I said.

'Where are you going?'

'To see if they'll offer a job to an out-of-work English teacher.'

There were now three Asian guys sitting passively upon the chairs by the wall. I went for the remaining spare seat but was promptly called over by the young guy behind the desk. He had a shaven head to compensate premature balding, but was not otherwise creepy in any obvious way, although I was not an attractive twenty-three-year-old woman. He gave me a frank visual appraisal. I liked to think I looked pretty good for someone in early middle age – I had kept my belly under control, and the archipelago of my widow's peak had yet to take the shape of an island – but I quickly grasped that were I some ordinary unemployed forty-something I wouldn't have had a hope. Until, that was, I opened my mouth.

'I'm English,' I said in Italian, 'but with permanent residence and the right to work in Italy. I'm looking for something immediately, and I'll consider anything.'

As expected, this changed everything. I had been no fan of Brexit, for obvious reasons, but I also knew it had improved the prospects for mother-tongue English speakers who had retained the right to live and work in the country.

'Take a seat,' he said.

'I'm sorry, I don't have a CV with me. I was just passing so thought I would pop in.'

'Don't worry. Now, tell me how I can help you.'

I explained that I was an English teacher married to an Italian. We had just moved to Bologna and I was planning to find work at a language school, but in the meantime I needed to begin earning immediately. Did he have anything in the hospitality sector, for example, where I might be able to use my language?

He opened his computer – a password, I made a point to notice: *pplmvr* – and clicked on a couple of files.

'Have you got a suit?' he said. 'I mean a smart one? Dark? Nice shoes?'

'I . . . yes.'

'Maybe get a haircut too. Look smart. We've got this event in the centre, starting tomorrow evening. There's an opening for an interpreter, but that's not really what they're looking for. There won't be any speeches. It's just to step in if their foreign VIPs have any questions. Do you think you could handle that?'

'Sure,' I said. 'No problem.'

'It'll be around five hours, at eight euros an hour. Okay?'

'Does that include tax or agency fee?'

He gave me a wry look. 'This isn't England,' he said.

'So no,' I said.

'I'm sorry, take it or leave it.'

'I'll take it.'

As I was going out, I stepped aside to let another Asian male through. He was followed by a white guy in a tight leather jacket and cowboy boots, who brushed by without acknowledging me.

'Last one,' he said.

Alba had moved a whiteboard into the boardroom. I drew a circle in the centre, which indicated Ryan's disappearance, then overlapped it with another, which stood for Len Ligabue. The shaded area between the two indicated both their contract and Ryan's last indicated position – in Len's office. As I talked the team through the current state of play, a pair of arrows sprouted from the respective circles and led to a further bubble containing Liana Benvenuto and Dante Millefoglie, the surviving members of the Triumvirate, along with *COUNTERFEIT TRUFFLES?* Another arrow led from Len to a Marco bubble, in which I wrote *MONEY WORRIES?* Floating between Marco and the Triumvirate was a final bubble, which included Count Malduce and Ishaan. Beneath the lot of them I drew a rectangular box, where I wrote *RYAN'S TRAIL*, although as I completed it, I realised it bore an unfortunate resemblance to a coffin. Anyway, I drew various lines indicating his engagement to the others, then taped a batch of snaps of the *jongi jeobgi* menagerie, which, along with a monkey, the saint and a pig, had now been joined by a couple of hawk-like birds that Jacopo had come across in the suburbs.

I stood back to look at the board, then turned to the Comandante.

'What do you think Alessandro knows that he's not telling us?' I asked.

The Comandante looked at me as if this was a stupid question, and I suppose it was – it went without saying that Alessandro would keep his cards close to his chest.

'The Special Operations Group focus on threats to the state,' he said. 'No doubt he welcomed our tip about the Ligabue case, but their bread and butter is broader stuff – terrorism, espionage, that kind of thing.' He indicated the Triumvirate bubble. 'Counterfeit truffles and mafia involvement would fit in this category – imagine the economic damage if it came out that foreign truffles were being passed off as Italian. It may be, as you suggest, that he has been steering the *Occhio Pubblico* reporter in Ryan's direction in order to distract from this whole issue, but remember, Daniel, he *is* a policeman – I'm sure he wants this young man to be recovered, if possible, alive.'

I shrugged. Although I had witnessed Alessandro's unorthodox working practices at first hand, I had to admit he had always kept his word – if not, then Signora Dolores Pugliese would not have been sitting around the table with us.

'He would have provided the address for good reason,' the Comandante continued. 'And the outcome of your visit seems to confirm that. I suppose this reporter may have tipped him off about the connection between Ishaan and Ryan, although I doubt it, but I also doubt anyone outside this office or the Triumvirate knew about the link with Count Malduce.'

'Which brings us to dodgy truffles,' I said.

'And the agency,' said Dolores, 'which connects the Count and Ishaan.'

'I've got the password to get into the system there,' I said to Jacopo. 'Do you think you could hack into the People Mover network? Presuming this is the agency that hired Ishaan, perhaps everything we need is there.'

'When do you need it?' he said.

'Before this event would be good.'

He winced. 'Look,' he said, 'hacking isn't like in the movies – I run a few programmes and I'm in. I'd have to penetrate their wireless network, and to do that I'd basically need to get someone in the office to download a program – let's call it malware, or a virus – which would then provide me with access. It wouldn't be a simple one either; it would need to be pretty complex. Even the most bog-standard PCs these days have firewalls and the like to prevent precisely this; in fact you don't really even need all this off-the-shelf stuff for your Windows PC any more, with its new inbuilt security settings.'

'So,' Alba said irritably, 'how come I'm always reading about people hacking stuff? Aren't you supposed to be the computer whizz?'

'The most effective form of hacking,' he intoned, 'remains, as it has always been, on site. Either someone has actually physically inputted a key into the USB that has basically farmed all the relevant information, or, like Dan, they have simply seen the password and logged on.'

'We're not going to be able to smuggle a key into the office and stick it in the console,' I said. 'At least, not in time. Well, let's see what we can pick up at the event – maybe someone will give us a lead on Ishaan.'

'We will have to force access,' said the Comandante.

Jacopo shook his head. 'No, Papà, you can't just "force" a modern firewall.'

'The premises had steel shutters, Daniel?' said the Comandante.

I nodded.

'Very well.' He picked up his phone while we all watched. 'Yes,' he said. 'Tonight . . . I know, I know, but then it always is, isn't it . . . A commercial premises . . . Excellent. Goodbye.' He placed the phone back on the table.

'The Nonnies?' I said.

He nodded. Jacopo and I exchanged a glance.

'Who are the Nonnies?' asked Dolores.

Chapter 23

The Comandante and I drove out to Casalecchio to meet Nonno Salvatore in the *pasticceria* on the main road. The town was a suburban appendage to Bologna proper, where many of the working – and criminal – classes had moved during the seventies and eighties to escape their gloomy homes within the walls for a taste of the countryside.

Once Casalecchio would have been almost as isolated as Boscuri, complete with a clay-grey river running through it; now major highways and rail links meant you could travel to the centre of Bologna in minutes. Of course, Nonno Salvatore, who had long since qualified for an elderly person's bus pass, despite never having paid a penny of tax, could have come to see us, but it only seemed polite for us to come to him at such short notice.

He had a mouth full of a *cannoli* when we spotted him at the table by the window, pastry crumbs clinging to the woollen tartan scarf knotted tightly around his throat. He still had his parka on, even though it was quite comfortable inside.

'Our TV star!' he said.

'Of course you were watching,' I said. 'That programme must be your highlight of the week.'

'Now, now,' said Salvatore. 'Temper, temper. You know you have to learn to keep your cool on television. You didn't come across well at all.'

'Since when were you an expert?'

Nonno Salvatore shot the Comandante a knowing grin. 'I have had my moments in the spotlight,' he said.

'He was a member of the San Lazzaro Crew,' explained the Comandante, 'as they were called by the press at the time. They broke into a number of minor banks across Emilia Romagna during the 1980s.'

'We were doing fine,' Salvatore said, 'until they put this one here in charge. Although if you ask me, Comandante, you still got lucky.'

'As you said on the programme.'

'It's on YouTube,' said Salvatore proudly.

'Are you on the programme?' I asked.

The Comandante shook his head. 'I declined to be interviewed.'

'He didn't want to admit he just got lucky,' said Salvatore.

'I would have been happy to admit that,' said the Comandante. 'Every action involves an element of luck. Take driving, for example. At some point even the best driver is going to be unlucky, even if it is through no fault of their own – another driver's mistake, perhaps. And that was all it was from my perspective, a matter of waiting. You might have got away with one job, three, but *seventeen*, Salvatore? Probability was against you. Your luck was always going to run out.'

'Bah,' said Salvatore. 'He always makes it sound like a science when it's an art.' For a moment his sour expression made me worry he was going to storm off – something he had been unable to do for five years after the Comandante had nabbed him – so I thought it best to change the subject.

'Where's Nonna Miranda?' A former brothel madam, she was usually the one to do the negotiating.

'Flu,' he said. 'In bed.'

'And Diego?' Salvatore rolled his eyes.

'Didn't you see the *Carlino*? Sent down.'

'I'm sorry,' I said.

'I warned him, dabbling in all this computer business. "It's the future, Uncle", and now *his* future is Christmas at La Dozza. Idiot. Stick to what you know.'

Despite the inconvenience of having his nephew incarcerated, Nonno Salvatore didn't seem overly concerned. In fact, he had brightened up. He winked at the Comandante. 'Still, *finishing school*.' Giovanni nodded as if indeed it was. 'So,' said the old con, 'tell me, how can we be of assistance?'

The Comandante filled him in on the requirements for the break-in, keeping the background oblique. As ever with the Nonnies, as with any criminals, it was important that things were on a need-to-know basis. Crooks were like water – they would flow into any nook or cranny given the chance.

Salvatore looked amused. 'Christ,' he said. 'If it wasn't for my legs, I'd do it myself.' He scrutinised me. 'Haven't you trained this one up?' He had a point. I'd done a lock-picking course and habitually carried a small set.

'The premises may be alarmed,' the Comandante said, I suspect to spare my blushes. The truth was we needed this done swiftly and efficiently, and Giovanni probably didn't want his son and son-in-law botching the job.

'All right,' said Salvatore with a knowing leer. 'I think I've got just the lad for you.'

I was driving back to Bologna along the old route, the winding road that had once been the only way to and from the suburb, when the Comandante said: 'You're looking tired, Daniel.'

'Well, it was a long night,' I said. 'And a pretty disastrous one, I have to admit. I'm sorry.'

'For what?'

'Letting the agency down. Really, *you* should have gone on.'

'I cannot interpret English, Daniel.'

'That wasn't a requirement, as it happens.'

'You weren't to know that,' said the Comandante.

'I should have. I was flattered, complacent . . .'

'We all make mistakes.'

'Is that your scientific method talking?'

'It's not science,' he said. 'That was just Salvatore's nonsense – merely an observation. We could not avoid appearing on the show. You did your best in the circumstances.'

'Well, it's out there now.' I glanced at him. 'Do you think Ryan's alive?'

The Comandante let out a long sigh. 'I hope so,' he said, his eyes remaining fixed upon the road. 'But amidst all this noise, I do worry that the lad may shortly be discovered floating in the Reno.'

'Suicide? An accident, even? A moment of madness? Bodies usually turn up pretty quickly if it's not suspicious. Floating, as you say, or the smell. There are just too many people about. The longer it takes, the more likely it seems that some form of criminality was involved. Let's say he *did* murder Ligabue – don't worry about motive for the moment – and disappeared under his own steam. He could have had it all planned out: a secret life, secret identity, secret funds . . .'

'If that *is* the case,' said the Comandante, 'then he will be found eventually. Although probably not by us.'

'That's not much of a vote of confidence, Giovanni.'

'What I mean is, if he really has gone to those lengths, then I suspect the time and resources required would exhaust the patience of even our clients in the Triumvirate. He would be far more likely to be tracked down via Interpol.'

'You mean he would have fled the country?'

'That's what I would do – particularly with Schengen in place. There are no border checks. And crime – regardless of how high-profile it might be in Italy – is almost always local. You look at the British newspapers on that phone of yours – have you seen any mention of Len Ligabue? Of course not. Slip over the border to Austria or France and it would be as if it had never happened. If he really *had* gone to those lengths, then that is what he should have done.'

'But you don't think he did murder Ligabue?'

'I think it is less probable.'

'And given that the non-criminal factors are also becoming less probable . . .'

'Yes, it appears more likely that he was taken against his will.'

'And more likely that he was taken by the killers of Len Ligabue.'

'It seems that way, yes.'

'But why?'

'Because, as you have said, he may have discovered or witnessed something he shouldn't have.'

'But in that case, why take him? If they were prepared to make Ligabue's death public, why not Ryan's?'

'It could have too obviously pointed to the truffle connection. Had Ryan's parents not been visiting, it may have taken a few weeks for them to realise that their son had disappeared and get in touch with us. Then even longer for us to join other dots. By that time *Occhio Pubblico* would have been and gone, the Ligabue case old news. And the longer it takes for an investigation to begin, the more time the perpetrator has to cover his tracks and for the trail to go cold.'

'So what I'm hearing is that you believe Ryan is dead.'

'It seems more probable,' said the Comandante.

'I'm beginning to understand why Nonno Salvatore got upset,' I said. 'Your logic seems irresistible, and rather depressing.'

'Oh!' The Comandante became unusually animated. 'But you are missing my point, Daniel. Quite the contrary – I was excited by the *extraordinary* just as much as Salvatore was. In his case, it was to reach twenty burglaries without getting caught, at which point he planned to retire – or so he lied to himself; in mine it was to solve the apparently unsolvable. The case of the San Lazzaro Crew was simple, although my colleagues didn't consider it thus at the time. Other cases much less so.

'My objective has always been to seek hope – of resolution, restitution – where previously there has been none. It may be *more* probable that Signor Lee has come to a sticky end, but until we have established that by eliminating the other possibilities, there is always the hope we will find him alive. I sincerely believe we may.' And he did look sincere, or at least as sincere as he did before he murmured a prayer of thanks before every meal.

'I can't help thinking,' I said, 'that I've just heard a pessimist trying awfully hard to sound optimistic.'

'I'm not a pessimist, Daniel. Simply a realist.'

'Isn't that what every pessimist says?'

Chapter 24

Ciro was a spindly, weasel-faced young man with a Campanian accent and one of those severe haircuts, almost a Mohican, favoured by Napoli soccer players and Camorristi. Here was a guy who had clearly grown up amid the clans, and I didn't have any doubt that breaking and entering was merely a minor accomplishment on his CV. He was a reminder, if any were needed, that despite the supposedly 'ordinary, decent criminal' credentials of the Nonnies – an established Bolognese crime family specialising in burglary, prostitution, gambling, and, of late, online phishing – there was really no such thing as ordinary and decent and they would have plenty of links with the multinationals south of Rome. In fact, probably the only reason set-ups like the Nonnies continued to be tolerated by the clans was to reassure the folk from the north that there was no real rush to reform. What happened in Naples stayed in Naples, that was the myth. Ciro here, and very possibly a dish of tagliatelle garnished with counterfeit truffles, was the reality.

I was surprised he had arranged to meet so early – it was 10 p.m., which seemed like a very public time to stage a break-in – but the Comandante hadn't batted an eyelid, so I wasn't going to ask. Meeting beneath the portico outside our office, we were able to walk to the venue, which also lacked the drama I would usually associate with this kind of activity, but I suppose that too made sense – it shouldn't be too much trouble to get into the agency, and as for a getaway car, well, parking in the centre was a nightmare this time of the evening.

The Comandante had wanted to accompany us, even if it only meant keeping watch, but I persuaded him to stay in the office. The clear, warm days were opening up the sky to an evening chill and we could do without him being laid up in bed like Nonna Miranda; though I had to acknowledge that this concern may in itself have been a symptom of my own submission to the Italian obsession with a *colpo d'aria* – the perils of 'a hit of air'. Soon I'd be going on about my *cervicale*, a mysterious zone between the shoulder blades and the neck that seemed to afflict every other native of Italy and was the source of discussion almost as feverish as that about food.

Fortunately, Virtus were not playing at the PalaDozza, so the street was quiet, free of the mammalian shadows that lurked along Bologna's ancient porticoes. It was illuminated instead by the even, limpid amber of any modern city, so there was little mystery about Via Ercolani, and neither was there anything apparently suspicious about the three of us, I hoped, strolling along, perhaps after an early dinner or a late *aperitivo*.

Jacopo and I stood, frankly nervous, our hands in our pockets, while Ciro knelt down and unlocked the padlock that secured the closed shutter as smoothly as if he had had the proper key, promptly sweeping the shutter upwards, apparently unconcerned about being detected or heard. He didn't even bother using a pick to open the old lock in the glass door, simply pulling out what looked like his own house key, rolling it around in his mouth until it was thick with saliva, and slipping it into the chamber, which clicked open immediately. He could have used a pick, I presumed, but for an almost mute operator like him, this was plainly a demonstration of his professional contempt.

'No alarm,' he said. He sat down on one of the chairs along the side, where previously the Asian guys had been waiting, and took out his phone.

'Shouldn't we put the shutters back down?' I asked.

He looked up – he was playing Candy Crush – and shook his head. 'You want to check the computer, right? Not lift it?' I nodded. 'The light will come through the shutters.' He slumped further down in the chair and went back to his phone. He wasn't about to grace us with further explanation, but I understood – better that it looked like we were in here working late than that someone came by, saw the light through the shutters, and realised what we were actually up to.

'Go on' I said to Jacopo.

Jacopo began to copy all the relevant files onto his USB stick while I poked around the office. It seemed little different from any other employment agency – plain, scuff-marked walls, cheap shelves with a few dusty manuals and directories. The only other desk was bare except for some cables tangled up on the top.

I sat down on a broken office chair, sunk to its lowest level, watching Jacopo silhouetted by the glowing screen. 'Almost done,' he said. My gaze dropped to something else outlined amid the nest of cables. It was like a little head, I thought, with pointy ears almost as big as its skull. I leaned forward and plucked it out. Was it some kind of paper animal? Meant to be a donkey, perhaps? Or a wolf? Only it had two front legs and no rear. I turned it upside down, so that in effect it was standing on its ears. This made no sense either, so then I used its front legs/ears as a platform and it looked like a sort of tree trunk, or perhaps simply what it was: a bit of mangled litter fashioned out of a receipt rather than the peculiar paper that had shaped the more lifelike models. Was I simply beginning to see things?

'Done,' said Jacopo.

Ciro pulled the shutter back down and reattached the padlock. Our goodbyes were perfunctory: I held out my hand, but he was already turning away with a half-wave. I wondered if he held the pair of us in as much contempt as he did the manufacturers of that lock.

We returned to the office, trudged back up the stairs. The only light was coming from the Comandante's office. The old man was rocked back in his upholstered chair, asleep, reading glasses slid down his nose, a volume open, face down, upon his chest. He opened his eyes as easily as a cat.

'Leopardi,' I noted. 'The Ispettore was also absorbed by the poet. You don't belong to a book group like Alessandro's wife? A secret policemen's club?'

'Well if I did,' he said drily, rocking forward and placing his glasses and the book upon the desk, 'I'm sure we would keep it a secret.'

'And Leopardi?'

'"Children find everything in nothing, men find nothing in everything." He was far more than a poet, Daniel. He was, arguably, the first existentialist. Schopenhauer was an admirer.'

'An existentialist is a surprising choice for a pair of such devoted Catholics.'

'Then you understand neither Catholicism nor existentialism.' He smiled. 'But what more could I expect from a Protestant?'

'As I have told you frequently, Giovanni, I'm not a Protestant. I had the same from Alessandro. Puritan, he called me. You Italians and your bloody labels. How can anyone truly say they're anything? There are no magic solutions; we all just muddle through. I believe in what's here, now. Rose, your granddaughter. Even you, you old curmudgeon.'

'Family,' said the Comandante. 'Well, *that's* very Italian. I'll consider it progress. We'll be getting you to Mass yet.'

'I'll go when your son does,' I said. 'Jacopo!' I called. 'How are you doing?'

'Give me a chance!'

I wandered through to the office he shared with Dolores. I had to admit, it had smartened up since the days when it was occupied by 'the bachelor boys', as Alba called us. Gone were the Styrofoam takeout coffee cups and piled-up paper plates, the Bologna FC flag and random gym stuff, discarded boxes and mysterious electrical devices. The leads that had once trailed across the office were now brimming from a box beneath Jacopo's desk, which was also startlingly tidy. Dolores's desk, turned away from his and set by the window, was clear except for the computer screen, a framed selfie of her and her late dairy cow, Desdemona, and a single red rose in an old glass vase. I wondered if she had bought the flower from one of the hawkers always pestering people in the evening, or had it been presented to her as a romantic gesture? Did Dolores have a new boyfriend?

I was about to ask Jacopo, but stopped myself. It wasn't just the office that had tidied up since Dolores had arrived. Jacopo had too – he had lost a couple of kilos, his nest of thick black hair had been shorn to a crop, bristles developed borders . . . I had no doubt the office clean-up could be attributed to Dolores; now I wondered if Jacopo's transformation could also stem from the same source. I didn't think Jac and Dolores were actually an item, but I hadn't exactly been looking out for it, either. Did Faidate Investigations have a workplace relationships policy? You had to be kidding! Up until now the whole workplace had been, literally, one big family. Should we have one? Was I forgetting what country I was in? They would think me mad.

'Problem?' said Jacopo, who had caught my shaking head reflected in his computer screen.

'No, no . . .'

'Look,' he said. 'Here are the employee files.' He clicked on a yellow folder, and hundreds of names were listed. He clicked on the first. Up came a file – an Italian, Sergio Castenno. DOB: 12/04/89. Address: 32 Via Malfiera, followed by his tax number. Profession: sales. Placement: Fones 4 U. Attached to the file was his photo ID, scanned on the back and front.

'Search Ishaan,' I said. Three immediately appeared. Jacopo opened each file, and we checked the photo.

'Bingo.' There he was – Ishaan Laghari. Unsmiling in the black-and-white photo, and with that haircut making him look as if he was born in 1940, not 07/09/97. Address: 117 Via Fosserella. The profession and placement spaces were blank, but there was a document attached. A scanned *permesso di lavoro* – a work visa – although it didn't say who the employer was.

'Save that,' I told Jacopo. 'I'll pay a visit to Via Fosserella tomorrow. Well done, by the way,' I added. 'You kept a cool head when we were at People Mover.'

'Easy-peasy,' he said. '*That* kind of hacking.' He closed the window and went to Facebook. Entered *Ishaan Laghari*. There were dozens of them, mainly from India, but also the US, Australia. None from Italy, but the presence of photos speeded matters up somewhat . . .

'Look familiar?' Jacopo asked.

'I *think* it's him,' I said. 'Although less quiffy.' He clicked on the page. 'Aurangabad.' The script was exclusively in Hindi, but the photos were exclusively of food, Italian food. No photos of Italy, however, not even any selfies. As far as the world was concerned, Ishaan Laghari was still in northern India.

'Friends,' I said. He hadn't chosen any privacy options, so there they all were – all 223 of them.

'Gold mine,' said Jacopo, scrolling down the list of exclusively Indian men and women until his mouse paused upon a paler face.

'*No*,' I said. Jacopo clicked on it. Up popped Ryan Lee.

'What happened?' asked the Comandante.

'There he is!' I prodded the screen. 'Our boy.' I slumped

back in my chair with relief. 'I was terrified this had all been a wild goose chase. That T-shirt seemed a mighty slim lead.'

'But I don't understand,' said the Comandante. 'You checked the account his parents showed you, and viewed his friends list.' I exchanged a look with Jacopo – contrary to common perception, Giovanni had actually been paying attention.

'That's because he had another account,' I said. 'This isn't Ryan Lee. It's bloody *Lee Ryan*.'

'Can he do that? Have two accounts?'

'He can,' I said. 'And he has.' I looked up at him. 'A secret life, secret identity . . .'

'Even secret funds?'

I rubbed my face. 'But that wouldn't add up – going to all the trouble to create a fake identity for nefarious purposes only to switch the names around and friend some guy you just met in Bologna.' I sighed. 'What it does indicate, however, is that they knew each other and were, well, kind of friends.'

'Virtual friends,' said Jacopo. 'It's not exactly the same thing.'

'Fair point,' I said. 'Let's see what we can find out about this Lee Ryan.'

But like that of his doppelgänger, 'Lee Ryan's' page didn't give much away either, apart from his residence – New York, New York. His photo was less a snapshot, as on his other page, and more of a posed selfie with a backdrop of Manhattan's skyscrapers. Other than that – nothing. Still, at least we now had a proper, solid connection between the two.

'Let's shake things up a bit,' I said, noting that 'Lee Ryan's' privacy settings, although not permitting friend requests, did allow us to send him a message. 'Drop them both a line . . .

whatever it takes to get some reaction.'

'Good job.' The Comandante patted Jacopo's shoulder. Finally, I thought, giving his son some credit.

'Thank Dan,' said Jacopo. 'He was the one that got the name.'

'Actually,' I looked at the Comandante, 'Dolores is the one to thank – she discovered the link in the first place.' He nodded thoughtfully.

We began to pack up. The Comandante returned to his office to call a cab – we were all going the same way, after all.

'Speaking of Dolores,' I said to Jacopo, 'the office is looking good. I never thought I'd see flowers in here.'

Jacopo shrugged and shut down his PC. I wasn't going to get anything more out of him. We picked up our jackets and went to meet the Comandante in reception. We waited in the stairwell as he switched off the lights and closed the *porta blindata* – the security door – then set the alarm.

'I'll meet you downstairs,' he said, thumbing through his key ring.

'What do you mean?' I asked.

'What do you mean, what do I mean?'

I looked at Jacopo, who didn't seem the least bit curious. 'How are you going to get downstairs, Giovanni?' I said. 'Fly?' Now Jacopo let out a laugh.

'Not at all,' said the Comandante. He found the key he was looking for and placed it in the lock beside the lift. The shaft lit up and the machinery yawned into action. Finally the rickety little cabin arrived at our floor and the door opened.

'How did you . . . Why are you . . . Should you be doing that?'

'I'd prefer not to take the stairs.'

'But isn't it dangerous?'

'Not at all,' said the Comandante. 'It's simply a new law, something about this generation of elevators requiring a safety certificate or some such rubbish. There's quite a wait for the inspector. In the meantime, Roberto,' he meant the caretaker, 'lent me a key.'

'Well . . .' I stepped forward, but the Comandante held up his hand.

'Oh no,' he said. 'That wouldn't be right – Roberto entrusted *me* with the key. I wouldn't want him to think I was offering free rides.' He got in, pressed the button, and looked at us impassively as the doors closed in front of him.

'I thought it would be something like that,' said Jacopo as we watched him descend. 'He always does what he wants.'

'He was kidding about the free ride, though,' I said. 'Wasn't he?'

'You would think so,' said Jacopo. He chuckled. 'But I wouldn't be so sure. In his heart, he's a man of the Po Plain,' he said. 'You know,' he rapped his forehead with the back of his thumb, '*testardo*.'

And it was true, I thought, seeing the Comandante waiting at the exit with that same neutral expression: he could easily have been one of those farmers out in the flatlands among the reeds and lakes, holding a broken shotgun and a string of waterfowl, dogs circling about his knee-high boots, perhaps a damp cigar poking from the corner of his clipped grey beard. The only clue as to whether he was about to snap his shotgun back and order you off his land, or invite you home to share a roasted bird and a bottle of the local Lambrusco, was the sparkle in those silver-grey eyes.

The cab pulled up outside.

'You managed all right, then?' the Comandante said. 'We don't need to ask Roberto for an extra key just yet?'

Chapter 25

Ryan Lee, or Lee Ryan, had been missing for seven days, although in defence of Faidate Investigations, we had only been on the job for five. But in that week, at least one thing had changed – summer had become a wistful memory and it seemed as if it had always been autumn. One morning we might be greeted by her brittle blue skies, the next a shroud of clouds, great dollops of rain hammering between the porticoes, which would be slippery underfoot and musty with their damp human traffic. Today was one of those days – of course it was. I had a funeral to attend later.

Occhio Pubblico was not returning our calls, and I hadn't bothered contacting Oriana. For my part, I had said everything there was to say, and despite the Comandante's insistence that we had to give it a go, it seemed futile to expect anything from them – the presumption was that what they did find out they would pass on to the police, presumably providing a film crew could be at the scene to record any action. *Bene*: at this point, if it led to our lad, what did we care? The important thing was to find him alive.

Via Fosserella 117 was not outside the walls, as I had

expected, but a quiet street off Via Petroni, which was saying something as Petroni was perhaps the noisiest street in the whole of Bologna, full of bars, kebab shops and *osterie* catering to the student crowd. A banner – *ONE LAW FOR THEM, ANOTHER FOR US* – hung limply from an apartment above a bar, placed there by residents lamenting the Comune's tolerance of the nightlife, along with the endemic drug dealing that went with it. Still, once off Petroni it was mainly residential, and more peaceful at this time in the morning, although that must have been scant comfort for residents emerging for work to find the detritus of the night before, including snoozing drunks and drug addicts, camped outside their homes.

Porticoes ran along both sides of the narrow street, but there was a gap between numbers 117 and 119. Although the homes looked identical to the others – yolk-yellow facades with green shutters – that gap made it easier for me to hang back in the gloom opposite, partially obscured by a column, and have a clear view of the comings and goings. I didn't want to make the same mistake as I had at the hotel kitchen when I went barging in after Ishaan.

On the surface, like so many other buildings in Bologna, Via Fosserella 117 seemed like a modest structure, in this case three storeys high and three windows across, but as the occupants opened and closed the double doors, I could glimpse a passage as deep as the building was tall.

For hundreds of years before Napoleon had led his armies into Bologna, the city had been the second most important of the Vatican State after Rome, and many of its *palazzi* would once have served as convents or monasteries – that pre-Napoleonic city had been a spiritual powerhouse as well as a major source of revenue, and required a large labour force to keep it ticking over.

The monks may have long since departed but now there were likely dozens of people living in number 117 Via Fosserella. A mix of students, immigrants and old people, as far as I could tell from the comings and goings.

I dashed through a veil of rain to press myself into the doorway and ring a succession of bells. After a short wait I received a crackly '*Chi è?*'

'NEO Electricity. Meter reading.' The door buzzed open.

I stepped into that tunnel-like corridor and examined the letter boxes. There was no *Laghari, I.*, that was for sure, nor any other Asian names. They were mainly Italian, in fact, although I suspected many were legacy addresses, the apartments long since rented out for short- or long-term lets, in the case of the latter almost certainly cash in hand. I hung the fake NEO ID around my neck and went to the first door.

I pressed the buzzer. An Eastern European woman answered. Behind her, a kitchen crowded with kids' things. I flashed my badge and asked her where the meter was. By the door, she said. I took out my phone and entered the numerals on the fake app Jacopo had made for me. Turned around. 'It's actually registered to Ishaan Laghari,' I said, searching for a flicker of recognition. None.

'I don't know. We pay all bills. Is problem?' Her dark eyes widened with real alarm, but I could tell it was simply the anguish common to any migrant afraid they might have triggered one of the many tripwires that could spell bureaucratic hell. I shook my head – I wasn't here to worry her – and moved on.

I performed the same routine at the apartments on the

three floors of Scala A, a mix of non-responses, bleary-eyed students, a surprised British tourist (to whom I pretended to be Italian – I didn't want to get waylaid by restaurant recommendations) and old folk.

I descended the first staircase and headed further into the depths, past a somewhat bleak inner courtyard cluttered with bicycles, garbage cans and dead potted plants, before dipping into the darkness of the hallway again and trying the first apartment looking on to this gloomy view.

The door opened – a slim young woman wearing a pale blue tracksuit and furry pink slippers. Her bleached hair was drawn back, her strong, attractive features bare of make-up and pinched red as if she had been working out. She leant in the doorway without saying a word.

'NEO,' I said. 'Meter reading.' She cocked her head. Looked down at the ID hanging around my neck, back up.

'So it says.' She had a thick Balkan accent. She seemed to consider something, then stepped aside. 'Here, by door.'

I felt her watching me take out my phone, already switched to the app, and make a show of entering the numbers. I hadn't been able to take in much – a clean, bare, basic kitchen. A mug of something steaming, an ashtray. The radio playing a pop station – Radio Lattemiele, Radio Milk and Honey.

I hesitated. This wasn't the kind of woman from the entrance – the harried mother, presumably wife of one of those ever-busy, underpaid *extracomunitari*, who probably subsidised the family income with cleaning or carer jobs; this was another category of migrant altogether, one who, for whatever reason, had clearly seen right through me. I could almost feel her stare against the back of my skull.

'Problem?'

I looked around. 'Ishaan Laghari,' I said. I looked her in the eye. 'Ring a bell?'

'You mean the kid that Norman gave you a beating for? You still looking for him?' Now I understood – she was one of the prostitutes from before. In fact, the one who had talked about 'Norman's' brothers.

'Norman,' I said. 'Funny name for . . . an Albanian?'

'Kosovan. Pristina is full of Normans,' she said. 'After Norman Wisdom. You're an English, no? Very funny man. Very, very popular in Kosovo . . . and Albania. Now what's it you want with the boy?'

'I'm looking into an immigration matter.'

'Well.' She raised a plucked eyebrow. 'We're all immigrants here, aren't we, darling. Have you got your *permesso permanente*? I've certainly got mine.'

'It's not you we're interested in.'

'What are you interested in exactly, darling? And who is this "we" of yours? Hold on.' She glanced towards the Bialetti on the stove. 'Before you fill me in, we're out of coffee. I was just about to go myself. There's a place around the corner – pick me up a pack of Lavazza and we can continue this conversation.' She seemed to think about it. 'Are you offering a finder's fee?'

'For decent information, yes.'

'All right.' She gestured towards the open door. 'See you soon.'

The store turned out to be further away than I expected, a little way down Via Petroni. A sparsely shelved grocer's with an exceptionally tall middle-aged man in a grey store coat behind the counter. I picked up the coffee and headed back up Petroni. As I shoved the receipt in my pocket and touched the origami tree trunk I'd picked up from the agency, I slowed to a halt. I took out both receipts. The items were different but the receipts identical. I headed back to the store.

I smiled at the shopkeeper and held up my phone, which was displaying a snap of Ishaan's *soggiorno di lavoro*.

'Guardia di Finanza,' I announced. 'I'm looking for this fellow. Can you tell me where he is?'

The shopkeeper's eyes bulged almost comically. 'I couldn't say.'

'But you do recognise him?'

'I . . .'

'Ishaan Laghari. He's currently working as a chef, a sous chef, so a rather good one. Do you know where he is? Come on . . .' I leaned closer. 'Look, it's not *you* we're interested in. I'm just trying to track him down — and I think he may have worked here. Or at least been put on your books in order to get his *soggiorno*. You made a deal with that crew from around the corner – Via Fosserella, right? Isn't that the truth? *Dai*, I know how it works. If you give me a tip, you won't get into trouble, I'll leave it at that.'

'What's this?' said a calm voice. An older man emerged from the back room.

'I'm looking for Ishaan Laghari.'

'And you are?'

'I'm looking for Ishaan Laghari,' I repeated, but instantly felt the ground shift beneath me. I had thrown in 'Guardia di Finanza' as a kind of shorthand, an 'open sesame' to ensure prompt compliance from nervous shopkeepers wanting to keep on the right side of the tax police, but I immediately sensed that, compared to the rather simple-looking Lurch-like figure behind the counter, this older guy, a full-bellied, balding Bolognese, was an entirely different kettle of fish.

'You're Guardia di Finanza?'

I tried to look as if I didn't have time for this. 'Any useful information you provide could garner a reward.'

'You've got a funny accent for a *guardia*.'

'I'm originally from Bolzano.' I rather desperately referred to the German-speaking city in Italy's far north.

'Can I see your identification?'

'A sizeable reward if the information proves really useful.'

He took out a phone, still looking at me, and made a call. 'Yes, put me through to the office of Capitano Bettini,' he said. 'Thank you. Hello? . . . Yes. I'm calling from Drogheria da Mario on Via Petroni. I've got one of your men here . . . What did you say your name was?'

'Really, that's not necessary.'

'Now will you show me your ID?'

I shook my head.

'I'm sorry. It looks like we have someone impersonating one of your officers. Probably a foreigner . . . What? . . . Yes, yes, I think we can. See you shortly.' He ended the call.

'Grab him,' he said. The big guy's eyes bulged again as he looked at me, but he didn't move. 'Go on.'

He shifted around the counter as if he had wooden legs, and cast a reluctant step towards me. I held up my hand. He froze. I could see that, although big, he was plainly harmless, and almost certainly more afraid of me than I was of him. I began to back out. The old guy barked at him again and he stuttered forward, hands outstretched but eyes pleading with me to get the hell out. I couldn't agree more. I opened the door behind me and stepped onto the portico. The old guy's eyes remained steadily on me, phone still in hand, as the door closed. Had he faked the call? I didn't think so. Was a Guardia di Finanza patrol car about to pull up? I doubted it, but I wasn't going to hang about to find out.

Still, there were those receipts, and the big guy had seemed to recognise Ishaan. It had been a bit of a leap, but not much of one, to suggest they'd hired him as a bogus employee – it was a common route to a work permit for *extracomunitari* and a source of income for struggling small businesses. I repeated that name – Bettini, Capitano Bettini – as I walked back up Petroni. If the shopkeepers were that close to the Guardia, they would have had to be in on it, too. A corrupt grey-jacket? Well, it wouldn't be the first.

Bettini: another one for our office whiteboard.

I was midway back along the portico of Via Fosserella when a beaten-up BMW with German plates sped past. It pulled up outside number 117.

I hung back as three men got out. They slammed the doors and the car moved rapidly off. They all looked pretty similar – on the short side, yet broad, hair shaved at the back and sides, fingers heavy with fighting jewellery. One of them I clocked immediately as Norman.

They went into the building.

I kept going, past 117 until I came upon a *vicolo*.

I ducked into it, keeping an eye out for a prowling BMW, and got the hell out of there.

Chapter 26

Not all of Bologna's porticoes are built to be high enough to accommodate a horse with a saddled rider, as is customary along the city's main thoroughfares. In fact, away from the *palazzi* that, albeit obliged by ancient ordinance to append the ubiquitous walkways to their facades, had done their best to ensure that at the very least they reflected their grandeur, other *portici* echo their more modest origins – whether appending the erstwhile homes of the middle class and clergy (where they reach a middling height supported by middling, plain stone columns) or, like the vast majority of Bologna's late-medieval dwellings, as part of lodgings constructed to squeeze in as many scholars as possible to what had been the Old World's academic Eldorado (and where you can feel the weight of centuries bearing down upon you as you walk beneath their flat, low ceilings).

These often wood-beamed porticoes could feel like catacombs, especially now, with the rain falling like a beaded screen in the street between, and we pedestrians their troglodyte custodians, scurrying along the higgledy-piggledy passages. But I finally emerged into a main artery – Strada

Maggiore – where, after pausing to knot my black tie in the reflection of a shop window, I caught a bus in the direction of the cemetery.

Standing room only. As we rocked along, enclosed by misted palm- and finger-smudged windows, I thought of sous chef Ishaan, a 'keeper'. Entrusted with eking out those treasured truffles, legging it down that scrappy, barren road, then . . . vanishing. At the time, I had had no reason to make the connection, but I realised he had probably sought refuge in one of those seedy camper vans.

Were the shopkeepers involved, too? This Capitano Bettini? They were well within their rights to alert the grey-jackets that a fake cop had turned up asking questions, but the big guy had seemed to immediately recognise Ishaan and the old man had appeared almost too well prepared – there had been no curiosity about why I should be looking for him, and perhaps a little too much readiness to call his contact, *Il Capitano*.

Liana Benvenuto came to mind, perfectly poised in the *salon dell' oca*.

In the past, it was a rather ad hoc thing. You'd have stalls in the local market passing off Albanian truffles as Boscurili . . .

I thought of the Eastern European turning up at the recruitment agency with the Asian guy – *last one*.

Ishaan in the hotel kitchen, shaving the truffles from that Tupperware tub. Was that it? Kosovan pimps, smuggling not only people, but truffles as well? Was that what Ryan had stumbled upon? Were these petty Balkan gangsters, rather than Italy's home-grown 'multinationals', behind the superfake?

I was prepared to believe anything, and nothing, as the bus juddered on, potential leads swimming before my eyes like sea anemones. The only thing I had to keep faith in as dog-damp passengers pressed against me, was that Ryan Lee, or Lee Ryan, as he also apparently liked to be known, was out there somewhere, still alive. Holding on, much like I was to this plastic strap.

Hang in there, mate. Just a little while longer.

I reached across the aisle, wiped the window and pressed the bell.

La Certosa, Bologna's mirror city. Behind those red-brick walls, cream porticoes re-created the city walkways the dead had once strolled, its galleries the salons where rich families had socialised, family tombs attempting to outdo each other with their opulence and piety.

It had been a stop on the Grand Tour – Byron, Dickens and Stendhal had all popped in to pay their respects – and the cemetery still impressed, albeit that subsequent generations of Bolognese had been obliged to occupy ranks of drawers set into marble walls like man-size safety deposit boxes, or were consigned to the lands around the former Carthusian charterhouse where once the monks had grown vines.

The Comandante was attending the church service, which he would later tell me had featured readings from celebrity chefs as well as Marco Ligabue, while I was to skip straight to the place of interment, outside the main galleries but not far from the grave of Bolognese singer Lucio Dalla, which had begun to generate its own contemporary cachet, attracting recently deceased celebs in much the same way as the nineteenth-century grandees had replicated their own exclusive soirées.

I would usually have paused at Lucia's own little spot – the well-kept family tomb in another part of the cemetery, a plain slab listing a dozen or so Faidate, which would in time, I suppose, also include me, but I was late, although it turned out that I need not have worried (when would I learn that the only things that ran on time in modern Italy were Englishmen?). From the shelter of the final gallery I arrived to see no one else save for a couple of workers finishing up arranging fake grass beneath a sodden black canopy.

I waited there, allowing my thoughts, and speculations, to catch up with me as the rain petered out and the sun began to brighten the spent clouds.

Oriana de Principe's florid perfume confirmed her presence at my side, although I had heard those heels cracking behind me from some distance. But I wasn't about to give her the satisfaction of expressing surprise, or alarm.

'No film crew?' I said.

'They're outside the chapel,' she said. 'Wouldn't let us in.'

'Poor you. And they asked you to stay away from the graveside, too?'

'Requested. The guys will keep a respectful distance, although I have the camera on this,' she pulled out her top-of-the-range iPhone, 'if need be. It's almost as good as the real thing.'

'I'm surprised to find you here, frankly. I would have thought you would have been on the trail of "murderer" Ryan Lee.'

'I'm sorry,' she said. 'Isn't that your job, to find Ryan?'

'I forgot, it's just your job to condemn him.'

Oriana puffed out her cheeks. 'Spare me the indignation. I just stated the facts. Maybe I provided you with some, too – it would certainly explain why he's disappeared.'

'Except he clearly had nothing to do with it.'

'Ah now, *caro*, I think you've become a little too close to the case – the evidence points elsewhere.'

'Where does the evidence point?'

'Well . . .' She checked her watch. 'Come with me, maybe I can show you.' I gave her a dubious look. She held out her hand like a challenge. I looked down at it. '*Dai*,' she said. 'I don't bite.'

'Now I know that's not true.' But I took it. It was rain-cold.

She led me back along the portico, past one great gallery after another, each stuffed with competing baroque memorials. On the way, she pointed out the renowned tombs of bygone Bolognese industrialists and inventors, writers and artists. None of them names I knew, or would remember.

'Of course it's Farinelli who always used to be the big draw,' she said, 'before Dalla. Did you know that history's greatest castrato retired here? After travelling across the known world, performing in the most opulent salons of Europe, he chose not Rome, Amalfi, Venice, but Bologna as his ideal home.'

'Yes, very nice,' I said. 'Now you were going to tell me something about evidence?'

Monumental Certosa seemed to go on and on, and was almost as labyrinthine as the city it served. Of course it would be – it had been designed to accommodate two centuries of Bolognese bourgeoisie before they had needed to break new ground. But I had never gone in this deep before – I usually took a shortcut to get to Lucia. *I* didn't come for the sightseeing.

Oriana pulled me down a narrow cloister consisting of the more modest walls of marble drawers, little photographs featuring deceased Bolognese at their best or most fondly remembered. Fresh flowers were hanging from many of them, even though their occupants might have passed away decades before – Italians remembered their dead.

There was a space between two blocks of drawers for a marble bench. Behind it, an arched opening with a view over the cemetery then the ring road beyond. Oriana sat down and beckoned me to join her.

'A good spot for spies,' I said. 'Very discreet.'

'And not only spies.' She reached behind my head and pulled my face towards hers.

I drew back. 'You're kidding . . .'

'You're not still angry, are you?' She stroked the back of my neck, leant towards me. Her mouth was inches from mine. Her breath smelt of cherries.

'Well . . .' She kissed me lightly upon the lips. Again, more deeply. Her tongue probed my mouth. My eyes must have boggled like that big shopkeeper's, but then I felt something else stir, too, and couldn't help but respond. I closed my eyes, heard the shift of material. Felt her hand on my shoulder, and she was astride me.

I broke off. 'Oriana . . .'

'What?' She was loosening my tie, unbuttoning my shirt.

'This is crazy.' I felt her begin to fiddle with my flies. 'Oriana!'

She pressed her mouth hard against mine and plunged her hand inside my trousers.

Game over – we fucked fiercely, quickly, in that tight space.

'Thanks.' She lifted herself off me and began tucking me back in.

'You were going to tell me something about a new line of enquiry?' I replied, determined to play it as cool as her.

'Oh *you*.' She flicked the tip of my nose. 'Really, you'll believe anything.' She shivered cheerfully. 'All this death,' she said. 'It really turns me on.'

'So I happened to be in the right place at the right time?'

She laughed, standing up and straightening her own clothes. 'Something like that.' She checked her watch. 'Come on, we should get going.'

We walked side by side, not touching, back along the cloister. 'Friends again?' she said.

'I'm not sure about that.'

'Quite right. You screwed me over the Ligabue link. You got precisely what you deserved.'

'Maybe so,' I said. 'But the parents didn't.'

She didn't reply. In the brief interval we had been away, the rain had entirely ceased and the sun had begun to break through. There would be a rainbow somewhere, I thought, although there was not one here. A crowd had gathered around the graveside, but it was in dark contrast to the sun, which spotlit the canopy, dazzled off the damp chrome poles.

Oriana waved at her camera crew and made towards them without so much as a goodbye.

'Hey,' I called. She looked over her shoulder, still moving

away from me but lit up as she was caught by the graveside's glimmer.

She blew me a mocking kiss and turned away.

The Comandante, standing in the second row from the back, gave me a cool look. He couldn't have possibly known what I'd been up to with Oriana, even if he had seen us emerging from the mausoleum. It was simply an old Carabinieri trick, I decided, to keep you guessing and get you to spill your secrets. I responded with a cordial smile.

'Sorry for the delay,' I said.

'Do you recognise anyone?'

I nodded. 'The front line, family – there's Marco, of course.' As pallid as ever, sporting black Wayfarer-style sunglasses although he was standing in deep shade. He looked like a man moments away from fainting. 'Aurelio and Stan.' They were on either side of Marco wearing suits they might have dug out from the back of the wardrobe, Stan's bush of grey-flecked hair pulled back and throttled by a ragged black ribbon, Aurelio's at least looking like it had had a comb run through it for once. They were staring dazedly into the grave as the coffin was lowered to the words of the priest, as if all their countryside confidence had been sapped here in the big city, by the shock of the tragedy and the intensity of press interest.

Scanning the crowd behind them, skipping over the national and local celebrities, I noticed Il Conte di Malduce lifting a well-tailored sleeve to discreetly check the time. A couple of unknowns over from him was the old lady, Lauriola, V., who looked like she made a career out of attending funerals.

Next to her, Liana Benvenuto beside a man I presumed to be
her husband or partner, then Dante Millefoglie. A few of the
restaurant owners I had come across during the investigation,
but no smoking gun – mafia type or Kosovan gangster – and
certainly no Indian Elvis or, God help us, our missing person
come to see his supposed victim planted beneath the soil.
Magari, as the Italians would say. *I wish*.

Dust to dust, the deed was done. The mourners were
forming a line to extend their condolences. I noticed Oriana's
camera crew upon a rise, filming from their 'respectful' distance. I would have loved to have melted away, but I girded my
loins and joined the rear of the queue, way behind Il Conte,
who I wanted to avoid bumping into given that I was due at
the truffle expo later: although the *palazzo* in d'Azeglio was
allegedly nothing to do with him, truffles most definitely were.

I arrived at Aurelio first, who looked at me hollowly and
without any apparent recognition. He automatically took my
hand, giving it a firm but perfunctory squeeze as if meeting me for the first time. Then Marco. Taking my hand, *he*
plainly recognised me. '*You*,' he said, still holding on.

'I am very sorry,' I said.

'Have the police talked to you? What were you even doing
at our home?' Everyone in the queue, and on the family side,
looked at me.

'As I said at the time, *signore*, we were following up a lead
about something and we wanted to talk to Signor Ligabue.'

'What? What did you want to talk to him about? This
missing supertaster of yours? I saw you on the television.
What did he have against Dad?'

A chilly silence took hold. The Comandante was standing

beside me but looking on as intently and silently as any of the others.

'Ryan Lee,' I said. 'I actually wanted to ask you how much you knew about him. Did your father mention him to you?'

'Now I recognise him!' I heard Aurelio say.

'About this man? Nothing. You tell me – why do you think he would have been there? You must know something. Where is he?'

'I wish I knew, Marco. We are looking for him as hard as everyone else. Are you sure your father didn't mention anything?'

He shook his head. 'Why would he?'

'You were his number two, right? And why wouldn't he charge the appointment to the company? Why did he have it invoiced directly to his home address?'

He finally dropped my hand. 'What are you saying?' I felt the mourners radiating hostility.

'Why would Signor Ligabue want to keep Ryan's appointment secret? Why would he want to keep it from you?'

Marco's mouth opened but nothing came out. He was still trying to form the words when I registered the murmur from the crowd, the volume of disapproval rising until the dam broke. It was an outrageous thing to ask. Shocking. Here it came – *maleducato*!

'You piece of shit.' A more earthy expression. Followed by a more earthy fist.

Fortunately, I saw Aurelio's haymaker coming, accompanied as it was by a rip from his too-tight jacket, and I flinched just enough for it to mostly miss its target. Instead it scuffed my temple.

There was a collective *oh* as the crowd expanded away from the violence then just as quickly contracted to frustrate it.

'Just go! Go!'

Stan was shoving me away while a trio of other women blocked Aurelio from further aggression. I stumbled across the turf onto the gravel path, accompanied by cries of '*Vergogna*!' – 'Shame!' – and more colourful words from Aurelio, all under the eye of the *Occhio Pubblico* camera crew.

I looked pleadingly towards Oriana, but she said something to the cameraman and he appeared to zoom in.

I picked my way back through the graves, trying to shield my face.

Chapter 27

'Thanks for stepping in,' I said when the Comandante finally arrived back at the car.

'Discretion is the better part of valour.'

'Is that what it says on your medals?'

The Comandante chuckled. 'Well, you survived . . .' He examined the mark on my temple. 'More or less unscathed. I'm not sure it was entirely necessary to confront Marco in that manner – I'm certain Umberto will be making the appropriate enquiries.'

'In his own time,' I said. 'The Ispettore's priority is to find the murderer, but Len Ligabue's not going anywhere; he's safely beneath the ground. *We* haven't got time for niceties. Say Ligabue hired Ryan because he was worried about something going on in his business – why else keep the appointment to himself? Why wouldn't he have mentioned it to Marco?'

'Because it was Triumvirate business?' said the Comandante. 'And remember, Ryan's list did not include any Antichi Artigiani del Cibo restaurants. He was researching the competitors.'

'And the firm's money worries,' I said. 'Oriana focused on Ryan for the programme because she had the scoop, but she was also hounding Marco over the company's balance sheet. Now *that* seems like a credible motive for murder. These things are just not committed by random guys like Ryan Lee.'

'But what of Ishaan Laghari?' said the Comandante. 'What could connect the three of them?'

'Food,' I said. 'Ishaan's a chef, Ryan's a taster, and Len was a restaurateur.'

'Although from very different cultures, backgrounds, circumstances . . . Still, we *do* know Signor Ligabue hired Ryan.'

'We also know Ishaan worked in a restaurant on Ryan's list, and not only that.' I explained about my morning and the link with the Kosovans. 'This *capitano* for the Guardia di Finanza . . . corrupt?'

'My contacts among the grey-jackets are more limited. I will have to ask Umberto what he thinks.'

'And there's also the Count – the event at the *palazzo* this afternoon.'

'It could simply be a coincidence. It *is* truffle season, the ideal time to hold an expo – whatever on earth that is.'

'Quite a coincidence, though – the agency with Ishaan on its books holding an event at Palazzo Malduce.'

The Comandante frowned. 'You will take care,' he said.

'I usually do.'

'What I mean is, any information Umberto supplies should always be treated with caution – as with a double-edged knife.'

'Hold on,' I said. 'He's your . . . he's our friend, isn't he? He wouldn't . . .' I was going to say 'knowingly put us in harm's way' until I realised how absurd that was. 'Place us at too much risk, would he?'

'Risk . . .' said the Comandante. 'We all have different

thresholds of what we would consider risky. I don't doubt that Umberto's bar may be set somewhat higher than our own.'

'There they are!' said Rose. 'Dad, are you all right?'

'What do you mean?' The rest of the family was waiting around the kitchen table, while Alba had some rigatoni on the stove. In Italy, school still ended at one o'clock, when the children would traditionally return to Mamma for lunch, despite the fact that in twenty-first-century Italy few *mamme* could afford to be home for their offspring, let alone supervise their afternoon's homework.

The Faidate household was something of an exception to this rule. With the *scomparsa* – literally, 'disappearance'; actually, 'passing' – of Lucia, the whole family had rallied around, and at least a couple of us would habitually make it home for lunch with Rose, although having a full house like this – the Comandante's presence was particularly noteworthy – was rare. It couldn't help but remind me of the old, early days after Lucia had gone, and I felt strangely moved and desperately sad about that. Perhaps that was what Rose had sensed.

'I saw you on the local news,' she said instead. 'Being chased away from the funeral.'

'It's already been on the news? It was only an hour ago.'

'It's all over,' said Rose, thumbing through her phone. 'Look.'

Occhio Pubblico *crew capture moment disgraced private eye Daniel Leicester gatecrashes Len Ligabue's funeral.*

There it was, taken from the rise, my hasty retreat from the graveside. The flailing arms of Aurelio Barbero behind a wall of women. Marco Ligabue looking devastated. Me stomping off with my head down. Then I look up, turning towards the camera, and sure enough, a close-up.

Thanks, Oriana, I thought. Thanks for nothing.

'What does it mean "disgraced", Dad? What are you disgraced about?'

'I've no idea,' I said. 'Maybe it's referring to the incident at the funeral.'

'Or maybe when you were on the programme. Or maybe—'

I cleared my throat. 'Are you all set for this afternoon, darling? Pencils, paper, all that?'

'Oh?' The Comandante lowered his *Corriere di Bologna*.

'Drawing lesson,' I said.

Giovanni nodded approvingly. 'You know,' he said, 'your mother was a very good artist.'

'Yeah, they closed the urban art course, our teacher got arrested,' Rose said.

'What?'

'Ah, lovely,' I said as Alba brought the pot over. *'All'amatriciana*, my favourite.' I took Rose's bowl as a means of getting between her and the Comandante.

'Yeah,' Rose was saying. 'He was in this rail yard when—'

'Did I tell you how I discovered Rose's new teacher?' I said to the Comandante. 'She was the woman that handed us the initial sketch of Ishaan. Compared to his photograph, it really is a quite amazing likeness.'

The Comandante was no fool – he could see what I was doing – but he gave me a curt nod and returned to the *Corriere*.

Stella Amore arrived as I was about to leave.

'Going to a funeral?' she asked.

'I went to one earlier.'

'Oh, I'm sorry.'

'Don't worry,' I said. 'It was mainly business.' I looked around at Rose, whose face had lit up. 'Let me introduce you to my daughter.'

'Howdy,' said Stella.

'Hey,' said Rose.

'Can I get you a coffee?'

Stella shook her head. 'Maybe a glass of water. So you're the artist, eh?'

'I was doing a graffiti course but the tutor got arrested.'

'Oh.' She looked at me. 'So I'm a substitute?'

'You're a fine artist.' I gave her a little bow. 'A *fine*, fine artist. I was saying earlier how incredible your sketch was.'

'Well,' said Stella, looking at Rose. 'You have to learn how to draw if only so you can forget everything you've learned. Are these yours?'

As Rose handed Stella her sketchbook, I pulled out the jug of filtered water from the fridge. I could see why she had been so excited to see her new teacher. Stella was clearly a 'proper' artist. She noticed me looking, so I had to say something.

'You're rather smart yourself.' It was true – she had ditched the DMs, that all-black ensemble from the bar, for a bottle-green silk blouse and bell-bottom trousers. Absinthe-green nails matched her blouse, while her dark trousers went with her curly bob. She looked like someone from another era, I thought. And she was quite beautiful, too, I realised, a little startled.

'Oh, I'm going to a *vernissage* after, at MAMBO.' She

meant Bologna's Museum of Modern Art. 'They're unveiling a door by Antonello Ghezzi that opens with a smile. Not the door – I mean, the door doesn't smile at you. You have to smile at it, and it opens. I mean, really, as if by magic. Some kind of hidden camera. What do you think?' She smiled. 'Will it open any doors?'

'Yes,' I said. 'I think it probably will.'

Chapter 28

The late-afternoon breeze that blew south across the city during the summer months like something from the Sahara had diminished to a geriatric wheeze, barely noticeable unless it was conveying woodsmoke, the din from one of the season's inevitable *manifestazione*, or, as now, the unmistakable aroma of truffle.

I had left little Via Paglia and was turning down Via Tovaglie when it hit me – that sweet, earthy, vaguely indecent smell, the kind of scent I imagined our world would be rich with had we had retained our olfactory senses to the degree of other mammals. On the other hand, at least we didn't spend all our time sniffing around bins.

At first, the aroma struck me as little different to that which had hung in the air during our visit to Palazzo Benvenuto, but as I stepped into d'Azeglio and became accustomed to it, I began to register a certain synthetic, chemical edge that had been absent at Benvenuto. The issue was its consistency – it remained determinedly the same rather than evolving into something more complex. It had one note, like cheap perfume.

I wondered, as I crossed the Bastardini's long afternoon shadows, if that was precisely the point – until now, I had thought of counterfeit truffles in a purely abstract sense, but in a crude way perhaps this demonstrated that inimitable differential the connoisseur, or supertaster, would detect between an imposter and the real thing.

I paused midway upon the steps of the Bastardini as this sank in, then continued downwards, crossing the road and carrying on along d'Azeglio to the great bulk that was Palazzo Malduce.

If the building had been constructed by a later branch of the Malduce family, it made me wonder how far back the Count could trace *his* origins. There certainly didn't seem to be a great deal new about it; it had little in common with the more mannered designs of the later Renaissance era *palazzo* opposite. It had clearly been constructed when the Malduce were most concerned about the likelihood of having to sit out a siege, with its high barred windows and thick stone walls cut to a diamanté design. A single arched gateway, wide enough to accommodate a bulky horse-drawn carriage, appeared to be the sole entrance. Its only concession to its urban setting was a flat stone seat running its length, presumably in order for the one-time petitioners to the family to have somewhere to wait.

There was a metal cylinder tucked away behind one of a pair of pull-up *TRUFFLE WORLD* banners standing beside the entrance. It was the kind of thing you could imagine being used to blow up balloons but was now almost certainly releasing that synthetic essence of truffle into the atmosphere.

I crossed the road to pass the *palazzo* and went to a nearby bar, where I ordered a coffee, checked my messages. Dolores was already inside the expo. I was betting she would be much less easily recognisable with her new look were she to bump into the Count. I, on the other hand, would presumably be a little easier to spot given my display at the funeral, and recent TV appearance.

I took another look at the entrance, which was guarded by a pair of burly bouncers. My plan was to wait until there was plenty of activity so my would-be employers would be too distracted to check my staff pass from People Mover and actually call someone to put me to work.

Lingering at the bar, my thoughts returned to Stella – 'It's *my* name' – Amore. *Star Love. Love Star.* To be fair, both names were reasonably common in Italy. But it was a startling combination. And not only her name. I shook my head. She was not at all like Oriana de Principe, for example, a classic Italian beauty who almost levitated with the confidence born from a culture in which the word 'beautiful' had not only form but substance – where it was a synonym for everything good.

Stella, with her angular, unconventional looks, would have probably been considered gawky as a child and teen, pitied by grandmothers until reaching womanhood, when she had grown into her looks, become almost a work of art in herself. Perhaps that was why she had been drawn to how things looked, and drawn them. She understood all too well how appearances could be deceptive.

Everybody is somebody else in Bologna.

And in Italy, I thought, noticing a crowd had begun to assemble at the entrance of Palazzo Malduce, for all its surface beauty, the truth could be as ugly as anywhere else.

I paid for my coffee and left.

Sure enough, by now the guards had their hands full and waved me through. Above – a hefty oak portcullis. Ahead – a crimson carpet leading into a courtyard surrounded by three floors of pristinely frescoed balconies. For an instant I was as disarmed by the splendour as any battle-weary *Landsknecht* who might have stumbled into this *cortile* during one of Bologna's many sieges, only to be cut down by a crossbow-man skulking behind a column.

The space was spliced between the light and shade of the descending sun. A couple of dozen people were milling about, flutes of Prosecco and canapés in hand.

'Welcome to Truffle World,' said Dolores. 'Can I offer you a glass of Prosecco, or would you prefer a soft drink? Our canapés are, of course, garnished with Boscuri white truffle.' She pressed a piece of paper into my hand, which I pocketed without looking at it.

'A glass of water would be fine.' I stepped off the carpet to stand in the shaded half of the *cortile*, and surveyed the crowd from the shadows – a mix of men with the same vaguely dis-reputable upper-class air as the truffle traders I'd encountered at the Grand Hotel, plus a smattering of attractive black-clad women young enough to be their nieces – for the most part, I presumed, hostesses like my own. Dolores reappeared and I took the glass. 'I should have told you,' I said. 'I prefer fizzy.'

'Then you can get it yourself.' She smiled sweetly.

'You should watch it, young lady,' I said. 'Your boss wouldn't appreciate that attitude.'

'Oh please don't tell my boss, *signore*. He's a complete twat.'

'You have my sympathies,' I said. 'You have no idea what idiots I have to work with.'

'You can't get the people these days.'

'So,' I said. 'Tell me.'

'That was the code for the restricted area. We were given it in the event any of these old creeps would like to cut a deal on the quiet. It also appears to be where the venue's truffle dishes come from. Certainly that's where they brought out the canapés, even though the kitchen,' she nodded to a doorway behind the line of drinks tables in the courtyard, 'is over there. It's where the immigrant staff are.' She anticipated my question. 'I couldn't see Ishaan, but no, I haven't had a chance to actually speak to any of them yet. What are you going to do?'

'I'll pop into the kitchens, have a word with the staff, then check out this restricted area.'

'It's at the far end of the hall.' She pointed along the carpet, which continued across the flagstones through another, lower arch. 'There's a door off to the right. A security guy.' She wiggled her nose, a sign I'd come to recognise as uncertainty.

'What?'

'I don't know . . . He didn't seem like the others.'

'What do you mean? Is he foreign?'

She shook her head. 'Italian, I'd say. But he's not a heavy like the others. Not typical. For security, I mean.'

'Maybe they've got manpower problems, too.'

'Just . . . be careful.'

I was tempted to respond with a quip, but this was Dolores – I'd begun to develop a respect for her instinct. I handed her back the water and placed the staff lanyard around my neck, walked around the border of the crowd with the intention of slipping into the kitchen unnoticed, but that didn't stop a Prosecco-quaffing Brit giving me his flute and ordering me to 'fill 'er up'. I gave a subservient nod and took his glass to the table, where I set it down with the other empties.

I passed through a narrow, arched brick doorway and down a dimly lit corridor covered from floor to ceiling with hexagonal red clay tiles. At the end, I pushed through a pair of dark wood doors.

The kitchen was a jarring mix of old design – large enough to cater for a medieval banquet, with long stone slab tables and a pair of huge empty fireplaces at either end – and modern convenience. Stoves and fridges had been placed along the sides of the chamber, electric sockets linked by cables were studded to the walls. Metal sinks had been crudely plumbed. Plastic storage boxes were stacked upon the tables.

A pair of Italian waiters were unboxing further bottles of Prosecco – one lamenting, 'Can you believe how much they're drinking?' The other, 'It's the British, they drink wine like it's beer' – while six Asian guys, a couple of whom I thought I recognised from the recruitment agency, were busy at the tables preparing food, mainly bread and the typical *salumi misti* – prosciutto di Parma, salami, mortadella – along with a selection of Italian cheeses.

I played it casual, approaching the first table with a quizzical look. 'Is Ishaan around? Ishaan Laghari?' The three guys looked at each other, then at me. I repeated, in English, 'I need to speak to Ishaan Laghari.' I showed them the photo but received blank looks. I went to the next table, and got the same reaction. But when I showed them the photo, it clearly chimed with the older guy. He said something in Hindi to the bloke opposite, who glanced up from breaking off chunks of Parmesan to check the photo. He replied, and they both chuckled.

'You know him?' I said. The man moved his head from side to side. 'Does that mean yes?'

'He's a cook,' he said, returning to hammering the cheese.

'Where is he?'

'I don't know.'

'Do *you* know?' I asked the man opposite.

'I don't know where he is.'

'Do you know where he lives? Where I could find him? There would be a reward in it.' The man looked at the photo again and nodded.

'I'm very sorry, *signore.*'

'If you do see him, can you ask him to contact me urgently?' I handed him my card. 'And ask anyone else to do so too. Remember, I am prepared to pay for information.'

'Yes, *signore.*' His workmate made a remark in Hindi and they had another chuckle.

'What's so funny?'

'Nothing, *signore.*'

I looked at them both. 'Are you keeping something from me? I told you, I'm willing to pay.'

They nodded their heads and got on with their work.

I removed my staff pass as I returned up that throat-red tunnel.

I walked behind the tables and through the arch Dolores had indicated, following the red carpet into a large hall. Frescoes swept along the walls – scenes celebrating the

Malduce clan's victories in battle, trade and marriage – while the vaulted ceiling was whitewashed, dominated by a trio of huge iron chandeliers, the kind of monsters you wouldn't want to be beneath during an earthquake if you valued your life.

Despite the dozens of stands on either side of the hall, the aroma of truffles was far subtler here than it had been outside, which was probably about right – these vendors were, allegedly, offering up the real thing.

All the big truffle enterprises were present. Right by the entrance was Benvenuto Truffles, although obviously no Liana – she had a pair of good-looking, elegantly attired young people to show off their display of whites, blacks, and various associated products like truffle-infused olive oil and cheeses.

I tucked one of their glossy brochures beneath my arm.

I passed stands by the famous brands of Piedmont, Umbria, Tuscany, Abruzzo, along with a handful of French companies specialising in black truffles. As I walked between the firms, each attempting to strike a balance between the rural origins of their product, its luxury status, and the limitations of the space, I even came across a 'New World Truffles' stand staffed by a comparatively inelegant team of Australian and American enthusiasts, clearly delighted just to be there.

'It's the first time, they've ever admitted producers from outside Italy and France,' the joyful American explained.

'Like New World wines?' I said.

His Australian colleague replied in a stage whisper. 'Don't mention that, mate!'

'But no Albanians, Bulgarians,' I said casually. 'Kosovans? They have truffles too, don't they?'

The American's face, which had been set on ecstatic,

suddenly turned serious. 'They trust us,' he said. 'They recognise we could represent legitimate competition but won't
– wouldn't, *couldn't* – play games with the provenance.'

'Or the tariffs,' added the Australian.

'So they figure "better pissing out than pissing in", as you
Brits say, right?'

'You haven't come across a Korean American chap on your
travels, have you? I'm thinking a supertaster . . .'

'You mean Ryan Lee?' said the American. 'Of course!
Ryan's famous – he helped us develop the chemistry, analyse
the soil and improve the mycorrhizal network. In fact, he's
here in our publicity.'

And there indeed he was. Looking fresh-faced and smiling, standing in a field in Tennessee in front of a curtain of
trees above a caption stating: *Soil and seeding was overseen by
renowned truffle supertaster Ryan Lee.*

'Have you seen him recently?' I asked. 'While you've been
in Italy?'

The two men looked at each other.

'Funny you should mention it,' said the Australian. 'We
were supposed to arrange a dinner, but he never got back to
us. Did you get any reply to your message?'

The American shook his head. 'With all the setting up, it
passed me by.' He frowned. 'Maybe I should try him again
now.'

'Actually, he's gone missing.' I looked around. No one
seemed to be paying us any attention. 'I'm a private investigator hired by his family to try and find him.' I handed them
my card. 'I'm working on it now, as it happens, so I'd appreciate it if you didn't mention to anyone else that I'm here.'

'You mean you suspect that people at Truffle World might be involved?' said the American.

'Oh no.' I tried my best to put on a reassuring smile. 'But I don't want to get kicked out for slipping in under false pretences.'

I made my apologies before they could bombard me with questions and continued on through the expo, which was beginning to fill up, the carpet running between the stands becoming crowded with groups gathered to sample wares or talk business. For all of Palazzo Malduce's grandeur, it didn't seem a very practical space to stage a trade fair – surely in this day and age it would be smarter to go to the Fiera district on the outskirts, or a hotel like the one where I'd met Oriana. But then I spotted Il Conte di Malduce, reclining in a black leather and chrome designer armchair at the Tuscany Truffle Association stand, apparently in deep conversation with a similarly attired gentlemen, and I thought I understood.

Truffle World was not really about practicality, it was about prestige. *Una bella figura*. The Anglo-Saxon presence here was little more than a token, I suspected. They wouldn't use a more practical space because they wanted to keep it exclusive, and Palazzo Malduce provided the perfect excuse.

I slipped past the Count, apparently without him noticing, and ducked sideways between a pair of stands. I put the pass back on, memorised the number Dolores had handed me and stepped back onto the carpet. I weaved my way towards the door at the far end.

Chapter 29

The dark-suited guard was sitting on a folding chair, legs crossed, checking his phone, looking . . . innocuous, relaxed. Dolores was right – he was no bouncer type. He was on the short side, with a shaven head and a thin, bony face. He looked like he did a lot of cycling. He could have been anyone – an accountant, a marketer, a lawyer – although probably not a security guy.

I nodded politely, but otherwise ignored him as I punched in the code, and he barely seemed to give me a second glance.

I pushed the unexpectedly heavy door open and stepped into a spacious anteroom. Afternoon sunlight streamed in from a high window, while around a pair of coffee tables, sitting in the same kind of designer seats I had seen at the Tuscan stand, traders were talking business.

A waiter emerged bearing a silver tray of vol-au-vents, their aroma hitting me as he whisked it towards the traders. I would have thought the Boscuri white pastries would have been irresistible, but the group ignored him and continued with their discussions. He headed towards the exit.

I went through the doorway from which he had appeared

into another, tiny room – an anteroom to an anteroom, the size of a scullery, which was what it may have once been.

There was a shudder, the sound of pulleys; a bell rang. A hatch was set into the wall. I opened it to find another tray of vol-au-vents loaded with cream of mushroom, white truffle shavings placed perfectly erect like fins.

A noise behind me. It was the waiter I had seen only moments earlier, now bearing an empty tray.

'That didn't take long,' I said jokingly, as if I was actually meant to be there.

'Fucking beasts,' he said. 'It's like feeding time at the zoo.' He picked up the fully laden tray from the dumbwaiter, and only then gave me a quizzical look.

'Oh,' I said. 'I was supposed to speak to the chef and they sent me this way, but . . .' I looked around. I couldn't see any other exit, only shelves.

'A-ha!' He reached around me and wrenched a handle hidden beneath one of the shelves. A doorway swung open. 'Doubled as an emergency exit in the old days.'

'Great, thanks!'

'And tell the kid to keep them coming . . .'

I descended a winding stone staircase, the kind I could imagine panicked aristocrats hammering down as the fortress fell. I paused: it looked over a broad corridor where they might have skulked while the *palazzo* was ransacked. Now it had been transformed into a modern fitted kitchen, with glinting stainless-steel appliances and blue-white surfaces.

It might have been a lonely place to work, but Ishaan Laghari seemed happy enough, his mobile phone plugged into the wall socket belting out Indian pop.

At the far end of the kitchen I spotted a fire exit. I hoped I wouldn't have another mad dash on my hands.

I descended the staircase at a measured, if careful, pace and got to within almost arm's length of the lad, singing happily along to the music, before he finally noticed me.

He started, but not unnaturally, in as much as anyone would have jumped had they been surprised like that. But most importantly, he didn't seem to recognise me from before.

I smiled apologetically.

'Sorry,' I said. 'I didn't mean to shock you.' I reached out and leant casually against the work surface.

He shook his head. 'It's all right.'

'How's the work going?'

'It's all right.' He looked down at the pastries. Then he looked back up, his eyes lingering questioningly on mine. They were extraordinary, I thought, almost black-brown, although it was those long lashes providing their oval frame that really brought them out. He was a good-looking kid, his slick, crafted quiff unique among the other kitchen staff I'd encountered. He seemed far more . . . sophisticated. And he appeared to have finally caught on.

I grabbed his forearm just in time.

'Please,' he said. 'Don't.'

'Don't what, Ishaan? I'm not a threat.'

'Then why are you holding me?'

'Because last time you ran.'

'What do you want?'

'I'm a friend of Ryan's.'

At this, he attempted to break free, but I managed to hold on, twisting his arm behind his back and pushing him down towards the counter.

'What is it?' I said. 'What's wrong? I don't want to harm you. I'm just trying to find him.'

There was a noise above. Ishaan's head twisted towards it. Two men were halfway down the stairs.

Ishaan shouted: 'I said nothing!'

The first man jumped the last three steps and came towards me. I recognised him instantly – one of the men I'd seen getting out of the BMW. I hesitated, but only for a moment.

I swung Ishaan towards them and ran the other way, slamming through the exit and out onto a fire escape. I pounded down the iron steps into a small inner courtyard. A car and a catering van were parked facing each other. Beyond, I could see that the rear gate was open, a busy street tantalisingly close. But there were footsteps close behind.

I darted between the car and the van, made for the gatehouse. I half expected someone to grab me as I dashed through the dark archway; the rear portcullis, even, to come crashing down in front of my face.

But in a few more steps I was through, outside – back into the fading light of the afternoon and the relative safety of the street, where I was hit by a bus.

Chapter 30

Specks swam against the black-blue sky – swallows, I finally realised, swooping to catch the insects rising on the late-afternoon breeze.

I thought, for a moment, I could just lie here watching them, at least until the sun set. But a woman in a pale blue TPER public transport uniform was looking anxiously down at me, saying ... something. Then a couple of others – an old lady, a pair of bearded students reaching for their mobile telephones.

'No pictures,' I muttered, inexplicably, reaching up to shield my face, though they were almost certainly calling for an ambulance.

I began to feel the cobbles beneath me, the throb of impact along my left side. I rolled onto my right.

A chorus of 'No!' But no one tried to stop me.

So I was on my side, beginning to test my body for breaks – that animal instinct to get immediately back up and scarper while you still can. But I wasn't running anywhere, not yet – not least because I was still trying to piece the jigsaw together and work out what the hell had just happened.

Looming above me was the red bulk of the bus, quite a crowd of passengers now coming out to take a look. The fizz of the overhead electric cable that powered it. Those busy swallows.

I was between the bus and the bus stop, I came to realise, which meant the bus must have been slowing as it pulled in. It probably hadn't been going faster than a few kilometres per hour, although that didn't entirely lessen the effect of being hit by it. I certainly felt as if my insides had suffered an almighty jolt, but so far, so good – nothing appeared to actually be broken. I eased myself into a sitting position as a pair of white-shirted municipal police officers joined the crowd, apparently as curious as any of the other onlookers.

'He just ran out in front of me,' said the woman in the TPER uniform, obviously, I now realised, the driver. 'You saw it, didn't you?' She was looking around at the crowd. There were a few non-committal murmurs. Curiosity was one thing; getting caught up in all the bureaucracy involved in an incident like this something else altogether.

The effect of being addressed like actual figures of authority appeared to animate the police officers into action. 'Why are you sitting up?' said the male officer. 'You should lie there, wait for the ambulance to come.'

'I think I'm okay,' I said, still exploring various parts of my body. 'It was just a knock.' I looked up at the driver. 'Sorry,' I said.

'Did you hear that? He apologised. He's saying it's his fault, right? That's what you were saying, right?'

'He's not saying anything,' said the female officer.

'He is – he just said sorry.'

'Sorry was obviously just a manner of speech,' she said. 'He's dazed.'

I looked up at the male officer. 'Would you . . .?'

He glanced at his colleague and the bus driver, who had begun to argue over what I had meant. 'You should lie down,' he said.

'Oh, come on . . .' I reached out and he helped me up. There was a twinge along my left arm.

'Are you all right?'

'Yeah,' I said. 'Probably just a bruise.'

'You didn't hit your head?'

I felt my face, my skull. 'Does it look as if I did?'

'You look all right to me.'

I heard an ambulance siren. 'I think I'm good,' I said.

'You need to go to the hospital, get checked out . . .'

It was only then that I remembered how I had actually arrived on the cobbles. I turned toward Palazzo Malduce, and sure enough, standing at the entrance were three hoods, Norman in the middle with his hands on his hips, watching.

'I need to go back in there,' I said.

'Is that where you came from?'

'That's right – those guys were chasing me.'

'Chasing you, you say?'

'Those guys, they're people smugglers, pimps. Probably involved in the dodgy truffle trade . . .' I rubbed my face. It was all coming back to me. 'They've got a chef in there I need to speak to – he might know the whereabouts of a missing person. . .'

'Are you sure you haven't hit your head?'

The ambulance had pulled up now, the paramedics in their blood-red uniforms getting out.

'What's he doing standing up?' asked the female officer.

'He said he was all right.'

'You shouldn't have let him.'

'You see,' said the bus driver. 'He's fine. Can we get going now?'

'Now just hold on . . .'

'Let's go,' I said to the male officer.

'What?'

'Come on.' I made toward Palazzo Malduce. For the first time, the Fosserella Gang looked a little perturbed. But then the cop had a hand on my shoulder.

'This way, signore.' He pulled me backwards, in the direction of the paramedics.

'I'm sure, with a police officer—'

'Signore,' he said. 'After an accident you need to be checked out.'

'But—'

'This way . . .' It wasn't going to happen – he wouldn't be persuaded. He was only a local cop. That pistol in his white holster had almost certainly never been drawn, at least not outside the shooting range. The extent of his remit was traffic accidents, public events and parking tickets. There was no way this guy was going to take on a group of hoodlums.

I allowed myself to be led to the ambulance and the waiting paramedics. As I looked back, I saw the hoods turn to go. Only Norman lingered. He caught my eye and his face cracked into a supercilious grin.

He drew an index finger beneath his chin, from ear to ear.

Chapter 31

I ended up being taken to the hospital – a moment of weakness, I thought as I sat in the assessment area being examined by the doctor; a waste of time. I should have broken free from the cop and walked away. No one would have seriously tried to stop me, but everyone had suddenly seemed very keen to do their jobs – the police to take down my details and write up the incident, the paramedics to load me into the ambulance – and I had been swept along. I should have melted into the crowd, phoned the office, enlisted some heavies to return with me to Truffle World and take on those thugs, even pulled some strings and got some assistance from our friends in the Carabinieri, but here I was sitting in *pronto soccorso* as the middle-aged medic with a rubbery downward cast to his face like an Italian Walter Matthau instructed me to look right, left, and said he would order an X-ray. That woke me up.

'Is everything okay?'

'Oh,' he said non-committally, 'you didn't hit your head, you say?'

'Not as far as I'm aware. It doesn't feel sore. I mean, I don't really remember. I mean – all I can remember is looking up at the sky, the birds . . .'

'Birds?' He looked alarmed.

'There were birds in the sky. Swallows . . .'

He wrote something down. 'So what you're saying is, you don't know if you hit your head.'

'No, I suppose not. But it didn't feel as if I had. I haven't got a bump, bruise, blood, or anything . . . There's nothing wrong, is there?'

That same grave look. 'You go and wait out there – you'll be called.'

I went to the waiting room as docile as a little lamb. Moments earlier I had been chastising myself for not slipping away; now I was terrified I'd done real damage. Hadn't this been how it had ended for Lucia? Knocked off her bike at a crossing – helmetless, naturally – her skull cracked against the side of the road by a reckless driver. Lying in that open coffin, she might have been sleeping, but you knew the instant you saw her that there was no one there. I couldn't let Rose see me like that.

My phone chimed.

Time for an Apero? A message from, of all people, Oriana de Principe.

I'm in hospital, I tapped irritably back.

What happened?

Why? Do you want to send a film crew?

Don't be silly! Are you okay?

I think so. I hope so. I don't know.

Which hospital?

***

Oriana was standing there as I came out of X-ray.

'What did they say?' she asked.

'Not much.'

'Well,' she gave me an appraising look, 'you don't *seem* injured.' She sat down beside me. 'What now?'

'Wait, I suppose.'

'Oh. Yeah. Of course, right.' She checked her watch.

'Really, don't let me keep you,' I said. 'Why have you come, anyway?'

She looked a little offended, then reached out and smoothed my hair. 'That's a silly question.' Her phone buzzed and she began to respond to a message.

The doctor's door opened. He stood there with that same grave expression and beckoned me in.

I got to my feet and Oriana rose too, accompanying me inside. Neither the doctor, nor Oriana, obviously, seemed to think there was anything out of the ordinary about this, and I wasn't in the mood to argue, not least because there wasn't – no one did anything alone in Italy if they could help it, and to crave otherwise was considered truly peculiar. Years previously I had fallen badly in a five-a-side soccer match and been accompanied to the very same waiting room *by both teams* while we awaited my X-ray results.

The doctor gestured for us to sit down. He opened the file upon his desk and began to carefully examine the contents.

'You have no history of head injuries?' he said. 'Knocks when you were a child, perhaps? Operations?' I shook my head. 'Cerebral disease?'

'No, Doctor.' He placed the papers down and gave me a long look. I wondered how I was going to break the news to Rose.

He said, simply: 'Then you can go.'

'I'm sorry?'

He frowned. 'What do you mean?'

'Are you saying I can leave? That everything's all right?'

'Oh yes,' he said, as if it was obvious. 'Everything's fine.'

'It's just . . .' I shook my head.

He stood up, held out his hand. Finally an amused smile lifted his rubbery lips.

'Don't worry,' he said in English. 'Be happy.'

'What *is* that?' I said. '"Don't worry, be happy"? That's not the first time I've heard it.'

'Oh, you know,' said Oriana, who was behind the wheel of her *Occhio Pubblico* white Volvo SUV. 'It's the title of that song, from the eighties . . . I think it was rather popular at the disco.'

Somehow I couldn't imagine the Comandante ever attending a disco. Nor the doctor, for that matter, but I suppose we were all young once.

'Where are we going?' I asked.

'Didn't you say you could do with a drink?' She turned the corner into a familiar slip road and pulled into the hotel car park. 'I mean, you've been given a clean bill of health, after all.'

'Actually, I could probably do with lying down,' I said.

'We could do that too.'

I shook my head. 'Honestly, haven't you had your fill of me today?'

'Ha! *Caro*, I don't know about you, but I was just getting started.' She switched off the ignition and turned towards me.

She held my face between her long, manicured fingers. 'I'll be leaving soon. We'll probably never see each other again.'

'Is that a promise?'

'Now I know you don't really mean that.' She leant over and kissed me. I drew in that cherry smell. Her hands reached down and pressed upon the top of my thighs. An increasingly familiar jolt ran through me – desire.

'Maybe just one drink,' I said.

Of course, we didn't stop at the bar – we went straight up to her room and fell onto her bed, but we only got so far before pain shot through my left side.

'What is it? Are you all right?' She turned on the light. '*Oooh* . . .' My left arm, ribs and hip had blossomed with bruises. 'My God,' she said. 'That must really hurt!'

I looked at her near-naked beside me and reached out. 'I'll get over it.'

'No no no.' She jumped up from the bed, pulling on a silk gown and pushing her hair back. She went into the bathroom and returned with a green first-aid bag.

'It's a little late for that,' I said. She flipped open the top and took out a jar.

'I get this from a little Chinese shop in Trastevere,' she said, unscrewing the top. 'Here,' she pushed me back, 'let me.'

She took out a dollop of the cream and began to rub it in. Although she was remarkably gentle, she could see that even her delicate touch hurt. 'I'm sorry, Daniel,' she said. 'I really should have taken you home. I was being selfish.'

'I'll live,' I said. 'Providing this stuff you're rubbing in doesn't poison me.'

She laughed. 'I hope not! I use it to remove blemishes.'

'I think it will take a little more than that . . .'

Lying on my side as she rubbed in the cream with those warm hands, I felt tiredness begin to get the better of me. Any more of this and I would be out for the count. 'You know,' I said, 'I hate to say it, but think I *had* better be going. I'm not going to be of any more service to you this evening, *signora*.' With some difficulty, I sat up and started to pull my clothes back on.

'I'll take you,' Oriana said.

'It's fine.'

'The least I can do.'

'Really, don't worry.' I spotted something resting on the top of her first-aid kit.

'My God, Oriana.' I held the knife up to the light. 'You weren't kidding, were you.'

'That's Israeli, too,' she said. 'Used by their commandos.'

I examined the carbon-black handle, the razor-sharp blade. I didn't know much about these things, but the weapon felt both extraordinarily light and extremely dangerous. 'You should be careful with this.'

'Oh, don't worry,' said Oriana. 'I know how to use it. I'm trained in that as well.' I laid the blade carefully back down.

'I bet you are. Don't you have to have a licence or something?'

'You only need one for guns.'

'But this *can't* be legal.'

She shrugged. I got it – in Italy, context was everything. A crime-fighting female reporter caught carrying a blade was unlikely to come in for any grief, even if she had planted it in the guts of a hood, which was precisely what she had meant when we had encountered Norman not so very far from here.

She took my face in those soft hands again, and gave me a lingering kiss.

'Can I ask you just one small favour?' I said. 'Can you try not to keep making me look so bad?'

'*Caro*,' she said. 'To do that, you'd have to stop doing it to yourself.' She walked me to the door.

'I suppose it's always a mistake to mix business with pleasure,' I said.

She looked genuinely surprised.

'Who's mixing?'

Chapter 32

Even intrepid gumshoes can enjoy a lie-in on a Saturday morning, especially when their left side is livid with bruises, although I actually didn't feel half as bad as I looked. I wondered if Oriana's mystery cream had had something to do with it.

I heard Rose leave for school, which was mainly sport on a Saturday. This would ordinarily have been my cue to rise, switch on Radio 4 and have my breakfast in peace. My solitary Saturday morning with the BBC was one of my few concessions to Englishness, despite the fact that listening to the litany of complaints that seemed to constitute the bulk of British news programming helped to remind me I was better off abroad. My adoptive country certainly had its shortcomings, but at least the Italians, despite their reputation, didn't appear to exist in a permanent state of indignation.

But not this morning. This morning I just lay in bed watching the very un-British Mediterranean-blue sky like a promise of paradise through the open shutters, feeling, frankly, *giù*, as I would say in Italian – *down*.

So I had finally got hold of Ishaan, quite literally, but not for long. Certainly not long enough to find out what had actually happened to Ryan, or how the two lads knew each other.

Who did Ishaan think *I* was? The police? Mafia? And where the hell *was* Ryan? To my despair, I still didn't know if he was even alive – or how he was connected with Ishaan.

I thought of Norman, that throat-cutting gesture. Was that aimed at me, Ryan, Ishaan? Had he and his mates flung Len Ligabue – and poor bloody Rufus – out of the tower?

Ishaan still felt like the key, but I had had my chance and blown it. I sat up: had the kid been bait? I thought of Dolores's warning about the guy on the door. It was certainly no coincidence that those heavies had come down to the kitchen after me.

The guy on the door, though, had appeared Italian. Was he Guardia di Finanza? Did he represent a link to a corrupt Capitano Bettini?

But I knew where to find Norman – either by day or by night. And I knew he was linked to Ishaan. I knew, too, that the time for working alone was coming to an end. We were not going to crack this without some serious muscle.

I swung my feet onto the parquet and rose. Finally had my breakfast, in silence. Went for a shower.

I had established a clear link between the hoods and, through Ishaan, Ryan.

I didn't know how much Ispettore Alessandro knew – usually a lot more than I did, in my experience – but there now also seemed to be enough to link Ryan to the Ligabue death for the police to get seriously involved. In fact, Alessandro might have been using me as a sort of battering ram, to stir things up a bit outside the usual channels.

We all have different thresholds of what we would consider risky . . .

Well, I had played my part and had the bruises to show for it – now Alessandro could play his.

I dried myself off and got dressed.

I heard the courtyard gates open, glanced down to see Rose returning, *Fedez* rucksack slung over her shoulder, singing along to Madame, the latest hot rapper. I put the kettle on, began to take out the food. Another weekend tradition: Saturday lunch together.

She belted up the steps, unlocked the door, gave me a perfunctory nod, her ear pods still audibly blasting rap, and flung the rucksack into the *lavanderia* as she shot down the corridor under the not-inaccurate assumption that an invisible hand would at some point unload and wash her sports stuff ready for Wednesday's beach volleyball (not at a real beach, you understand, but an indoor court in Casalecchio). I was quietly hoping that at some stage in the not-too-distant future she would become self-conscious enough about my handling her laundry to begin doing it herself, but we had yet to arrive at that milestone.

I had got the orecchiette in the pot, ready for our usual broccoli *pazzi* with olives, capers and peperoncini – something her mother used to prepare – when the doorbell went. She dashed out in a T-shirt and sweat pants, her hair shower-wet.

'It's Stefania,' she said. 'We're watching *Amici*.'

'Has she eaten?' I said.

'I said she could eat here.' She pressed the entrance switch.

'You could have told me before . . .'

'Don't worry,' she said. 'We're both on diets.'

'You don't need to go on a diet,' I said. 'You're shooting up!'

'Well Stefi does, so I said I would too.'

'Stefi doesn't either. Does her mother know?'

'She's the one who suggested it. Which reminds me, can you buy some kale?' There was a knock at the door. Rose opened it.

'Dad says . . .' she stopped. 'Dad.' I looked over but couldn't see from the stove who it was.

'What?'

'You'd better come.'

I wiped my hands on a tea towel and went over. A pair of Poliza di Stato were standing there in their dark blue jackets and forage caps.

'Signor Daniel Leicester?'

'That's me.' No sooner had I confirmed my identity than the other cop had grasped my still-wet hands and cuffed me. Rose screamed.

'What the hell is going on?' I said.

'You're coming with us. We're arresting you on suspicion of murder.'

'What? Who?'

'You can't do that!' Rose yelled. 'You can't take him. You can't! We're . . . *we're Carabinieri.*'

The one who had cuffed me laughed. 'That's not going to help you now, *signorina.*' He began to pull me along the balcony. Rose came after us, her voice becoming increasingly squeaky.

'Dad . . . *Dad.*'

'Call Grandad,' I said in English.

I saw Jacopo emerge from the balcony opposite our apartment, a towel around his waist.

'Make sure she's all right!' I shouted in Italian.

They took me down the stairs and into the courtyard. The gate opened. A pale blue police *volante* was parked outside. Standing beside it, Stefania. Her mouth dropped open.

'Hi, Stefi.' I tried to say it as if it was perfectly normal to see your best friend's father being hauled away by the police. 'There's pasta on the stove.' They opened the car doors. 'Make sure you turn the gas off, okay?'

Stefania nodded emphatically. I felt a heavy hand on the back of my head and was pushed into the car.

Chapter 33

'Where are you taking me? What the hell is going on?' I was pressing myself against the grille separating me from the cops in the front seats, but they ignored me.

I sat back, glaring at the backs of their heads.

Whatever was happening, I knew that one way or another I was in the soup, not least because, as had been made abundantly clear to my daughter, these were not 'our' people. They were Polizia di Stato.

While Italy is not the only European nation to have both military and civil police forces, typically it is the only one to have successfully resisted their meaningful reform or merger. Indeed, the nation appears to have delighted in police proliferation, beginning with the financial police – the Guardia di Finanza – along with various other bodies commissioned to police municipalities, forests, penitentiaries, the postal service, mortuaries, coastlines . . . the list goes on. In short, anywhere there is anything to police, you will usually find a distinct police service, often with its own uniform. But the two principal forces of law and order remain the Carabinieri, founded under the King of Piedmont before he came to rule the whole of Italy, and the Polizia di Stato, established at the time of the Unification.

While the Carabinieri – 'Riflemen' – remain the military's senior service, the Polizia di Stato is strictly civilian. But the differences mostly end there. Both have a roughly equal number of officers on the streets, investigate anything from petty to serious crime, and are constantly looking over each other's shoulder to see what the other lot is up to. Over the years, politicians have frequently mooted merging the two in an effort to streamline services and cut costs, but have just as smartly backed off. Given that any reform would most likely mean the Carabinieri being absorbed into the Polizia, such a move would prove deeply unpopular – there are too many statues in town squares memorialising heroic *carabinieri* who died protecting the locals from foreign aggression or in the line of duty, and it remains one of the institutions in which Italians have most trust.

But as you can imagine, this doesn't sit well with its younger sibling, the Polizia di Stato, which lacks the Carabinieri's legendary status, or its Napoleonic-era dress uniforms.

And uniforms are important to Italians.

I had expected to be taken through the centre of the city, directly to Polizia headquarters at the Questura, but instead we had gone on to the Viale and were swinging around the city before turning out towards the suburbs.

I knew this route – we were heading towards the outer ring road. We passed old factories, a new data centre; a furniture showroom, a couple of wholesalers. African and Gypsy encampments. Cargo areas for the nearby airport and lorry parks. I began to feel a little sick.

We turned down that slip road. For a brief moment I thought we might keep going – that they were going to try and pin the death of that pimp, Norman, or one of the prostitutes on me – but no, we pulled into the hotel, drove right up to the entrance.

The one who had cuffed me now turned around to peer through the grille.

'Big enough clue?'

'What's happened? Oriana . . . is she . . .' But they were getting out. They opened the back door.

I was led through the lobby as staff and guests looked on. I felt their eyes stay on me as we waited for the lift.

'Oriana's . . . *dead*?'

The lift was empty. We stepped in, one on either side of me, a hand upon each arm. The lift ascended to the fourth floor.

The doors opened. Instantly, the panoply of a crime scene. The corridor crowded with equipment, white-suited forensics crews. Bustling and idling police. All orientated towards the room along the corridor – Oriana's room. One of the cops left us and went over. Without crossing the threshold, he called in.

While I waited, a member of the forensics team, looking like a polar bear in her hood, recognised me – it was Massima, a contact.

'*Mio Dio,*' she mouthed. My God. I shook my head, as if it would somehow confirm that I had nothing to do with this. She made a discreet telephone gesture – did I want her to call anyone? I shook my head again.

A plain-clothed officer finally emerged from Oriana's

room. Her straw-blonde hair was cut in a functional bob.
Smoker's lines were drawn around her mouth, her quick grey
eyes. She had the hard set to her jaw of someone who had had
to endure a career of condescension within a macho hierarchy,
although to be fair this could be true of almost every Italian
woman of rank. In any case, I knew better than to try it on.

'I'm Daniel Leicester,' I said. 'A licensed investigator with
Faidate—'

'I know who you are.' There was a slight Neapolitan edge
to her accent.

'Is it Oriana de Principe?' I said. 'Look – just tell me.'

'So you know her?'

'Of course,' I said. 'I was here last night.'

'You admit it?'

'I'm not *admitting* anything. Let's not play games. You've
already dragged me here in front of my daughter. I've got
nothing to do with any crime. Oriana's a friend.'

'A friend?'

'Yes . . . well . . .'

She gave a hawkish nod to the cop beside me.

'Suit him up,' she said.

They led me to a storage area where the Police Forensic
Science Unit had installed themselves along with their kit.

Massima gave me a sympathetic, and desperately curious,
look but otherwise tried her best to behave discreetly. The
cop uncuffed me and I stepped into the forensic suit. I held
out my hands as a pair of synthetic gloves were slapped on.

'Put a mask on him too,' the detective called. 'We don't
want any droplets.'

'There you go,' said the cop, tying the mask behind me himself. 'Nice and tight.'

I stepped back into the hallway, doubtless looking as if I was dealing with some kind of viral outbreak, and was walked back along the corridor to the room. The detective, her only concession to the crime scene a pair of pale blue surgical gloves and plastic shoe covers, was leaning in the doorway looking down at her phone.

I suspected hauling me here was against the rules, but I was unsurprised by the *laissez faire* attitude of the police. What might seem like grounds for an appeal now, could easily be dismissed by an irascible judge with a stroke of the pen. In Italy, laws are regarded not so much as rules as guidelines, and all the more so among the arbiters of those guidelines.

'Right,' said the detective, and went in. I was given a little shove by the cop, and followed her through.

From the entrance to the room, little seemed to have changed. The bathroom immediately to my left looked pretty much as I remembered it – a little untidy, but nothing out of the ordinary. Ahead, I could see the TV on the wall, facing the bed. Through the windows a view over the tennis courts, and probably the mini golf course as well, had I been inclined to look.

The end of the bed was a little disordered, the azure-blue cotton cover scrunched up, mostly on the floor. But that, again, was how I remembered leaving it. I stepped forward and looked up the bed, where everything had changed.

The white sheets where we had lain, where Oriana had tended to my bruises, were now heavy with blood, congealed like soup between the creases.

There was a sideways swash to those sheets, and seeing the bare foot sticking crookedly upwards from beyond the other side of the bed, it was as if she had been propelled across it, then tumbled off but tried to pull herself back up again.

I followed the detective to where she lay. Yes, her left leg was supported by her raised right knee, both twisted bedward. Her dressing gown was open, her right hand reaching upwards, lost in the sheets. Her breasts were exposed but otherwise unmarked, her long white neck; her face, too, although smeared with blood, was not injured, although I noticed a blackening above her eyebrow. Her eyes, her mouth, were wide open. I understood why they used to think you could capture the image of a murderer on the victim's pupils – Oriana looked as if she had been frozen in the act of yelling their name. At least there was no fear in her face, in fact no acknowledgement of death whatsoever, as if she had been fighting too hard to notice.

'So, you walloped her,' said the detective. 'I don't know – two, three times, around the head? She stumbled backwards to the bed, where she reached for the knife – see?' I saw the upturned first-aid box, pills, bandages, plasters scattered across the floor, that jar of ointment rolled beneath the desk, then followed the detective's pointed finger to the space beside Oriana's body and the blood-blackened blade. 'But you got there before her and . . . well, you know the rest.'

I had avoided looking, but now I forced myself – the mess between her sternum and pelvis. A frenzied stabbing that had left her middle a crimson sash, half a dozen puncture wounds like angry, irregular mouths, their fleshy lips still gleaming beneath the wash of dried blood. There would have been no way she could have plugged them all – there were just too many, it had happened too quickly.

'I didn't do this,' I said quietly.

'So you're saying she did it to herself?'

'I didn't—'

'So now you're saying you *weren't* with her last night?'

'No.'

'Good – because we have witnesses. Come on, son. Make it easy on yourself – you had an argument, you whacked her and stabbed her.'

I shook my head.

'So if we test that knife, we won't find any of your DNA? Fingerprints? It doesn't look to me as if it's been wiped clean. "A moment of passion", isn't that what your type usually plea?'

'I . . .' I thought about the night before. 'I promise you, Officer. I didn't do this. The real killer is still out there somewhere.'

She gave me a pitying look. 'Oh come on, Signor Leicester. You asked *me* not to play games, but isn't that precisely what the real killer would say?' She nodded to the others. 'All right,' she said. I felt a hand on my shoulder.

As they began to lead me away, I took a final look at Oriana. She had become the single thing she would have hated most of all – a victim.

Chapter 34

The *volante* pulled into the street beside the Questura, probably the most unapologetically, and appropriately, some might say, fascist-era building in Bologna. I was taken through a side door and immediately down to the custody suite. It was there, in the depths of the building, standing before the admission desk, that my apparent celebrity status became known.

Polizia gradually drifted down to take a look. Eventually it seemed like half the cops in the building, male and female, had gathered to watch as samples were taken from beneath my nails, my hair, saliva, then I was fingerprinted.

Finally came the moment I had been dreading – and they had all been waiting for – the inevitable strip search.

In fact, I knew very well that there was nothing inevitable about it – they had to have reasonable grounds to believe I was concealing something – and I didn't doubt that conducting it in front of a crowd of police officers of both genders, along with a cheerful commentary concerning my attributes, was contrary to procedure, but as with the crime scene, so at the Questura, especially when they had a member, irrespective of my actual civilian status, of the 'opposing team' in custody.

The custody sergeant snapped on a fresh pair of surgical gloves.

'Now, *signore*, if you will bend over.' There was a huge cheer.

'Is he a virgin?'

'He won't be for long!'

'Has anyone got a spare battery?' I heard the sergeant say. 'I think I might need something stronger.'

'Make sure you don't get sucked in,' someone shouted.

'We'll have to send in a search party!'

'Count me out!'

I straightened up. The sergeant walked around to face me as if we were on stage and he the master of ceremonies.

'I'm not sure he finds this funny. Aren't you English all jokers?'

I wondered if any of this would end up online or – heaven forbid – *Occhio Pubblico*. It usually wouldn't be worth the risk. There were limits, even within the elasticity of Italian law and order – but for a case like this . . .

Finally I was handed a pack that included fresh underwear, plastic sandals, a pair of too-wide and short jeans, and a sweatshirt that was too small. I already looked like I was in prison, I thought.

I was led to a cell. There was a tray waiting for me upon the slim blue vinyl mattress.

'*Buon appetito*,' said the sergeant.

The minutes became hours; the hours passed. I would glance intermittently at that closed pale blue cell door, more often than not seeing a cop's face pressed against the glass porthole as if I was in an aquarium. More photo opportunities, I presumed.

So I began to spend most of my time on that hard mattress turned to the wall – the only place, I quickly realised, where I would be able to get any privacy, for now and, I feared, the foreseeable future.

On the surface, I was fucked. All right, with a good lawyer I stood a fair chance of clearing my name, but when? The Italian justice system was a byword for inefficiency. I might be locked up for years before the trial process – in practice, three separate trials – was complete, and of course there was no guarantee that at the end of it I would be found innocent.

Fucked. They would find my prints and DNA all over that knife, and there would be no wriggling out of that one on a technicality. They could excuse the lack of other samples – blood samples from Oriana, at least – on my body by the fact that I'd been able to clean myself up.

I thought of Oriana lying by the bed. Her face fixed in that silent shout, her body twisted, still trying to wrench herself up.

I hunt murderers.

Her girlish smile as she had sat astride me, pressed her nose against mine; that concerned, almost maternal frown as she dabbed her expensive cream onto me.

I heard the cell door open. I lowered my hands, clasped as if in prayer in front of my face, and turned around. A cop stood there.

'It's time,' he said.

Chapter 35

TRANSCRIPT 0098745KLQ Polizia di Stato, Questura di Bologna, 20.02

Commissario Rita Miranda: Interview with Daniel Leicester in connection with the murder of Signora Oriana de Principe. Signor Leicester, you have been read your rights, for the tape recording, yes?

Daniel Leicester: Yes.

CRM: *Bene.* Now, you don't deny you spent the evening with Signora de Principe?

DL: I spent an hour or so with her in her room before going home. I had had an accident. She . . . wanted to take care of me. When I left, she was fine.

CRM: What time did you leave?

DL: Around seven. At least, I was home by seven thirty.

CRM: And you've witnesses?

DL: My daughter. There must also be some CCTV?

CRM: Of you leaving the room? It was not a prison, *signore*, it was a hotel. But of course, your daughter will say whatever you have drilled her to.

DL: Just leave my daughter out of it.

CRM: It's a little late for that. Anyway, so your story is that the *signora* tended your wounds and sent you on your way.

DL: I wanted to leave, but that's about it, yes.

CRM: It seems a little odd that you were so friendly with the *signora* after you had had this very public row on TV.

DL: It was . . . is . . . complicated.

CRM: How so? Are you saying you weren't embarrassed? Annoyed?

DL: Oriana and I . . . we had an . . . odd relationship.

CRM: A sexual one.

DL: Yes.

CRM: And then she filmed you at the funeral, where you got in a fight, no less. You're clearly a violent man, *signore*.

DL: Aurelio Barbero threw a punch at me, I didn't respond.

CRM: Then up she pops, ready to tend your wounds. Yes, it certainly was an odd relationship. Was it a violent one? Sadistic? Masochistic, maybe?

DL: No.

CRM: But 'odd' can mean many things, can't it, *signore*. For example, it seems odd to me that you were having any kind of relationship with her after the fool she had made of you. I mean, come on, that really must have hurt!

DL: Look, I know what you're trying to do, but it won't wash. I'm telling the truth and the real culprit is still out there. And it's probably the same one who killed Len Ligabue.

CRM: Oh, the celebrity. Well, that's a Carabinieri matter. Naturally we will discuss it with them in due course, but for now we have our own celebrity corpse, and we have *you*, Signor Leicester. Look, Daniel. I know the truth can be stranger than fiction, but I really don't need the kind of conspiracy story you've been cooking up while you've been stewing in the cells. In my experience murder is almost always more banal. You know – the elephant in the drawing room. You want CCTV footage? We've got something better – we've got national TV footage of the *signora* humiliating you in front of an audience of millions. That must have stung! Oh Daniel, Daniel, you wag your head, but *I* would have been furious . . . and you *were* angry, right? We've already spoken to producers. 'Judge, jury and executioner.' That's what you said – and then you decided to take the role yourself! Oh . . . *please* . . . for the recorder.

DL: I did not.

CRM: But you have to admit, from our perspective, you must be the prime suspect?

DL: I can understand why you might prefer it that way.

CRM: What does that mean?

DL: Clearly it would make your life easier.

CRM: If I was interested in an easy life, Daniel, I wouldn't have become a police officer. Look – you have the motive. You were at the location, and there's physical evidence connecting you to the act.

DL: Physical evidence?

CRM: The knife, Daniel.

DL: I picked it up when she was treating my bruises. It was in her medical bag. If you powder the ointment jar, you will probably find my prints on that, too.

CRM: So what were you doing with the knife, Daniel? What's your story?

DL: I don't have one. I saw it there and took it out. She had mentioned it before. I hadn't believed her, and there it was. I took a look at it. She told me it was Israeli. I put it back.

CRM: You're good at thinking on your feet, I'll give you that. Okay, let's say I do believe you, Daniel. Look at it from my perspective. How could I explain your story to the judge?

DL: From your perspective, I would want to get the people actually responsible. The judge would, too.

CRM: But based on where I'm sitting now, the judge would be saying I'm already looking at the person, right? Now, it frankly appals me to say this, as there are few things I hate more than killers of women. But I also have to bear in mind that, although you will most definitely be convicted, you will try to string this out in the courts for as long as possible and, frankly, I can think of better ways to spend my time. You're going down, son. Be a man for once in your life and confess. You know – something like 'It was the heat of the moment, she drove me crazy with her taunts about my cock' – that would do the trick. You'd likely be out in ten, by which time you would have just about exhausted the process in any case. What do you say?

[Knocking sound. Door opening. Muffled female voice.]

CRM: Hold that thought! Interview with Signor Daniel Leicester in connection with the murder of Signora Oriana de Principe suspended at . . . 20.34.

I was left alone in the interview room but didn't for a moment *feel* alone – I could sense the activity behind the mirrored screen if not see it. I was excruciatingly conscious that an entire day had passed since Oriana's body had been discovered, and although time had been passing dreadfully slowly within the windowless basement of the Questura, outside it would have been moving much more quickly: the death of a celebrity, albeit a minor one of Oriana's calibre, would be massive national, even international, news: a journalist on *Occhio Pubblico* struck down investigating a story, a murder linked to another celeb? And how long before they got my name? I shook my head; it was almost certainly already out there. I would be all over the news, the web, every crevice of my personal life and history was probably already being pored over. Christ, some joker might at this moment be posting a video of my strip search . . .

There would be serious pressure on Commissario Miranda, serious pressure on everyone from the Prefect down. Judges would be chomping at the bit to have a go, grasp their moment in the limelight.

The door opened. It was not Commissario Miranda or an investigating magistrate, but Ispettore Umberto Alessandro.

'Stand up,' he said. 'You're coming with me. Well, don't look so surprised – get a move on.'

I followed him out of the room. The next door was open and Commissario Miranda was standing there, arms crossed – behind her a tinted window looking on to the interview room, and another two detectives, smoking fiercely – her resentment well hidden behind her frosty smile.

Alessandro nodded.

'Commissario.'

'Ispettore.'

We carried on along the corridor, plain-clothed and uniformed cops collecting in the doorways to watch in silence.

We pushed through a fire door and went down a set of steps into the car park. There was a dark blue Carabinieri limo pulled up, its engine running.

'Get in the back and lie down,' said the Ispettore. 'Pull the blanket over your head.'

I did precisely as I was told, pressing myself against the soft black leather as the car pulled smoothly away.

Chapter 36

'You can sit up now,' said the Ispettore.

I knew this place, I thought as the graffiti-riddled metal gates opened automatically and the limo rolled inside. We were in Bolognina, the Special Operations Group's hideaway on the wrong side of the tracks. There were two other cars parked in the yard outside the abandoned factory – my Punto and the Comandante's Lancia.

I got out. Rose flung herself into my arms, sobbing. As I held her, the others emerged from the factory. All, I noticed, were smoking, even Alba. I could see the strain on their faces.

'What happened?' Rose shrieked.

'Nothing,' I said. 'It's all a misunderstanding.'

'It's on the news! That reporter!'

'I know, I know. But it's a dreadful mistake.'

'They won't put you in prison, will they?'

'Of course not, darling. I'm here now, aren't I?' She looked at me, plainly unconvinced. At that moment, dollops of rain began to fall. They splashed on her upturned face. I wiped them away.

'We had better get inside,' said the Ispettore.

The workshop was much as I remembered it – the machines

long since removed, only holes remaining where they had once been bolted into the concrete floor. Chipped and scarred wooden benches, broken windows, scene-of-crime stickers from when the place had been seized by the Carabinieri . . . beyond, the strip of wasteland leading to the new blocks of flats, where they had apparently made some progress since last I was here – there was a *SI VENDE* banner strung hopefully across the front. Soon residents would be looking down at what the SOG was getting up to, and it would have to find somewhere else to conduct its activities out of the public eye.

I felt wretched having Rose here, at a place that had originally been a mafia torture den – not to mention whatever the Ispettore's mob got up to – but I understood why they had brought her. That irresistible Italian sentimentality: regardless of the crisis, family always came first.

A half-dozen plastic chairs were set in a circle as if this were a meeting of some kind of encounter group. I took one. Rose insisted on staying on my lap and draping her arms around my neck, while the rest of the family, plus Dolores and the Ispettore, took the others.

'Well,' said the Comandante, looking intently at me through a swirling cloud of blue smoke. 'What happened?'

I told them as matter-of factly as possible, although I left out the gory details with Rose there. 'I want to thank you,' I added to the Ispettore, 'for getting me out.'

He gave me a pained look. 'I'm afraid it's not that simple, Daniel.'

The Comandante said: 'Umberto had to pull strings at the very highest level for you to be released into his custody for a brief period.' He looked at the Ispettore. 'Twenty-four hours . . .'

Alessandro checked his watch. 'Now twenty-three.'

' . . . before you are formerly charged with Signora de Principe's murder. The Polizia were dead against it, of course, spitting, but the Prefect . . .'

'Let's just say he was more forthcoming,' said the Ispettore. For the first time I began to appreciate his penchant for fostering influence in high places. 'But it is a small window,' he continued. 'And needless to say, the Polizia will be counting on our failure to resolve the issue.'

'If I can get hold of this pimp, Norman . . .'

'Is that going to be enough, though?' said the Comandante. 'From what you say, these are hardened criminals. They're neither likely to crack or be enough for Commissario Miranda.'

'Ishaan, then.'

'Again,' the Ispettore waved his hand, 'immigrants . . .'

'I'm an immigrant myself.'

'With links to the Carabinieri,' said the Ispettore. 'And I must say, I can see the Commissario's point – judged by any ordinary measure, you are logically the main suspect.'

'Ryan Lee,' I said. 'That's where it all began. Then Ligabue, Oriana . . . If I can find Ryan Lee . . .'

'We've already spent a week looking for him,' said the Comandante. 'What makes you think you'll be able to crack it in a day?'

'Ispettore,' I said. 'Can you have a team ready to release Ryan?'

'But you don't know where he is,' said Alessandro.

'I think I know how to find out.'

The hardest part was taking my leave of Rose.

I had had the chance to change into my own clothes, a jumper, casual jacket and jeans, and Jacopo had returned with a stack of pizzas, so sitting there – even Alessandro in his tailored raincoat and double-breasted suit with a carton containing a five-euro Margherita open upon his lap – gave the lamplit setting a strange sense of domesticity, as if we were on some kind of outing and simply sheltering from the still-falling rain.

But we were up against the clock. We soon polished off the pizzas, and now we were standing up.

'No!' Rose shouted, clinging on to me.

'Don't worry, love,' I said. 'Whatever happens, I'll be fine, I promise you.'

'Just stay.' She looked up at me. 'Five minutes longer?'

I squeezed her tight, tried to detach her. 'Then it will be another five, and another. I have to get going precisely so we can spend lots more time together.'

'Don't die,' she said.

'Of course I won't die, love.'

'Mum did.'

A terrible quiet swept over us all.

'Well, *I* won't,' I said firmly. 'That I promise you. Now,' I unprised her fingers and held her by her bony shoulders. 'Let's have some of that British bulldog spirit, heh?' She tried to smile and it broke my heart. 'That's more like it. I need you to look after the rest for me, okay? Make sure they stay on the ball. Can you do that?' She nodded through her tears. 'Good.' I summoned all my courage, and not a little of my cowardice, and turned my back upon her.

I walked out of the factory beside the Ispettore without looking around.

**

The rain had stopped as suddenly as it had begun. Beyond the yard gates, an ambulance siren neared then faded away. A full moon made us silver.

I got into the Punto. Alessandro knocked on the passenger window and gestured to be let in. I reached across and opened the door. He pushed back the seat, looking oddly out of place in the position usually occupied by Rose or Dolores. He gave me a frank look.

'Why the mystery?'

'The fewer people involved, the better,' I said.

'That sounds like the sort of thing *I* would say. You know, you and I, Daniel,' he gave my elbow a squeeze, 'we go back. We don't need to keep secrets from each other.' I recalled a surprised-looking corpse in a churchyard. The Ispettore's still-smoking revolver.

'It's not about secrets,' I said. 'But it *is* personal. Just make sure you're ready to go.'

He gave me another searching look, dug into his pocket. 'This is a burner.' It was an old-fashioned numerical mobile. 'No password and only my number. When you've used it once, dispose of the SIM and phone separately.' He paused, seemed to make up his mind. He pulled out a Beretta not dissimilar to the Comandante's.

'Don't tell me,' I said. 'Also a burner.'

'Something like that.'

'Has it only got one bullet?'

'Hardly.' He handed it to me. It felt weighty. 'A full magazine. If you do use it, throw it into the river. A deep part.'

I was still looking at the gun as he got out of the car. I leant over and put it into the glove compartment.

Chapter 37

The Beretta knocked insistently against the glove compartment door as the Punto rattled along those shimmering streets. It had certainly extended my options, but it had also raised the stakes. *Umberto's bar may be set somewhat higher,* perhaps by providing me with the pistol he expected me to comport myself as he or one of his fellow professionals might – judiciously, discreetly, surgically . . .

In a sense, I was flattered. Had he been taken in by my British reserve? Because I was conscious that my current state of mind was neither judicious, discreet, nor surgical. I continued to cradle that crystal-hard anger that had taken hold ever since I had seen Oriana's body.

I had always considered fury a phenomenon that flared but would assuredly pass. This, however, sat behind my eyes like magma. I had begun to understand the mindset of the murderers I used to watch in the court dock from the press gallery. More often than not I had considered them monsters who had just got carried away, usually after a night out, alcohol and drugs perhaps dissolving what tenuous synapses ordinarily suppressed their violent urges. But now I began to understand them a little better, what it meant to carry all that unconsummated rage. The necessity to manifest it, regardless of the consequences.

But there remained one difference between them and me: they were puppets to this imperative, whereas I was not – at least not yet – that far gone. I knew what was happening. I had an objective. Nonetheless, I sensed this as a quality separate from my usual, largely pacific nature; as something I would need to channel like a soldier, precisely because, unlike Norman, apparently, I had never actually been one. Anger, viciousness, malevolence were woven into the fibre of scum like him, which was presumably how he kept his girls in line. When I confronted him, I couldn't fake it – he had to understand *I* would not be another one of his victims, unless I wanted to become one. On the contrary: I was Oriana's vengeance.

I doubted he would be packing a pistol. Why would a pimp need more than a knife? I also had one other advantage. Surprise. That didn't mean he wouldn't be keeping an eye out for me – it probably came as second nature for someone raised in a culture of vendetta – but, presuming my name was already out there as having been picked up by the police, he certainly wouldn't expect me to have already been let loose.

I pictured him drawing his finger across his throat.

I imagined him on his knees at the point of my gun.

I avoided the slip road by the hotel leading up to where the prostitutes plied their trade. Instead, I went around the other side and parked my car in the industrial estate beyond the underpass where we had initially guessed Ishaan had fled.

I removed the pistol from the glove compartment.

I was a hundred metres or so from the underpass. Above it ran a railway line, the electric cables crackling with the damp. Rather than venturing down the tunnel, first I would climb up the slope with the intention of gaining a better view.

I tried to pocket the Beretta, but it wouldn't fit into my jacket. Instead I stuck it in my waistband, something I thought only occurred in the movies, before beginning to clamber up the slippery embankment, my shoes struggling to find a purchase on the damp shingle. I slipped forward, digging my fingers into the gravel, before finally grabbing hold of the slick rail and pulling myself up to a squat.

Below were three camper vans set at intervals along the road, pools of lamplight along the pavement between. Only one girl, however, on display. Her head down, examining her phone. Of course – it was late on a Saturday evening. Prime time, I imagined, for lonely bachelors. Speaking of which . . . A pair of headlights rounded the corner, snailed along the road. The girl looked abruptly up from her phone, straightened herself and turned with her hands on her hips. I couldn't see her clearly, but despite her bleached blonde hair, she looked to be squeezed into her white vinyl hot pants and boob tube, her breasts pushed forward, stomach sucked in. She wasn't the woman I'd encountered at Via Fosserella.

A maroon Jeep SUV stopped in front of her and she made to lean into it, but before she could do so, it had pulled away. It continued to the end of the road until it reached the roundabout, then came back again. The woman, who had let her stomach out and her breasts in, adopted another hopeful pose, only this time angled towards the opposite side of the road. But the car continued on until it turned out of sight.

A whisper upon the tracks. I looked right, left – a pair of white dots rapidly expanding. I slid back down the embankment as the Trenitalia Frecciarossa screeched above, streamers of blue current pursuing it like ghouls.

I considered scrambling back up for another look, but there had not been much to see. No sign of Norman, certainly, although he could be in one of the vans – if not in the back, then in the warmth of the front.

The underpass was broad and sloped downwards. Perhaps the original intention had been to provide a road linking the two sides beneath the railway track, but instead now a solitary concrete bollard sat in the middle, indicating it was for pedestrian use only. I couldn't see why. Perhaps they had just run out of money. In any case, it plainly also served as a public toilet, occasional homeless refuge, and canvas for graffiti, although why artists would bother scribbling here in the unlit dank was anyone's guess.

I had only walked a couple of metres inside when I stopped, stepped back into the shadow. At the other end of the underpass I had seen the orange flare of a cigarette – Norman, where we had encountered him that time before; the vantage point from which he kept an eye on his investments.

I pulled out the Beretta, stepped forward . . . then stopped. Something was holding me back. Was it Oriana's hand on my shoulder? The Ispettore's? Either way, standing there in the dark, I instantly understood Norman would never take me seriously, even if I had a gun in my hand. I could see it already, how he'd say: 'Then shoot me.'

He would step closer – 'Come on, English, *shoot me*.'

And grab the gun.

The Beretta wasn't a magic wand, and regardless of how I might pose with it, this wasn't the movies.

I had to mean to fire it. And he had to believe I would.

The approach of another train. As it screamed overhead, I began to back out of the underpass.

I opened the car door. Tossed the pistol onto the passenger seat. If I couldn't persuade Norman – didn't even have the courage to try at the point of a gun – what the hell *could* I do?

I checked my watch.

Twenty-two hours.

I started the engine, pulled out. My mind was empty. I had no clear ideas, certainly no plan. Even that anger I had been so certain would see me through had now, apparently, vanished.

It's personal. Who the fuck did I think I was? I was just as phoney as one of those damn truffles.

I got back on the main road. The *faux*-Liberty bulk of the hotel was lit up to my right. I thought of Oriana standing in front of it as if she was in a perfume ad, the pair of us cycling along that slip road.

I did a U-turn, headed back from where I'd come. Only this time, I took the hotel exit.

I drove slowly past the hotel, continued along the slip road as if I was trailing the pair of us – me in my suit and she with her silver dress hitched around those firm, muscular thighs.

There it was – the first camper van, where we had encountered the prostitute, then the next. That girl in white vinyl was still waiting, gamely adopting the pose as I drew near.

I slowed down, but not as much as the maroon Jeep, and took a look. She was young and quite obviously anxious. Her eyes were not so much come hither as pleading to me, and I hated to think what Norman did to motivate his girls. I continued along the road, past the other camper vans, their grimy windows aglow behind tatty curtains, until I arrived at the roundabout.

I came back the other way, cruising now at around thirty kilometres an hour.

I switched my headlights on full so Norman wouldn't get a good look at me, but I saw *him* for an instant, holding a hand flat against his eyes, dazzled by the light.

Which was when I jerked the steering wheel towards him.

The car barrelled down the slope, shaving the concrete bollard before crashing into him full on.

An animal thud reverberated through the vehicle's tinny frame as he was pitched first onto the bonnet then against the windscreen, cracking the glass.

He windmilled out of sight.

The car carried on, scraping the side of the underpass in a spray of sparks and screeching metal before I remembered to brake.

It heaved to a halt, the seat belt snapping against my chest. A kind of shudder ran through the vehicle – and me – before it was properly still.

I stayed sitting there, my hands glued to the steering wheel, blinking at the blood-flared windscreen.

Finally I began to fumble for the door handle, stopped. In the wing mirror I checked the silhouette lying still on the ground.

I reached for the Beretta. Only it wasn't on the passenger seat. I scrabbled around in the darkness until I found it wedged against the door. I plucked it out by its barrel, turned it the right way around, and finally got out.

As I edged closer to Norman, I heard a clacking sound. I looked up – it was the girl in white vinyl, tottering uncertainly towards us. I meant to wave her away, but she let out a yelp and ran off, as best she could in those heels. Of course – I had waved the gun. Now I pointed it unsteadily at Norman.

He cut a lurid figure in my ruby brake light, although I couldn't tell how severe his injuries actually were. In any case, I wasn't going to take any chances.

The pimp was lying on his back, legs and a single arm splayed outwards. I looked for his other arm and realised he was lying on top of it. His nose was smashed, his mouth splashed with blood. He was breathing, though, and his good arm now reached up towards me in a kind of defensive gesture, or one of surrender.

'I think I've dislocated . . . my arm . . . shoulder,' he said. 'My ribs, it hurts . . . when I . . . breathe . . .'

'Why did you do it?' I said. 'Kill Oriana. Who paid you?'

'Who?'

'What do you mean,' I said, '"who"?'

'Who's Orana?'

'Don't give me that shit.' I raised the gun so it was pointing towards his head.

'Whoa . . . please . . . Now I see you. You're that snoop. You mean the girl? The one you were with that time?'

'Look familiar?' I made a throat-cutting gesture.

'Man, I was just fucking with you . . . really.' He tried to move, gasped. '*Really.*'

'Who ordered you to do it?'

'I haven't done anything, I swear. Whatever it is that happened to this girl of yours . . . it had nothing to do with us.'

'I don't believe you.'

I glanced at the gun. I would have liked to have cocked the hammer, but I realised I had no idea where it actually was.

'Who ordered it?' I repeated. 'Capitano Bettini?'

'Who's he?'

'Don't give me that. The Guardia di Finanza are in on it, this racket you've got going. Immigration . . . work permits . . . truffles . . . He's the one behind it.'

Now he looked me in the eyes. Did he see something there to be afraid of, after all? Whatever it was, he began to nod.

'Him. Yeah. But I didn't do nothing. I didn't kill no one. Not your girl . . . this Orana . . . Never . . . I promise you . . .'

'Ryan Lee,' I said. 'Where is he?' Norman shook his head, as much in pain, I think, as denial.

I spoke through gritted teeth. 'You *will* tell me – where is Ryan fucking Lee?'

'Look, man, I promise you I don't know who you're talking about . . .'

In the distance I could hear a siren. I waited, waited . . . it was getting louder. This one wasn't going to pass by. 'Ishaan,' I said. 'The Indian cook . . . No more bullshit, Norman – I *know* you know him. Now tell me where he is, or so help me God . . .'

That was when I saw it – a slide mechanism worked discreetly into the flat top of the gun. I brought my other hand over and snapped back the Beretta's hammer.

'The Count,' said Norman. 'Malduce. His place, in the hills.'

Chapter 38

My car gave out about a kilometre from the destination. I was surprised it had managed to get that far – the entire right side was wrecked, with one headlight out and the bonnet concertinaed upwards. The wheel arch was grinding against the tyre and the passenger door warped shut. I had thought the tyre might give out first and was ready to run on a flat, but something went in the engine and the thing just conked out, smoke pouring threateningly from its exposed innards. Fortunately I had time to pull into the corner of an unlit car park outside a private hospital where no one would notice it, at least until morning.

I had managed to pull out of the underpass just as blue lights began to sweep the other side. As far as I could tell, it was an ambulance rather than the police. In any case, no one came after me.

As soon as I was far enough away, I called Alessandro. Shared what I'd found out.

'Hold on,' he said. He spoke to someone, then gave me an address. 'There?'

'How should I know?'

'Meet us there. How quickly do you think you can make it?' My car had already begun to play up, but I thought I would be okay.

'Half an hour,' I said.

Thirty minutes later, I was sitting behind the wheel of my broken Punto, looking through the starred windscreen as smoke hissed upwards. I knew that I should get out and begin to walk, but something kept me there. The adrenalin that had been pumping through me had drained along with the lifeblood of the car and now, as I looked down at my hands, I noticed they were shaking. I felt nauseous, faint, and from somewhere at the back of my skull a little voice informed me I was in shock. Then it reminded me, almost politely, that this wasn't over yet. I was still against the clock, which was counting relentlessly down.

I opened the door, swung my legs out, and pulled myself to my feet. Hanging onto the Punto's roof, I drew in the fresh hill air.

I walked to the fringe of the car park and broke open the phone, extracting the battery and SIM, then threw the separate parts into the woods. I returned to the Punto, leaned in and removed the Beretta. Still holding on to it, I began to head up the narrow road.

It had hardly registered until now, but of course I knew this place, I knew it well. The Count was virtually a neighbour. I used to drag Rose up here for a countryside walk when she was under the illusion I was still in charge – we would cross the Viale, pass the church of Santissima Annunziata, and head up the main road into the hills before it spliced into more minor tributaries like this one.

This road would end at the entrance to Villa Ghigi, as the countryside park was known. It was here that Count Malduce lived, not in some pre-Renaissance *palazzo* but one of the Brutalist-style concrete houses set back from the road with only their garages and entrances – shaped as you would imagine the entry to a nuclear bunker – fully visible from ground level. Above, one could glimpse grey walls and the bottoms of wide, frameless windows fringed by ivy and concrete tubs cascading with ferns.

Although they couldn't seem more removed from the buildings in the city below, these houses in fact balanced conspicuous consumption with self-defence as much as any city-centre *palazzo*. I had always imagined their wealthy occupants living a kind of Kubrickian existence up here among concrete walls, late-period Picassos and fuzzy black-and-white CCTV, ready perhaps to greet any *Clockwork Orange*-like visitors with a machine gun.

Now I knew.

As I neared the Count's address, I placed my pistol back in my waistband, but it began to chafe, so I tucked it around the back.

Chapter 39

I was too late, or something had gone wrong – a dark blue Carabinieri van was parked outside the house. Next to it stood a paramedic's luminous yellow motorbike.

A pair of uniformed *carabinieri* were stretching a cordon across the road. The first seemed about to stop me, but the second said: 'That's the guy,' and I was allowed through. Up ahead, about a dozen of their tough-looking blue-bereted colleagues were milling about as if they were spoiling for a fight. When they saw me, they looked ready to have one, but someone said again: 'That's the guy,' and everyone relaxed. I passed through them towards the light – a raised garage door.

Sitting on the concrete floor was Count Malduce in his dressing gown, covered with blood.

A medic was crouched beside him, but he didn't seem particularly galvanised, despite the gore. Where had the Count been shot? Surely he wouldn't just be sitting there cross-legged, sobbing?

Then I saw it – the folded fawn and black German Shepherd beside him.

'Daniel,' said the Ispettore. It was the first time I had

seen him in a uniform other than his Napoleonic parade dress. This was how his colleagues must have perceived him, regardless of his usual immaculate plain clothes – in the braid-heavy epaulettes and peaked cap asserting the authority of his formal, rather than functional, title – *Colonnello*. 'What kept you?'

'What happened?' I said.

'We're not at your beck and call,' said Alessandro. 'These men are on overtime. We heard some movement in the garage. We thought it might be your man. We opened it up and . . .'

'It was the dog.'

'The boys were surprised. It came at them. They shot it.'

We looked sadly at the Alsatian.

'Then the Count came down?' I said. Alessandro nodded. 'Have you checked the rest of the house?'

'There doesn't seem to be any sign of your American boy.'

'I'm sorry. I thought . . .'

'You did well to get this information so quickly.' The Ispettore gave me a wry look. 'I presume in doing so you haven't dug yourself into a deeper hole.'

I thought of Norman lying in the underpass. He hadn't looked like he would want any more trouble. 'Have you noticed?' I said.

'Certainly,' said the Ispettore. The walls of the garage were stacked with plastic tubs, a couple of which had been opened – they were full of white truffles.

'Not Boscuri, I take it.'

'I would be extremely surprised,' he said. 'I doubt Boscuri could produce that many in a year.'

The medic stood up. 'He seems to be all right,' he said. 'Although we should get him to hospital, just to be sure.'

Alessandro looked down at the Count, who had grown quiet. 'You don't need to go to hospital, do you, Cesare?'

The Count mumbled, 'No.'

'Cesare?' I said.

'Caesar. His parents always had high expectations. And to his credit, he tried to meet them – bit of cheque fraud here, impersonation there. That was how we first bumped into each other, wasn't it, Cesare? When I nabbed you for not paying a hotel bill. Said you were the son of a duke that time. I was genuinely pleased for you when you became the real thing.' The Ispettore looked at me. 'He wooed and married the old countess. Made her happy, I'm sure, in her final years. Inherited the lot.' He shook his head. 'I never thought we'd bump into each other again – you had your hobby and everything seemed legit. So how does this work?'

'The truffles must come through the Kosovans,' I said. 'He uses the kitchen staff to substitute the legitimately bought ones for the counterfeits and sells on the Italian originals – maybe even back to the restaurateurs.

'The kitchen workers – they're all terrified of getting into trouble with the authorities, whether they're legally here or not. But something went wrong – somewhere along the line a superfake got mixed up with the genuine truffles he was selling on.'

I plucked one of the truffles out of its tub, held it up to the light. 'It looks pretty ordinary to me. Tell me, Cesare, how did you do it? Make these superfakes?'

'Answer the man,' said the Ispettore.

'But I don't know what he means,' said Cesare. 'Make?'

I held the truffle in front of him. 'Fake Boscuri whites. You couldn't just pluck them off the Balkan hillsides. Truffles like this have to be nurtured, created. But when you got caught out, you snatched Ryan Lee.'

The Count looked up at Alessandro. 'I didn't have anything to do with Mr Lee, honestly, *signore*. I was as shocked as anyone else. And these . . .' he nodded at the truffle, 'they're ordinary. All right, they're from the Balkans, but normal enough – found, not made. What the Englishman says about that is true – we replace a percentage of Boscurili with the Balkans but retain enough of the original whites in every dish to maintain flavour and appearance.'

'I must admit,' Alessandro said to me, 'that seems more like Cesare. And this gang of yours – they don't exactly appear the scientific type.'

'But they're not alone,' I said. 'There's also Capitano Bettini of the Guardia di Finanza.'

'What about him?'

'He's behind it.'

Alessandro frowned. 'How do you mean, Daniel?'

'I asked . . . my contact who tipped us off about this place. And he confirmed Bettini was the one pulling the strings . . . What?'

'The Capitano is my brother-in-law.' Alessandro smiled. 'And although I would not ordinarily hold that against him, I happen to know that for the past three months he has been in the United States on a course. He is actually due home shortly.'

'But Norman . . .' I thought of him red and crooked in the brake light – Norman had been terrified.

'*You* then,' I said to Cesare. '*You* killed Oriana. She was about to expose your business, all your damn pretensions. You wouldn't have it. You turned up at her room, attacked her—'

'I swear . . .' The Count held up his hands. It was true – he didn't exactly look the type to overpower Oriana . . .

'If not you, then who? Come on, out with it, you bastard.'

'Daniel . . .' The chatter of the *carabinieri* had ceased. Their cigarette smoke hung in the air. I had been shouting. 'My friend,' said Alessandro. 'How about you take a look around the house.' He indicated the concrete steps leading upwards. 'Before you go . . .' He reached behind me and removed the Beretta from my waistband. 'Perhaps I should hold on to that for now.'

The steps led straight into a kitchen, the kind of space that features in interior magazines – all concrete and rust-treated ironwork with ivy-draped shelves displaying gleaming pots and pans. The view beyond the wide windows was thick with trees.

I ventured further into the house. In the hallway I found myself facing the same kind of neon-red question mark I had encountered in Len Ligabue's apartment. A coincidence? Sometimes a pipe is just a pipe, as Dr Freud might say, although I could well imagine Count Cesare seeking to emulate the tastes common to his milieu.

I entered a vast living room with a view above yet more trees, their canopy swaying silently like a brooding night-time sea. Beyond were the twinkling lights of the city, its hexagonal defensive shape clearly visible from up here, Asinelli winking away low-flying aircraft.

It was like a penthouse, I thought, or perhaps a very grand tree house.

The *soggiorno* also looked like it had been pulled from a periodical – black leather designer sofas, Persian rugs spread upon the glossy concrete floor. A modern open fire with wood piled high either side. One interior wall was carpeted with a soft, moss-like organism, another was almost entirely glass – looking onto a concrete basin flush with moulds, packed with ferns and palms.

On the final wall, where I might have expected some form of modern art, or perhaps a large mirror to enable the Count to admire himself in this setting, was a figurative painting from over a century past: a group of Victorian-era folk, the central figure sporting a top hat, a woman linking her arm through his – only they, along with the half a dozen others beside them, were clearly sporting masks. Not the sparkling if faintly sinister Venetian kind, but rather of grotesques – pallid human faces distorted into purposeful vulgarity. I instantly recognised it as a work by Ostend painter James Ensor, who had been inspired by the city's rather bawdy carnival. I had once spent a couple of weeks there investigating the expat smuggling business, and his house had been open to the public. Could the painting be original? I doubted it, but it was definitely a good copy.

I left the room and went up the solid concrete steps. Immediately to my right was a master bedroom with a king-size bed, at the end of which was the only aged item of furniture I had seen thus far – an eighteenth-century dressing table with a speckled mirror. Along with an array of colognes and hair creams was a woman's brush set and, in a silver frame, a wedding photo of the younger Cesare with his new bride, who must have been thirty years his senior.

An ample mahogany wardrobe was fitted into the concrete wall. I opened it. Naturally, it was full of expensive suits, shirts and accessories. In the final panel there was a collection of dresses, presumably also the late Countess's. I pulled them aside and began testing the wall behind in case there was anything hidden, then threw Cesare's suits onto the bed and did the same, but . . . nothing.

I stepped back into the corridor. Across the way was a guest bedroom, as neatly made up as a hotel room. I gave it the same treatment before continuing to the final room along the corridor. The door was open – of course, the police had already given it a perfunctory search – but it had clearly been lived in. Or rather, was *being* lived in. The duvet was partly pulled back. I pulled further and laid my palm flat upon the sheet – it was still warm.

I looked around. The room was neat. As neat as a room occupied by Ryan Lee? Not quite. There were some clothes draped over a chair. On the bedside table a glass of water, a couple of paperbacks. A well-thumbed Italian cookbook, and a novel – *The White Tiger* by Aravind Adiga.

I checked beneath the bed. Opened the wardrobe – a couple of shirts hanging up, a purple T-shirt, *SUN KIL MOON* emblazoned across the front. I looked around for further hiding places, then went back into the corridor. Nothing in the bathroom, although I noted the solitary toothbrush and a pair of flip-flops. I walked to the end of the landing, where there was a window and small terrace. The window had been pushed closed. I opened it and leaned over. This part of the house looked onto woods rising upwards, hence it was only a six-foot drop down.

I climbed over the railing and dropped.

Although my landing wasn't hard, neither was it quiet – I hit a bed of leaves and slid down the incline beneath the terrace. But I saw that there was another set of skid marks, and scuffed-up leaves. I scrambled up from beneath the terrace and took in the wooded landscape. Monochrome faded to black beyond the illuminated borders of the house, the trees dissolving into a charcoal mass. It didn't become much clearer as I moved forward, leaving behind the police chatter, the clumping car doors.

Was Ishaan watching me? I had to believe it. Would I catch him this time? I had my doubts. I ventured deeper into the woods, the house becoming an isolated spot of light, the trees standing tall around me, perfectly content to observe this little drama being played out.

'Ishaan,' I called. 'I promise I'm not here to hurt you. I want to help.'

Nothing.

'I work for the parents of Ryan Lee. He's disappeared; we're trying to find him. I promise you won't be harmed, we'll protect you.'

A crack, far closer than I had expected. I realised Ishaan could only be metres away.

'I promise,' I said. 'This has nothing to do with you, your immigrant status, anything you might be involved in. It's just Ryan we want to find – for his parents.'

'Who are you?' A voice to my right.

'A private investigator, Daniel Leicester.'

'Then you're not one of them?'

'Who are "them"?'

'The others . . .' He began to emerge from behind the tree. No wonder he was willing to give himself up – he was naked except for a pair of underpants, and visibly shivering. I took off my jacket, placed it around his shoulders.

'Who are the others?' I said.

'You know – you *must* know. The rivals.'

'Rivals?'

Ishaan began to cough with the cold.

'Come on,' I said. 'Let's get you inside.'

We made our way back to the house, but I couldn't find a way open at the rear, and no one answered my knocking, so we had to come around the side and walk a little way back up the lane to the garage. The paramedic had now departed. The cops were for the most part sitting in their van, idling out their overtime, but the Count was still cross-legged on the ground, mournfully stroking the head of his dead dog.

'Romeo!' said Ishaan. The Count looked up. Their eyes locked for a moment, then Cesare looked away.

'You found your boy, then,' said the Ispettore. At the sight of the uniform, Ishaan shied away. 'Don't worry, son,' said Alessandro. 'I've no interest in your resident status.'

I heard a car pull up outside – it was the limo. Jacopo and the Comandante began to get out. 'I thought you could do with a lift,' said Alessandro.

'I'm running out of time,' I said.

'Well, you're not going to get very far on foot.'

'What about the kid here?'

Before the Ispettore could answer, Ishaan said: 'Take me with you.'

Chapter 40

It didn't take Ishaan long to pack – the couple of books, a pair of jeans, trainers. He pulled on the *SUN KIL MOON* T-shirt and went to the bathroom to get his toothbrush. He returned to the bedroom and took a final look around. 'I'm ready,' he said.

I followed him out, down one set of stairs, then another. Back through the garage past the Count, to whom he didn't give a second glance, and over to the waiting car. We got in the back.

'Is this him?' said Jacopo behind the wheel.

'Ishaan, yes.'

Jacopo turned the car around and we began to head down the hill, Ishaan looking out at the concrete houses passing by.

'First things first,' I said. 'Tell me about the T-shirt.'

'What T-shirt?'

'The one you're wearing, that belonged to Ryan Lee.'

'Ryan gave it to me.'

'Why?'

He shrugged. 'Present.'

'I don't understand,' I said. 'How did you meet Ryan Lee?'

'The Count introduced us.'

'Where?' I said. 'Why?'

'For a test.'

'A test? What test?'

'He wanted to see who was best.' He smiled at the recollection.

'What do you mean?'

'The *truffles*,' he said, as if it was obvious. 'The Count wanted to see who was the better taster – myself or Ryan.' He chuckled to himself, shaking his head. 'Ryan was better.'

'The Count used you to mix the Balkan truffles together so no one would notice.'

He shrugged again. 'I can taste. I mean, I've got good taste. The Count was always boasting about me, so when he met a professional, I suppose he wanted to see.' He turned to me. 'But I knew I would lose. I can taste like a chef, not a supertaster. It was a silly competition.'

'And they . . . the Count, Norman . . .'

'Norman?'

'The Fosserella Gang.'

'Fosserella?'

'The gang, you know – the Kosovans. The people who smuggled in the truffles.'

'*Them* – I owe them money.' Ishaan frowned. 'Seriously bad men. It cost me, my family, ten thousand euros for the last part – over the border. Then I had to work for them, but,' he looked indignant, 'it's been too long. Three years, and they always say my debt isn't paid. They say, you're special. You're well treated. Look what a great house you have, and if you make trouble . . .' He drew a finger across his throat, a gesture I had seen only too recently.

We turned into Via Mirasole. I noticed a RAI broadcast truck parked at the far end, but otherwise there didn't appear to be any lurking paps.

The Residence gates opened and we drove into the courtyard. I looked up at the surrounding balcony – the lights were off. Alba would be up there with Rose, I knew. I just hoped this wouldn't be the last time I'd come through these gates while my girl was still a girl.

The four of us went to the Comandante's place on the *piano nobile*. It might have been the more prestigious apartment, with its broad entrance and mosaic floor, large spaces designed for dancing and dining, but it lacked the familial cosiness of our home above. I'd always found it strange to imagine Lucia growing up among these austere corridors with their blackened paintings, her stockinged feet upon the cold floor. Certainly when our time came, as the Comandante liked to put it, I had no intention of moving down here.

Giovanni switched on the lights in the gloomy dining room with its extravagant blood-red Murano chandelier above the dining table, rarely used save for Christmas and Easter. Jacopo went to the kitchen to make some coffee.

'And how are you?' The Comandante gave me a searching look.

'Me?'

'Yes, you, Daniel.'

'Fine, just fine.'

'You seem a little . . . agitated.'

'Do I?' I looked at Ishaan. 'Well . . .'

'You should get some rest.'

'Rest?' I checked my watch. 'I have less than twenty hours.'

'After we've wrapped this up, you should get a few hours' sleep, otherwise you will be no good.'

'We'll see.'

'That's an order.'

'An order?' Jacopo had arrived with the coffee. '*We're* not in the Carabinieri, Papà.'

'But I remain boss.'

'A few hours, then.' I looked again at Ishaan. 'So, you're from India.'

'Aurangabad.'

'And how did you get into Italy?'

'I flew into Tirana; they were waiting for me. I was there for a few days, then they took me to Italy.'

'How?'

'Lorry.'

'And then what?'

'I was working for them, like I said.'

'That simple? How did you get on to the database for the employment agency?'

'It's for the paperwork . . . just like in India. I need someone to give me a job, then I can get another. The government think I'm doing one job, but I'm not. Not that job, anyway. Lots of jobs, but no taxes. And then there's him.'

'The Count?'

He nodded. 'He thinks he is a better man than them – I mean the criminals. He thinks he is doing me a favour, but I am like his dog . . .' His voice broke. 'Romeo. A pet. I'm not sure he really sees me as human.' He nodded. 'It is a gilded cage.'

'So you met Ryan Lee, you got to know him.'

'It was like a glimpse of another world,' he said. 'His grandparents were immigrants, you know – to America. Now *that* is the land of opportunity. In one, perhaps two generations . . . I could imagine my son travelling the globe like that.'

'And you met him where?'

'The Count invited him home.' He smiled. 'Naturally, I cooked.'

'And that's when you had the test? When was this? What day, I mean.'

Ishaan thought about it. 'Two days before he disappeared. That was why I was afraid – I thought you were them.'

'*Them* – who do you mean? These "rivals" you mentioned?'

Ishaan shook his head. 'I don't know. But Ryan told me that was why he was here: to find this truffle. Not our own cheap ones, but this special truffle someone had made that wasn't Boscuri, it was . . . *almost*, but not quite . . .'

'So you really don't know anything about these special truffles, Ishaan? These superfakes?' I said. 'You know, you can tell us – we're not the police. Our only interest is finding Ryan.'

He looked down, ashamed. 'I just prepare the cheap ones so they taste like expensive ones. I don't know anything about the others you're looking for. Honestly, I doubt I would have been able to tell – that's the difference between me and Ryan.'

'And when did he tell you this? At the Count's?'

'Oh no, he didn't want to speak about work at the Count's, although I think that's why the Count really invited him.'

He hesitated, shook his head in acknowledgment. 'Ryan is no fool. He didn't say, but I could see he didn't really trust the Count.'

'But he trusted you?'

'He's . . .' he looked down at his hands, 'a nice boy. He took me to dinner.'

'And the Count didn't object?'

'I don't think he would usually have let me, but he said all right.' He thought about it. 'He asked me to see if I could find out more about Ryan's work.'

'So did you? What else did Ryan tell you at dinner?'

The door opened. Rose was suddenly wrapped around me. 'You're alive!'

'Of course I'm alive, darling. I told you I would be all right, didn't I?'

'I saw the cars. Why didn't you come up?'

'I thought you would be sleeping – you *should* be sleeping.'

'I can't sleep! How could I?'

'Well,' I said, looking guiltily around the table, 'you should. Why don't you go up? I'll be there in a few minutes.'

'Your father needs to get some sleep, too,' said the Comandante.

'Who's he?' Rose was looking at Ishaan. 'Is he the murderer? Does this mean you're free?'

Ishaan looked alarmed.

'He's not the murderer, darling. He's just helping us with our case – to find the *real* murderer.'

'So you haven't found him yet? But you've only got . . . nineteen hours!'

'That's plenty of time, my dear,' said the Comandante.

'We've almost cracked it.' Although Rose would usually buy whatever her grandfather was selling, this time she didn't look convinced.

'Len Ligabue,' I said to Ishaan. 'A reporter – Oriana de Principe. Do those names ring any bells?' He shook his head. 'They've both been murdered.' He looked blank. 'Were there any other people the Count mixed with? Invited to his home? Anybody·else who could be connected to the business?'

'I was surprised he invited Ryan,' said Ishaan. 'The Count was usually a very private person. He loved his dog . . .' He paused.

'Did something happen to his dog?' said Rose.

'Nothing, darling.' I could feel fatigue beginning to overwhelm me. 'Is that it? There's nothing more you can tell us – maybe about Ryan?'

Ishaan frowned, then his face lit up. 'He makes these beautiful paper models.'

'Oh yeah,' I said wearily. 'This bloody origami.'

'*Jongi jeobgi*,' said Rose.

Ishaan nodded. 'He made one when I was there, at the restaurant. Excellent truffles, although they were from Piedmont, not Boscuri as they had advertised. That was why he created a monkey. Did you hear about the drought?'

'Hold on,' I said. '*That* was why he made a monkey? What's a monkey got to do with Piedmont?'

'It's a slow monkey,' said Ishaan. 'Something about the food being slow . . . but the service was good,' he added collegiately.

'Slow food,' said Jacopo. 'Piedmont is where the slow food movement was founded – you know, in reaction to McDonald's fast food.'

'It wasn't a monkey, Dad,' said Rose. 'It was a sloth!'

'What?'

'You know – a *sloth*. Slow!'

'A sloth . . .' I thought about its unsettling smile. Jacopo shoved his phone in front of my face with, indeed, a sloth.

'So,' I said. 'What about the others? There was the model of St Francis of Assisi.'

'Umbria,' said the Comandante. 'Umbria is another major source of truffles.'

'He showed me how to make a simple one,' said Ishaan. 'A dog. I tried, but forgot . . .'

'The bird, then? Hawk?'

'Oh.' Ishaan remembered. 'Yes, he told me that if he found any Albanian ones, he would make an eagle.'

Jacopo's phone again. A black eagle against a red background. 'Albanian flag.'

'And the pig?'

Ishaan looked up. 'You found a pig?'

'Yes, why?'

'He said he only made a model when the origin wasn't Boscuri. And if he found one of those special ones – superfakes, did you call them? – he would create a pig.'

'A pig, why?'

He shrugged. 'Because that's what they use to find them where he believed they came from.'

'Where?' I asked. 'Somewhere else in the Balkans? Serbia? Kosovo?'

'Oh no,' said Ishaan. 'Your "superfakes" come from China.'

'What?'

'That's what he told me. He said the taste was *almost* Boscuri, but there was something acid . . . I don't know.'

'Indians, Kosovans . . .' said the Comandante. 'And now Chinese?'

I shook my head. 'No,' I said. 'I suspect the source of our superfake is somewhat closer to home.'

Chapter 41

Jacopo took Ishaan to his apartment, while I went upstairs with Rose. It was one o'clock in the morning, perhaps my last morning of freedom for many years. I had eighteen hours left. Part of me was straining to get on with it, the other part knew there was little I could do at this time of night; and anyway, the Ispettore was right – fatigue clung around my head like a hood. I really needed some sleep. Rose, on the other hand, hadn't let me go since she had turned up at the Comandante's and appeared to have no intention of doing so now we were back in the apartment. Meanwhile I could hear Alba's satisfied snores from my bedroom.

'Come on,' I said. 'You really should get some sleep.'

'What about you? Where will you go? I'll kick Alba out.'

'Don't do that, darling. The couch will be fine.'

'It's too uncomfortable. You haven't slept there since Mum died.'

'You remember that?' It was true. For the first couple of months I hadn't been able to face our bed and had slept in the *soggiorno*, creeping back into our bedroom in the morning before Rose woke up – until one morning she had found me there.

'Don't leave me,' she said.

'Come on, then.' I took her through to her own bedroom. 'Would you like me to read to you?'

'I'm not a kid!' She climbed into her single bed. 'I solved the crime!'

'You did too.' I sat down beside her. 'You'll make a crack detective.'

'Maybe,' she said, as if this was simply stating the obvious. 'Although I might become an artist.'

'Ah,' I said. 'Like the glamorous Signora Amore.'

'Look.' She leaned over and produced her sketchbook. 'She told me not to bother with pretty things but to "capture the beauty in the ordinary". That's my big toe.'

'It is!'

'And that's my keys on the table.'

'It's true.' I was genuinely impressed. 'You've made it beautiful. There's something you've done with . . . the light.'

'Less is more is what Stella says. Or rather, more of less. She says the mind fills in the gaps.'

'A bit like detective work.'

'What do you mean?' she said.

'You're always seeking the truth in the spaces between. The danger is in filling them in the wrong way, putting in too much detail and drawing the wrong conclusion. Sometimes the truth can be staring at you all along.'

'She's single, you know.'

'What?'

'Don't worry, I didn't ask her outright. I just asked her some questions about her life and *deducted* it. Like a detective.'

'What about Oriana? Weren't you just in the process of relocating us to Rome?'

'But she's dead,' she said matter-of-factly.

I looked at her.

'What? You said it wasn't anything serious!'

'I know, but . . . Show me some more pictures.'

I can't say who fell asleep first, but thank goodness I was propped on the edge of her single bed, half sitting up with one arm wedged against her bedside table, because I hadn't set my alarm and otherwise might have woken up way into the morning and lost more precious minutes. Instead, at around six, an inner alarm began to tell me that my arm was numb and I woke to find myself draped half on and half off the bed. Rose was curled away from me, nestled around her sketchbook. I eased myself gently up and crept out.

The corridor was already hazy grey with the morning light. I paused by my own bedroom – I didn't want to wake Alba, so I was going to slip by and go straight to the bathroom, but I saw a glow and glanced in. She had already woken and was looking at her phone.

'Dan! I didn't realise . . .' She made to get out of bed.

'Don't worry,' I said. 'Although I could do with some clothes, if that's all right?'

I opened the wardrobe. 'Thank you so much for looking after Rose.'

Alba ignored the remark – it went without saying. 'And you – how are you?'

'Well,' I said. 'Frankly, I've been better.' I checked my watch. 'I've got fourteen hours.'

Now she did get up. 'I'll fix you some breakfast.'

'Really, it's no . . .' But she was already in her dressing gown: much as for the British a cup of tea is the universal panacea, for Italians it's food, any food.

I came into the kitchen fifteen minutes later, showered and in a fresh change of clothes, to fried eggs, grilled tomatoes, a couple of slices of prosciutto, toast, fresh orange juice and even a dessert dish of diced fruits. I had no idea where half the stuff had come from, but then I realised Alba must have brought it up from her apartment.

'Like an English breakfast, no?'

'It certainly is,' I said. 'A miracle. Only missing the baked beans.'

'What are they?'

'Never mind.' I sat down. 'The condemned man ate a hearty meal.'

'Don't say that!' Tears sprang to her eyes.

'Just kidding,' I said, but I couldn't help thinking I might have spoken more truthfully than I'd intended.

'I'm sorry,' she said.

'For what?'

'Giving you a hard time. You know – over . . . women.'

'Don't worry about that!'

'Maybe it's true that I get a bit jealous of your protégée . . .'

'Dolores? Are you saying that you'd like to do more . . . active work? You know, out on the streets?'

She shook her head. 'Oh no,' she said as if she couldn't think of anything worse.

'Then why? Why should you be jealous?'

'Oh, you know,' she said. 'She's young.'

'You're young, Alba,' I said.

'I'm thirty-five,' she said. 'And single.'

'Oh come on,' I said. 'The thirties are the new twenties. Anyway, look at me – I'll be forty-four next birthday, and even *I* don't think I'm old.'

'That's different,' she said. 'You were married. You have Rose.'

'I thought you were seeing that guy, from the internet.'

'The internet's a waste of time.' Her words could not conceal the hurt on her face. 'They say they're serious because that's what they think you want to hear, but they're not. We're all just . . . disposable.'

'I'm sure there's someone out there for you,' I said, and I meant it. There *had* to be a good man on whom Alba could lavish all the energy she expended on Famiglia Faidate.

My phone buzzed. A name from Alessandro, along with an address.

'I have to go,' I said.

'Of course! I'm so sorry, keeping you here with my stupid complaints.'

'Don't be silly,' I said. We hugged, and she kissed me fiercely on both cheeks.

'Come home,' she said.

Chapter 42

I parked the Lancia outside a bar just off the Viale. I was on the north side of the city, at the far end of Via Pratello. It came as a surprise that the proprietor of Epulum lived in the same street as one Dolores Pugliese, but when I saw the apartment block – a 1950s building set back from the main medieval drag, I got it. It was a comfortable alternative to the kinds of places most Bolognese of that generation would have grown up in, and saved moving further away from the city centre where they had their business.

I went into the bar and ordered an espresso at the counter – it was just past seven. Thirteen hours to go, I noted sourly.

I downed the coffee and crossed the road. The glass-fronted emerald-marble entrance with its shining bronze bell plate and potted plants was consistent with the respectable, petit bourgeois values of the residents. I ran my finger down the names until I came to Bessani. I hesitated for just a moment, then pressed, making sure I held it long enough to attract attention. The response came almost immediately.

'Yes?'

'Carabinieri for Bessani, open up.'

'What?'

'Carabinieri. Open up!'

The door buzzed. I stepped into the hallway and checked the letter boxes to ascertain the floor number, but before I could find it, I heard a door opening perhaps two floors above. I took the stairs.

'What is it?' The old man was standing by the open door in his pyjamas, his white hair hastily combed. 'Has someone broken into the restaurant?' As I neared, he saw that I was not in a uniform, and with the exception of my friends in the SOG, *carabinieri* were almost always uniformed. Perhaps he even recognised me. In any case, he began to retreat and tried to close the door. I caught it just in time.

'I'm with Faidate Investigations,' I said.

'The Comandante's son . . .' He released the pressure on the door. I noticed his wife looking worriedly on in her dressing gown, her hand on a telephone receiver.

'Son-in-law. I need to know where you got the fake truffle from.'

'The what?' He looked genuinely surprised.

'The fake Boscuri white truffle you put on the plate of Ryan Lee, a Korean American. The guy who left the paper pig.'

'I don't sell fake truffles, young man . . . Who do you think you are, accusing me of selling fakes, calling at this hour of the morning impersonating a *carabinieri*!'

'I'll call the real Carabinieri,' said the wife in a scene that was beginning to seem unsettlingly familiar.

'Bullshit,' I said to the proprietor. 'You sold a fake Boscuri truffle to Ryan Lee and he left that model as a little token of proof. Now Ryan has gone missing and there's a line of bodies linked back to him.'

'Now I know you,' said his wife. 'You're the one on *Occhio Pubblico*. The one who murdered that reporter!'

'Look, if you don't want to get dragged into this, old man, you'll tell me where that fucking truffle came from.'

The man looked confused. 'But they were all Boscuri . . .'

'Who's your supplier?'

'Benvenuto. We've always gone to Benvenuto . . . always . . . Hold on . . . but no, it couldn't be . . .'

'What?'

'We were unexpectedly busy – last-minute bookings. We ran out, so I nipped around the corner to buy a batch. But that would be unthinkable!'

'Who's around the corner?'

'Antica Macelleria. But I know the place well – it's part of—'

'Antichi Artigiani del Cibo.'

'That's right. But I know the Ligabue, we go back . . . Aurelio was my number one supplier before he went in with his brother-in-law and the restaurants. That was why I switched to Benvenuto, otherwise—'

'So you got this truffle from an AAC outlet.'

'Unless you're suggesting Benvenuto are selling duds.'

I noticed the wife was still standing in the hallway, receiver in hand. 'You can put that down,' I said. 'I'll be on my way.'

'Wait,' said the old man as I turned away. 'Are you saying that the Ligabue are selling duds?'

'I wouldn't worry too much,' I said. 'No one else seems to have noticed.'

Chapter 43

Boscuri appeared as sleepy as ever – I imagined the truffle hunters had only just returned from a night creeping around the hills, torch in one hand, shotgun in the other – and there was no other traffic on the lane leading up to Il Cacciatore.

This time I wasn't going to risk calling in the Carabinieri until I was sure what I was dealing with. Having seen them in action, I didn't want any more dead dogs, let alone supertasters.

I parked in a lay-by a couple of hundred metres from the restaurant before approaching on foot. The sun was full in the azure sky, but there was little of the city's warmth up here. Despite my jacket, I shivered in the morning chill.

I saw the bulk of Il Cacciatore ahead, paused. To the side I noticed a gate onto a downward-sloping field that skirted the property. I climbed over and followed a path along the side until it began to lead away, so I crossed the ankle-length dewy grass back towards the property.

Just before I reached the treeline, I encountered a rusty barbed-wire fence. It made me think about the others who must have come this way before with mischief on their mind

– truffle hunters, poachers. Sons, grandsons, of partisans, who would have known a thing or two about stealing around the woods. I wasn't their equal, nor that of Aurelio, in countryside craft, but there was one craft I was beginning to learn. As Oriana might have put it – *how to hunt murderers*.

I painstakingly lifted the wire and eased my way through.

I moved slowly through the trees, tearing off a branch to probe the tangled ground in front of me – Aurelio Barbero was just the type to lay animal traps, although not only for animals – until I glimpsed the roof of the farmhouse through the outline of the trees, then the high fence of the dog pound. I began to move to the side and up the gradient so I could get a good view of the compound.

I squatted behind a boulder.

Below, the Lagotto were beginning to rove, snuffling, shitting, but otherwise muted. As far as they were concerned, there weren't any humans, or truffles, nearby to get worked up about.

My thoughts returned to Aurelio. Of course – Ryan had stayed here, been trained by him, so would have trusted him if Len had. He would have been the first person he would have turned to when he discovered the dud truffle – perhaps wanting to alert Aurelio to the discrepancy before he went to the client. But if Aurelio had been in it together with Len, why had Len ended up going out of the window? An argument? And how had Ryan been involved in that? I pictured Aurelio and Len arguing, Aurelio losing his temper as he had with me, lashing out . . . A struggle, fall? Then the dog? It seemed pretty callous, especially for an apparent dog lover. Hadn't Dolores bumped into him coming to visit the damn mutt?

The dogs were barking. Stan Ligabue was at the gate of the compound, the dogs crowding excitedly on the other side of the fence.

She opened the door, slid in, pulling a trolley with what looked like a steel milk churn. The dogs jumped around her as she dragged it further into the compound.

'Go on then!' she shouted. 'Go go go!' Despite their anarchic welcome, the dogs dispersed, though still full of barks, and retreated to their kennels. They watched, only their eager heads visible, as she dealt out a line of metal trays onto the ground in front of them and then began to tilt the trolley, pouring out what I took to be their food. The Lagotto were remarkably restrained. Now and again one would begin to venture pensively forward, perhaps make it a third of the way to its bowl before, without turning to look, Stan would call: 'No!' and it would sheepishly retrace its steps. Did she have eyes in the back of her head? I hoped not – otherwise I'd really be in trouble.

Something was licking my hand. I flinched and lost my balance, toppling back against the tree. Suddenly there was a pair of paws upon my chest, a round woolly face bearing down on me. A brown and white Lagotto was looking into my eyes as if expecting a prize for having discovered me; or perhaps he just meant blackmail.

A door slammed below and he was just as quickly gone, bouncing back down the slope and out of the trees. I saw Aurelio turn the corner and begin to walk between the house and the compound. He shouted something inaudible to Stan and headed in my direction.

I shrank behind the boulder. I shouldn't have been

immediately visible because I had chosen a position at a right angle from the path, camouflaged by foliage. But, of course, the dog had already detected me.

Sure enough, the Lagotto scampered ahead as Aurelio moved swiftly up the path. As he reached my level, I ducked completely down.

I heard the dog pause, waited for it to come crashing through the undergrowth and jump all over me. But then it was gone, and there was only the sound of Aurelio ascending behind it.

I waited until I was sure he had passed by before I began to pick my way cautiously after him, careful not to take my eyes off that grey mop of hair of his as it moved between the trees.

I arrived at another boulder, apparently suspended in the act of rolling down the hill by the roots of a tree, and realised that, instead of heading along the path between the rocks, Aurelio had swerved sideways across the slope before taking a ragged course further up. I did the same, clambering over tree stumps, clinging onto branches and scrambling upwards, frequently on all fours, as I tried to keep up. Then I was tumbling down a dip, landing deep in a bed of damp leaves. By the time I'd clawed my way out, Aurelio had disappeared.

I pulled myself out of the dip and up against a tree. To hell with it: I launched myself forward.

The wood became ever denser, the roots of pines, ferns and oaks exposed between the boulders like tentacles. I scrambled over them, trying to keep going, but as I continued up that natural assault course with no sight of Aurelio, I began to face the obvious – the bastard had, quite simply, disappeared.

I finally wedged myself between a rock and a tree while I gathered my breath, and considered my options.

I could head back down the slope and confront Stan. But what was I going to get out of that? Presuming she knew, she wasn't simply going to point me the way to Ryan Lee. And I hadn't forgotten that shotgun.

No – I would cut my losses, work myself back down the hill to the car and call Alessandro. It might well result in another wild goose chase, worse, some kind of bloodbath, but – I checked my watch – it was my last damn throw.

I was lowering myself from my perch when I heard the bark. Distant but distinctive enough. There again – further up the slope, towards an outcrop that appeared to have been cleaved out of the rock.

I moved diagonally towards the grey carbuncle, trying to work out where the sound was coming from. As I neared it, I realised it wasn't coming from the surrounding trees at all, but from within the stone itself.

I moved closer. Saw that, hidden from the vertical sight-line, there was another one of those leaf-filled dips. As I approached, I peered down and saw a space between the ground and the rock large enough to crawl into, and which looked as if it had been frequently used to do just that.

I descended into the dip, crouched beside the hole. Took in the cool, damp air. I shone my phone light inside: it was a kind of cavern. There were voices, too, indistinct but clearly some kind of conversation.

I slid through, lowered myself to the ground. My head scraped the cave's ceiling, but I could just about stand upright. On closer inspection, I realised that what I had taken for natural spidery patterns upon the rock were man-made – initials, names, dates. The size and shape of the markings changed, but there was a consistency to the dates, which ranged between 1943 and 1945. It was an old partisan hideout. Of course – perfectly concealed up here and almost impregnable.

I moved the light across the graffiti, which for some must have constituted a final testament before they emerged to fight. Alongside the signatures – *MATTEO, DOMENICO, I. H., T. P.* – was a heart-shaped declaration of love, a hammer and sickle, a slogan: *FUCK NAZI BASTARDS.*

I shone the light on the boulders apparently forming a solid wall at the back of the cavern, got closer. One boulder in particular cast a long shadow, and I realised it concealed another opening.

It had once been some kind of natural entrance but had been enlarged by cutting tools – I could clearly see their perpendicular marks upon the sides as I peered into the darkness. I crouched down and squeezed through, shuffling along the smooth stone floor, which gradually gave way to firm dirt. I directed my light upwards. The rock had been replaced by a series of wooden props. The space began to grow higher and wider around me. The stone outcrop itself had come to an end – the partisans had dug directly into the hill.

I was finally able to stand properly straight. I realised that they had constructed an entire bunker in here, with passages and rooms running off the entrance, albeit that most of the openings appeared to have collapsed, their soil ceilings caved in. One passage ended abruptly in rubble; another was barred by fallen beams. I swung the light above my head – in this main chamber at least the ceiling seemed solid enough.

I hesitated, then switched off my light. Ahead, a leak of daylight drew me forward.

There was a clang of metal against metal. The clink of crockery. I ducked as I entered another wood-shored passageway, measuring every careful step. Then: a hanging curtain of ivy. I edged closer. Through the leaves, I saw a kind of cave terrace, more ivy covering the walls. The dirt floor faded back into stone. And there was a view, stretching across the hills and churches of the badlands.

In one corner – a camp bed with a blue sleeping bag laid flat. There was a gas stove next to it, along with a small pile of books, an upturned torch and a candle holder.

A man in a Barbour jacket was sitting with his back to me at a folding table, a moka placed on a ceramic tile in front of him.

'How's the kid?' he said.

He looked around.

Chapter 44

'Hold on,' Dante Millefoglie said agreeably, apparently not in the least perturbed to find me standing there. 'What have you done with Barbero? Barbero!' he called.

'In here!' came the response from behind a curtain seemingly concealing another passage.

'Everything okay?' Dante shouted.

'Kid still won't eat,' came the reply.

Dante looked at me conspiratorially. 'Stubborn, these Asiatics.'

'He's American,' I said softly.

'Be that as it may . . .' Dante reached for the shotgun on the table. Even though he had made it seem like the most casual of gestures, he still had it pointing at my belly before I had taken two steps forward. 'We're off hunting after this. Not for truffles, obviously – wild pig! They're also in season, you know.'

'Is someone there?' said the voice behind the curtain.

'Don't worry!' Dante called back. 'As I was saying – stubborn, these Asiatics. A characteristic they share with the British. You know, your Brexit did my firm no favours.'

'I've heard some excuses,' I said, 'but that takes the biscuit.'

Dante chuckled. 'You're right. I might have a hard time convincing a judge, although the red tape, the taxes, none of it helps!'

'Why?' I said. 'Why kill Oriana? Ligabue?'

He shrugged. 'Simply a question of logistics, Daniel. Of moving goods from A to B . . . One has to eliminate barriers.'

'But *Oriana*?'

'Ah, poor Signora de Principe, a fine investigator. Rather too fine, as it turned out. She was definitely a few steps ahead . . .'

'So you killed her.'

'She got in the way. You know – barriers . . .'

'I saw her body. Vicious, spiteful. Just like flinging the dog out of the window. That's what troubled me – Aurelio might have killed his brother-in-law, but the dog? He loves the damn things. But you, you're fake to your fingertips. Behind that urbane exterior, you're full of rage.'

Did I glimpse a spark, an infernal flicker behind those calm brown eyes? Regardless, Dante's tone did not change.

'Really, Daniel. I can assure you, it was nothing personal.'

'The mafia say much the same, which, incidentally, you mentioned to throw us off the scent. But it was you all along – the Albanian truffles, and now this.'

'Oh! Albania! We can't all be born with a silver spoon in our mouth like Liana, especially here in Italy where everything, *everything* is stacked against the small businessman. A few shortcuts are expected.

'It certainly began by helping those hoodlums get their people over the border. Then I happened to notice that along with human traffic they had begun to smuggle their cheap

Balkan produce too. At that point I didn't want to have anything more to do with them – vulgar people – but it did excite my interest in the business potential.'

'These superfakes, you mean? The ones that ape Boscuri?'

'Do you know, in China they use pigs instead of dogs to find them? Then there's their venerable tradition of copying – as their scientists explained it to me, be it a reconstructed temple or a truffle, in their culture the perfect copy is every bit as authentic as the original, which is why they take such pride in getting it right.

'In any case, I knew that Aurelio here . . .' I looked around – Aurelio Barbero was standing dumbfounded behind me – 'had been having some issues with recent crop yields.'

I looked at Aurelio. 'Issues?'

'It's not raining,' he said gruffly.

'What?'

'Autumn comes later every year,' said Dante. 'It turns out there may actually be something to this global warming. Liana's having the same problem. They're investing massively in irrigation, but not everyone can do the same. The true, forest-found Boscuri white is arriving later and getting smaller every year. So I came up with the idea to source them from elsewhere. It turned out our Chinese friends, after applying a few tweaks to the soil chemistry, were able to produce the perfect copy.' He glanced in the direction of the curtained-off passage. 'Or at least so we thought.'

'And you went along with this?' I said to Aurelio. 'You've been packing AAC outlets with these?'

He shrugged. 'They seemed identical. *I* couldn't tell the difference.'

'Did Len know about all this? I thought that was why he didn't ask Ryan to check the stores.'

Aurelio snorted. 'The blathering idiot never guessed. On the contrary, he was certain he was getting the real thing. He wouldn't listen when I tried to explain how hard it had got up here, and he would try to screw me over the price. He part-owned Il Cacciatore and would say he was keeping it afloat for us, like he was doing us a favour! Prick. He could stuff his truffles up his arse.'

'Country folk,' said Dante.

I looked at Aurelio. 'You were there, then? When Len was killed?'

His mouth crinkled beneath his bushy beard. He shook his head.

'Aurelio tipped me off after the boy got in touch,' said Dante. 'He had wanted to share the news with his rustic pal before going to Ligabue. They had certainly built a bond of trust . . . Anyway, I made sure I was there for the meeting with Len. To be frank, I didn't have a plan worked out in advance. I just wanted to be on the inside track. It only came to me as they were sitting there discussing it.'

'To kill Len and take Ryan.'

'It was the only way, I realised – frankly, him or me. Not a hard choice. I managed to lure Len to the open window and, well, it was all over in a moment. Ryan was the tricky one, struggled a bit, but I managed to subdue him with the help of one of my trusted men.'

'The guy at the expo?' Dante looked blank. 'You know, sitting outside the reserved area, where they tried to grab me.'

'Oh yes, that one. I thought you might show up, and my Kosovan friends wanted a word, so . . .'

'And you want Ryan to help you develop your truffles.'

'If he doesn't starve himself to death first!' said Dante. 'But enough of our chitter-chatter.' He cocked both shotgun barrels.

'No,' I heard Aurelio say.

'I'm sorry, old man,' Dante said. 'You know it has to be done. No going back now.'

'Enough!' Aurelio stepped between us.

'Do we really need the drama?' said Dante. 'Look, we've got this far—'

'And no further!'

'Aurelio—'

We all heard it – the *thwop-thwop-thwop* of a helicopter.

I thought quickly. 'You didn't imagine I just turned up?' I said. 'Everyone knows where I am. That's the police.'

Aurelio looked desperate. 'Police?' He made to grab the barrels of Dante's shotgun. The other man rammed it into his belly, but he somehow managed to keep a hold.

I wasn't going to hang around. The pair were between me and the exit. I made for the curtained passageway instead.

I pushed through the drape and found myself in an earthen cavern, exposed tree roots hanging above like half-finished wiring. A weak glow emanated from a lamp sitting on a crude shelf crafted in the soil wall.

On the camp bed below, a sallow form was visible in a sleeping bag. He turned towards me, his face stone grey, black eyes wide with fear. Of course – Ryan Lee had no idea who I was.

And I didn't have time to explain. 'Another way out?' I asked in English. No answer. 'Ryan,' I said, 'I'm here to help you.' Now that face I'd seen in photos these past days came alive, and he twisted towards a shadow, a narrow opening in the rock that just might lead somewhere.

'Who are you?' he said.

I drew back his sleeping bag. He was still in the T-shirt and trousers he had disappeared in, *sans* jacket and shoes. His hands were cuffed. I tried to lift him up but he looked down and I realised one of his ankles was attached by a metal cable to a dumbbell beside the bed.

'Can you make it?' I began to help him up off the bed, but even with one arm over my shoulder as I hauled him towards the opening, I realised he couldn't move more than a few centimetres at a time; the bell must have weighed thirty kilos, and judging by Ryan's silent anguish, every step hurt like hell. It didn't take much to imagine that cable biting into his ankle. No doubt this wasn't the first time he had tried something like this.

From the cave beyond the curtains I heard an almost melancholic 'oh', then the thump of someone falling onto the turf floor.

'I'll be back,' I said.

I lowered Ryan back down. Too quickly – the bed cracked, then collapsed under him. The last I saw was the kid rolled onto his hands and knees, reaching out for me.

I plunged through the opening, more a crack in the earth – narrow, low – soil whispering in my wake as I went, my arms outstretched like the suddenly blind. A dozen or so metres along I found the way blocked by some kind of wooden prop.

I dared to switch on the screen of my phone: two directions, but from neither did I get any sense of an escape, hint of light or fresh air. The left appeared even more abandoned than the right. Some kind of counter-instinct had me choose it. Sightless again. I moved forward until I tripped over some rubble, reaching wildly in the darkness before hitting the floor. I picked myself up but soon discovered I could go no further – my way was blocked.

Then I heard it – the clunk of metal on stone, a hollow ring that could only be the sound of a shotgun barrel. Another clunk followed by a cough. A pair of tentative steps.

'Daniel,' called Dante Millefoglie. 'There's no way out. Only dead ends. A bit like your investigation,' he laughed. 'As I said, the girl was *way* ahead of you.' There was a pause. He had to be listening.

Torchlight flared against the wall like the beam from a distant lighthouse. A scratching sound. Something moving, fast.

A flash, a deafening boom. The world turned to dust.

Chapter 45

I stopped my mouth and nose against the peppery debris.

A weak light wobbled through the haze. I had the sense that Dante, too, had paused at that fork between the two passages.

'Oh dear!' came his voice. 'What have I done? It's one of those . . . what do you call them? No, not rat . . . These are much cuter. *Coypu*, that's it. Did you know, they're another foreign import? Escaped from the fur farms decades ago. Now the countryside's *infested* with them. Well, that's one less.'

There was a crack, the sound of another couple of slugs being loaded.

'But of course, I'm looking for somewhat larger game . . . Come out, little piggy, wherever you are.'

His light dimmed to nothingness. He must have ventured into the right-hand passage. But in that brief interval, he had exposed something else through the dust – the rubble I had tripped over marked the remnants of another caved-in tunnel. And at the top of the pile appeared to be a hole. A human-sized rabbit hole.

I picked my way painstakingly up the mud and stone pile,

painfully aware of every shift of the shingle; straining to hear Dante turn back.

I pushed my outstretched arms through the hole, but I could see I would need to widen the entrance. I began to ease out a large stone. It came slowly, like a loose tooth. With some effort, I laid it gently behind me. I dug my fingers into the slackened earth again and continued trying to excavate a gap broad enough for my head and shoulders.

I was almost there when something gave beneath me. Not much, but it was enough to trigger a mini slide. I had no choice – I began to scramble through the opening. I heard Dante thudding back along the other passage.

Shafts of light began to illuminate my progress, brighten the clay grey around me. I felt the chill of emptiness beyond.

I heaved myself through and into thin air.

I felt it as I fell, even before I heard it – the blast quite literally hot on my heels. Dante would have had me if he hadn't aimed high. Instead, the hole collapsed behind me as I dropped, spat out along with a mouthful of mud, gravel and stone.

I hit the earth palms first, rolled onto my side in a cloud of dust and debris. I fumbled for my phone and shone the light up to the hole. It seemed blocked, but as I lay there I could clearly hear the sound of scraping – Dante hadn't given up by any means. How long before a pair of shotgun barrels forced their way through?

I swung the phone around.

Light bounced off the silt-sparkling air. I was on the floor of a passage much like the others, although it seemed even longer abandoned. Roots, moulds, even colonies of mushrooms occupied earthen shelves that would have once served as spaces for partisans to sleep, sit, read, write under candlelight.

I picked myself up and began to move into what seemed like it had once been some kind of communal area – part stone, part earthworks, part parlour.

An oak kitchen table, carried up here from someone's house, no doubt, sat in the middle. A dirt-darkened credenza stood beside it, its doors hanging open, fungi colonising its empty shelves. Half a dozen cane café chairs were piled, for some inexplicable reason, beside the items of furniture. At the peak of this pile, atop an upturned chair leg, hung a rusty German Second World War helmet peppered with bullet holes.

Tracking my light along the webbed beams, I found further names, initials, crude hearts and political declarations, among them: *L. L., A. B., 1982.*

Perhaps Len Ligabue and Aurelio Barbero had not always been at each other's throats.

Then – sounds. Coming out of the dark beyond this open space, from another vegetation-thickened passage. I cast my light towards it but couldn't penetrate the ominous tangle of roots and foliage.

Had Dante found another way in?

I edged back in the direction I had come, praying I wasn't about to find him there instead, crouched in the darkness, looking down the double barrels of that shotgun.

Hello, piggy . . .

But no, the path remained empty. I switched off my phone, sank into the darkness. Waited, just waited, as those ominous, indistinct sounds continued and I began to face the fact that this time I really was trapped.

'Daniel!'

Not Dante's voice, that much was clear.

'Daniel! Where are you?'

Ispettore Alessandro's.

I made my way back to the parlour and stood at the mouth of that blocked passage. Began to wrestle a path through the roots and foliage pungent with soil, rot, and even, nestled between tree and earthen wall, the heady tang of a most expensive tuber.

But that would be someone else's mystery to solve.

I finally managed to force my way through the vegetation and arrived at another pile of rubble, a partially collapsed entrance. I clambered over it to emerge into a clearer passage lit by the milky light of day and made haste towards the source.

I pushed through the ivy screen onto a silent scene – I was back where I had begun, only Dante Millefoglie was now standing against the backdrop to the badlands, shotgun in hand.

A crescent of machine-gun-toting *carabinieri* faced him. Aurelio Barbero stood among their ranks – for the moment, spectator rather than suspect.

'Drop the gun,' came the instruction from a sergeant. 'No one needs to get hurt.'

Dante gave me a look of acknowledgement before gently laying the gun upon the cave floor.

He straightened up, made a brief, if florid, bow to his audience, then took two steps backwards.

Chapter 46

Ispettore Umberto Alessandro joined me with the others looking over the cliff edge. Below, Millefoglie's body was clearly visible, broken and unmoving upon the rocks.

'How did you know?' I said. 'When I heard the helicopter, I said something about the police, but I was clasping at straws.'

'You didn't think I'd give you completely free rein, did you? If you'd disappeared, either by fair means or foul, the Polizia di Stato would never have let me forget it, let alone the Prefect.'

'Of course,' I said. 'That truly would have been a tragedy.' The Ispettore grinned. 'Tell me, then.'

'We placed a bug in the Lancia. When we saw where you were headed, we worked it out.'

'You didn't think I could handle it on my own, then?'

'I never had any doubts, Daniel.' He patted me on the shoulder. 'None at all.'

Ryan Lee's voice came from behind the curtain: 'Help!'

I drew it back – there he was, sitting where I had left him, only now leaning back against the collapsed canvas bed, his legs outstretched, one trouser leg rolled up beneath the knee, where he had clearly been having another go at the cable. His cadaver-grey ankle was red raw.

The morning sun that had lent a kind of cruel beauty to Dante Millefoglie's view across the badlands now illuminated this forbidden chamber. Ryan's grimy, tear-streaked face seemed awfully young in the light, and he struck a forlorn figure sitting there in his week-old clothes.

'Help me,' he said, yet I didn't, I couldn't move. It had been a long road here, and now that I had arrived, I felt terribly tired. And also, I realised, somehow bereft – I shouldn't be the only one standing here.

Damn it, Oriana, I thought. Just . . . damn it.

A *carabiniere* pushed past me. He knelt down beside Ryan and sprung the cuffs. He called out and another officer arrived with a bolt cutter to snap the cable.

I forced myself to go over.

'Are you all right?' Ryan asked.

I laughed. 'Shouldn't I be asking *you* that?' Between me and the *carabiniere*, we helped him to his feet and walked him out into the cave where he spotted Aurelio, apparently chatting civilly to one of the officers.

'It was him!' he said. He gave me an anxious look. 'Where's the other one?'

'Don't worry about him,' I said.

'He's mafia,' he said, meaning Aurelio. 'My family . . .'

'He isn't mafia,' I said. 'That was just to scare you.'

'Mom, Dad?'

'They're fine,' I said. 'They're the ones that hired me.'

'You mean you're not the police?'

'I'm a private investigator.'

'You're not Italian.'

'No,' I said. 'I'm not Italian . . .'

We gave Ryan a bottle of water and a couple of energy bars. The Ispettore asked him a few rudimentary questions but Alessandro didn't appear to have much interest in holding onto him – he seemed more interested in exploring the cave complex.

'Battlefield archaeology has always been a passion of mine,' he said before ducking through the curtain.

The *carabiniere* helped me take Ryan back to the entrance and out through the gap in the rock.

We picked our way downhill, finally arriving at the rear of the farmhouse, where the Lagotto greeted us with their usual enthusiasm. Stan was in the courtyard, an extinguished hose still in her hand, a female *carabiniere* standing beside her.

'What's *he* doing here?' She was looking at Ryan. Her surprise seemed genuine.

'You didn't know about any of this?' I said. She ignored my question.

'Aurelio?'

'He'll be coming down shortly, along with the police. I suspect you'll have some catching-up to do.' I thanked the *carabiniere*. 'I can take it from here.'

I walked Ryan out, past Il Cacciatore, and down to the car.

For the initial part of the journey, as we travelled along the twisting hill roads, Ryan Lee didn't say a word, and why should he? Moments before, he had been a captive, his fate uncertain, and now, just like that, he was free.

I took my eyes off the road briefly to check on him – a little colour had returned to his dirt-smeared cheeks.

'You're okay?' I asked.

'I . . . Is this a dream?'

'I'm sorry?'

But Ryan looked desperate. 'You'd tell me, right?' he said. 'If this was a dream? I mean, I'd *know*, right?' He slammed a fist down on his thigh, once, twice.

'Whoa.' I pulled the car over, unclipped the belt. Grabbed hold of his wrist – this, too, I noted, was ringed red from the cuffs. 'It's all right,' I said. 'You're free. It's over.'

'Really?'

'Really.'

He dissolved into tears. I held him against my chest as he let loose, rocking him like I might my daughter after a nightmare. 'Shush,' I said. 'It's not a dream. You're awake. You're free. Really.'

The kid finally appeared to calm down, although even as we carried on along the country roads, I could tell that he wasn't entirely there. It was only once we reached the *autostrada* that I think it really began to sink in.

Ryan rolled his tongue around his mouth as if he was testing a truffle against those extra-special taste buds of his. Finally, he nodded to himself. This was no dream. He looked at me.

'Thank you,' he said quietly.

'You're welcome.'

'You know,' he said, 'when I saw Dante kill Mr Ligabue, I was afraid after that . . .'

'He would kill you? You were right to be scared.'

'But I never thought . . . I mean, hell, I'm just a food taster.'

'Food's a serious business in Italy.'

'Too serious. How did you find me?'

'Well,' I said, 'that's a long story, but in the end, you have Ishaan to thank.' Ryan looked surprised. 'Your friend,' I said. 'The young guy, the chef.'

'Ishaan?' He shook his head in wonder. 'Of all the . . .'

'Why so surprised?'

'He's a genius, you know. I came across him cooped up at that creepy count's. Cooked this fantastic meal, but didn't say much. It seemed . . . I don't know . . . weird, so I asked him if he wanted to join me for dinner the next night. Poor guy – he said he had to ask the Count for permission.

'Anyway, he got it, and it turns out the guy's a damn encyclopedia on Emilian cuisine. I think he wanted me to see if I could get him a gig as a taster – that was what we were up to at the Count's, it turned out – and really, he wasn't so bad, but, I mean . . . people like me, we're genetic freaks. Ishaan, though, he could be a truly special chef.'

Ryan smiled, probably for the first time in at least a week. 'Man, that was quite an evening. I don't usually drink, like to keep the palate pristine, but he insisted I try the wine. We went back to my hotel for a nightcap and ended up riffing half the night until at some point I must have passed out. I woke the next morning to find him heading off to work.'

'You gave him your T-shirt.'

He thought about it. 'Yeah, that's right. What's so funny?'

I turned on to the Viale, merged with the mid-morning traffic.

'Lucky break,' I said.

***

The Residence gates opened and there they were – the Lees alongside Dolores, Jacopo. The Comandante with his hands resting upon Rose's shoulders.

As Ryan got out of the car, Mrs Lee rushed towards him as if he was a rock star, smothering his filthy face in kisses.

'My boy, my boy.' Mr Lee was crying too, although standing at a dignified distance.

Now Rose clung onto me. 'You're not going to prison, then?' I shook my head, looked over at the Comandante.

'Carabinieri one, Polizia di Stato zero.' He seemed satisfied.

'Did you know they had bugged the car?' I asked.

'*I* bugged the car,' he said.

I noticed Ishaan materialise between Dolores and Jacopo. He waved sheepishly at Ryan, who grinned back.

'You need to get out of these clothes, have a shower,' said Mrs Lee. 'My God, you seem half starved. Let's get some food into you!'

'And get you back home,' said Mr Lee. 'To civilisation. Oh,' he added. 'I'm sorry, I didn't mean . . .'

'Don't worry,' I said.

The Lees asked us to call a cab. Ryan went over to embrace Ishaan and chatted easily with the other kids, despite just an hour earlier having been trembling in my arms. The resilience of the young; if only you could bottle it.

I turned to the Lees, who were looking like they had won the lottery.

'I guess we can say our business is concluded,' I said.

'Thank you so much,' said Mrs Lee. 'And I'm sorry if I was, you know, rude that time before at the television studio.'

'It was understandable,' I said.

'That awful reporter,' she said. 'Ambushing us like that. You were right to be wary of her from the start.'

'Yeah.' I sighed. 'I was certainly right to be wary.'

'I'm sorry, did I say something wrong? I didn't mean to upset you.'

'Not at all.' I heard a car pull up outside, a horn sound. 'That must be your ride.'

We gathered to say our goodbyes. As the Lees got into the cab, I pulled Ryan aside.

'Just one thing,' I said. 'Lee Ryan.'

'What do you mean?'

'Your other Facebook account. Why?'

'You saw that?' he said quietly.

'It's how we confirmed your link with Ishaan. Why the two accounts? The alter ego?'

Ryan shifted uncomfortably. He glanced at his father in the cab before leaning towards me. 'They don't know? *He* doesn't know?'

I shook my head. That boyish smile returned.

'Well, hey,' he said, 'we've all got to have some secrets. Why do you think I moved to New York?'

I thought back to my first meeting with the Lees. *Girlfriend? Boyfriend?* 'Okay,' I said, 'but why friend Ishaan there and not on your regular account?'

He looked over at Ishaan and their eyes locked. Something passed between them, although quite what I couldn't say. Ryan looked back at me. 'Like I was saying,' he smiled, 'we've all got our secrets.'

He climbed into the cab and it began to pull away.

As we turned back inside, I noticed Ishaan still standing there, examining something tiny cradled in his hands. 'Ryan gave it to me,' he said. Crafted from a till receipt, it was a perfect paper eye, lying oval like a leaf in his palm but looking up at me with an intricately folded pupil in its centre.

'It is the third eye,' he said. 'That's what it means – Ishaan – Lord Shiva's third eye. He sees through all artifice. He sees only what is true.'

Chapter 47

Piazza Santo Stefano, 'the Square of the Seven Churches', has been the spiritual centre of Bologna almost as long as Piazza Maggiore has been its secular font.

But while Maggiore boasts the signature buildings of Bologna's late-medieval boom, Santo Stefano much better reflects the dimensions of the city before it swelled with wealth and grandiosity.

Like Maggiore, it grew out of the Roman era, beginning with an octagonal second-century temple to Isis. In the fourth century, the site acquired a small, boxy church next door – Santi Vitale e Agricola – which, around a millennium after its construction, would have to be bricked up following a rumour that St Peter himself had been interned inside and the complex became overwhelmed with pilgrims.

But by that time there were plenty of other reasons to visit the piazza. After Isis had been converted to Christianity, the rounded temple acquired walls and was transformed into a simulacrum of the Holy Sepulchre of Jerusalem for those pilgrims unable to visit the real thing. It was possible to crawl inside in imitation of the original and venerate the bones of Bologna's former bishop and patron saint, Petronio. Prostitutes were permitted to worship at the site on Easter Day and uttered secret prayers, while pregnant women were encouraged to sit upon what was left of the saint, presumably for good luck.

In the meantime, further churches had been built upon the complex in fulfilment of Petronio's desire to bring Jerusalem to Bologna.

The churches sit at the far end of the cobbled piazza as you approach from the two towers. On either side you have porticoed medieval *palazzi* – as ever with Bologna, architecturally somewhere between Ancient Rome and the Renaissance – while along the *portici* themselves some traditional businesses cling on, like legendary ironmonger's Pezzoli Enologia, and Gianni the barber, although these days new openings usually feature expensive bars or bistros.

But it would have been boorish to turn down the invitation, and I had to admit that, having gone through so much on their behalf – albeit indirectly – I had never actually visited an Antichi Artigiani del Cibo restaurant. And this one, as Marco Ligabue had been at pains to point out, was a bit different.

For a start, there was no *antica* in the title, nor any artificially aged signage. Instead, a smart ebony sign above the door simply proclaimed in silver art deco lettering: *LEN*.

And although the menu described itself as traditional Bolognese, it was divided into two options – 'city' and 'mountain'. While the city menu featured the usual *cotoletta alla Bolognese* and *tagliatelle al ragù*, the mountain focused on more earthy fare like *spezzatino di cinghiale con polenta* – wild boar with polenta – and *cervo con patate al tartufo* – deer garnished with truffle-infused potatoes. Naturally, I wondered about those truffles, although not too much. Hell, I wouldn't be able to tell the difference anyway.

But the biggest difference was the interior. There were no hanging pork shanks or wheels of Parmesan on display at LEN. Instead the setting was comfortably contemporary, with big windows looking on to the piazza and booth-like seating amidst contemporary art, while a simple counter along the far wall separated diners from the kitchen and its furious activity.

As we came in, Ishaan was overseeing the work of a cook bent over a pot of polenta, but he nevertheless looked up and gave us a cheery, if somewhat anxious, wave. As the head chef on opening day he didn't have too much time for niceties.

The rest of the kitchen staff, I noticed, were mostly Italian. In the publicity for the new restaurant, Marco had said he wanted to 'lift the veil' on the business and 'bring the diner into the kitchen'. He had made a big deal about Ishaan's expertise. But he was also a businessman. Out of the fifteen or so staff at work behind the counter, I counted three, including our friend, who were non-white, plus, out of the half a dozen waiting staff, a single woman of Eritrean extraction who was almost certainly native to Italy.

Still – baby steps.

'The Ispettore's brother-in-law had to pull some serious strings to get the lad exceptional leave to remain,' said the Comandante, looking dubiously at the booth before, with some effort, sliding in. 'He will probably be expecting an invitation too.'

'Over there,' I said. At the far side of the restaurant sat a grey-haired, grey-uniformed *capitano* of the Guardia di Finanza, with a very elegant, rake-thin lady who could only be the sister of Ispettore Umberto Alessandro.

I looked at Alba. 'Dolores?'

She rolled her eyes. 'Important appointment. Something about a beauty parlour.'

'You're kidding,' I said. 'That's so not Dolores.'

'You think you know women?' She exchanged a look with Rose and they both set a suitably reproving gaze upon me.

'Normal service has been resumed, I see.'

'There she is!' Rose pointed to an unfamiliar figure coming through the door and heading towards us. 'Wow!'

'You like it?' said Dolores, whose hair was bleached white. 'I decided this was more my style.' She shot me a defiant look, the Comandante, I noticed, one a little less bold. But the old curmudgeon seemed amused.

'It suits you, dear,' he said. 'Very modern.'

'It would be even more modern,' I said, 'if you stopped calling every woman "dear".'

'I think it's sweet,' said Dolores. The women all looked fondly at the Comandante. I could do no right, it seemed.

Now Jacopo arrived. He was holding a chocolate-brown Lagotto in his arms, the mutt looking sheepish with a transparent plastic cone around his neck and his two front legs sticking over Jacopo's forearm in splints.

'Oh. My. God,' said Rose. 'Is that *Rufus*?'

Jacopo perched himself at the end of the booth, the dog sitting docilely upon his lap.

'He's so cute!' Rose crouched down beside him.

'The surgery said he was ready to come out,' I said. 'But the truth is, he's a bit of an orphan.'

'What do you mean?'

'His owner's dead, obviously. The couple who might have cared for him – Aurelio and Stan – well, it's not exactly a good time for them. And Marco doesn't want him around; he says he reminds him too much of his dad.'

'So what's going to happen to him?'

I looked around the table at the rest of the family. Rufus began to lick Rose's outstretched hand.

'What's going to happen to him?' she repeated.

I shrugged. 'No idea, to be honest. I suppose,' I looked at the dog, 'there's adoption?'

'People are always on the lookout for a Lagotto,' said the Comandante.

'Except there's a problem,' I said.

'He's got no sense of smell,' Dolores told Rose. 'That was why Len took him in the first place.'

'But it turned out he was very good in front of the cameras,' I said. 'Still, those days are over, aren't they, old boy. It's the doggy orphanage for you.' As if on cue, Rufus gave Rose an especially winsome look.

'Couldn't *we* take him?' Rose asked.

I sighed. '*This* conversation again? And who's going to walk him?'

'I—'

'And whatever happened to the bulldog? I thought you wanted an English bulldog, out of patriotism or something.'

'You said it was cruel! Their breathing, noses, everything ...'

'I don't know . . .' I looked around the table at the remarkably straight faces. 'It would be a huge responsibility . . .'

Rose gasped.

'And a responsibility that would be entirely *yours* . . .'

'Oh Dad!' She put me in a headlock, inflicting a series of kisses before releasing me to crouch back beside Rufus, who seemed to have sensed what had happened and assumed a definitely more cheerful expression.

Well, you landed on your feet after all, I thought.

Later that afternoon, I left the pair of them on the sofa in front of an *Amici* – aptly named – special, the dog curled up beside Rose as if he had been there his whole life, my daughter absently running her hands through his woolly hair. His tail responded with a somnolent wag.

As always at times like this, I took a mental photograph.

I stepped quietly out of the apartment and went down to the courtyard, where there was a patch on the grass where our little Punto had been parked. I was seriously thinking about giving in to Rose on that other matter, too: an SUV, or *Soov*, as the Italians more excitingly put it. A small one, at any rate. These days they seemed so ubiquitous, they were almost as anonymous as Puntos, although a darn sight harder to park. Anyway, for now I would have to make do with the limo. I wasn't trailing anyone, and where I was going, parking was not usually a problem.

As expected, there was plenty of space at La Certosa this time on a Saturday afternoon – Sunday was the traditional day for a visit – and I walked the familiar route to Lucia's resting place, that mental snapshot still fresh in my mind.

As I sat on the wall beside the tomb, feeling the weakening rays of the sun upon my face, I replayed my memories for her benefit. I usually didn't have much of a problem sharing them with her and often inserted her figure beside me, creating a mini fiction; even, upon occasion, adding a bit of dialogue. I thought I knew Lucia well enough – what she would have approved of, laughed at, hated – but this time I found myself at a bit of a loss. I honestly had no idea what she would have thought about Rufus. We had never had a pet before, never even discussed it. Would she have liked him? Hated him? She might even have been allergic to animals. I had no idea. I realised with a jolt that we had never got that far. The spell was broken – I found myself looking only at a cold inscription as the sun continued on its way and my face fell into shade.

Feeling a little lost, I went walking. I had nothing much to return to, after all – I suspected Rufus would be quick to win the struggle for my daughter's affections. Hell, he had already. So I walked, and walked – back through those avenues of stone, the ghostly porticoes, galleries where the bourgeois had sought to outbid each other yet now lay anonymous and, for all their investment, forgotten.

I found myself back in that little corridor lined with the drawers of the dead, the flowers marking their old bones as fresh as ever. Inevitably, I drifted to the stone bench.

I smiled at Oriana's impetuosity, my own malleability.

The evidence points elsewhere, she had said.

Where does the evidence point?

Maybe I can show you . . .

And this time, I actually looked. There was nothing inscribed upon the drawers, stacked one atop the other, to give the game away – at least no names or faces that I recognised. Neither was there anything carved on the stone bench.

Finally I gazed eastwards through the arch, across the cemetery towards the ring road. And what lay in between? I saw it now, as clear as day – those four red parallel lines bordering the roof of a cargo depot, the trucks neatly lined up – Millefoglie SpA.

Signora de Principe, a fine investigator. I could agree with Dante Millefoglie about that, at least.

I thought I might pluck a flower or two from the surrounding drawers to lay upon our seat, only to realise why they always seemed so fresh – none of them were real.

A bell chimed.

La Certosa was closing. I continued along the marble passage until I found some steps leading to the exit. A doorkeeper was waiting at the gatehouse, impatiently checking his watch. What would happen if I were to be trapped inside? Well, I suppose one day I would find out – I would take my long rest here beside Lucia. Who knew? The pair of us might even come across the spirit of Oriana as we drifted between the Certosa soirées. Among the entourage of the divine Farinelli perhaps, or belting out a ballad with Lucio Dalla.

But that excitement could wait. For now I walked alone along the cypress-lined path to the car, and headed for home.

Afterword

It began with Paolo Ghezzi's grandfather, Enrico, who lived in a town in the Emilian hills not unlike Boscuri and, having fought as a partisan during the war, enjoyed rearing Lagotto Romagnolo as part of his peacetime hobby truffle hunting. In those days, truffles were mainly a local delicacy, and indeed Paolo's grandmother Agnese used to get so fed up with Enrico's hobby – which he was all too successful at – that she would fling the excess fungi through the open kitchen window. Paolo remembers that there was always quite a pile outside as he was growing up.

But one day the young Lagotto Enrico had been painstakingly training to sniff out truffles over the preceding couple of years went missing. He never found it. Instead, Enrico, a stoical 'man of the mountains', got hold of another pup, which he began to train, only for this one to go missing a year or so later. He gave it one further go, but the next dog only lasted six months before it was snatched. At which point he gave up – the Nazis might not have defeated him, but the Lagotto poachers had. Truffle mania had taken over and Agnese's pile had long since been spirited away. Things had got out of hand.

The truffle trade now dominates Paolo's hometown, and it inspired him to use the essence of truffles in his artwork *Respiro di tartufo*, together with his collaborator Nadia Antonello of Antonello Ghezzi. Paolo's reminiscences, and artwork, surely planted the seed that became *The Hunting Season*.

So to Paolo – and his *nonni* – I owe a huge debt. And then there is fellow author Antonio Laurino, who has patiently sat through my monologues about the novel's ups and downs, and in particular helped me come up with the 'fake Laurea' scene, along with Glauco Miranda, whose enduring positivity has so often simply kept me going.

Then I must thank Russell Norman, not only one of my earliest readers but also the person who taught me how to cook my first Italian dish – appropriately pasta with 'Bolognese' sauce – all those years ago in that little galley kitchen at the top of the fire escape. *Who knew?*

I'd like to thank Michael Atavar, Chris Bailey, Mike Bailey, Nick Cobban, Ruth Davison, Nino Guiffrida, Michelle Lacy, Nick Lawrence, Gordon MacMillan, Marco Settembrini, Matthew Stradling and Mark Warner for their continued support, and the Debut 20 group of writers, who helped me feel a little less isolated during the time of Covid; in particular, founder Polly Crosby, Trevor Wood for inviting me to join and facilitating so many of our activities, and Philippa East, Louise Fein, Charlotte Levin and Frances Quinn for going out of their way to offer me a helping hand, although to be honest often simply a kind word from one of the other members has gone a long way to lifting my mood. I would like to thank my old English teacher,

Alistair Darbey, who encouraged me in the single pursuit in which I showed any early promise, and Louis-Ferdinand, creative companion, *enfant terrible* and cat.

Then, of course, the serious stuff – you would not be reading this at all were it not for the faith and support of my agent Bill Goodall and the clear-eyed enthusiasm of Krystyna Green and Hannah Wann at Constable. To Amanda Keats I owe a particular debt for steering me through editorial straits towards publication, as I do to copyeditor Jane Selley and proofreader Joan Deitch. I would also like to thank Clara Diaz for helping garner those all-important reviews and add how much I have appreciated the enthusiasm of Bettina Hartas of Trip Fiction, who has really helped spread the word.

Most importantly, I must thank my wife, Lea, and all my family here in Bologna – Silvia, and *nipoti* Simone, Luigi, Massimo and Elena. *The Hunting Season* is dedicated to their father, Rino, who died as it was with the editor, and who will be warmly remembered by all who knew him.

Tom Benjamin
Bologna, May 2020